The Runaway Man

KELLEY TANTAU

CRANTHORPE
MILLNER
PUBLISHERS

First published by Cranthorpe Millner Publishers (2023)

ISBN 978-1-80378-148-8 (Paperback)

www.cranthorpemillner.com

Cranthorpe Millner Publishers

For Mum & Dad

ABOUT THE AUTHOR

Kelley Tantau is a 28-year-old Kiwi author and an award-winning journalist living in rural New Zealand. She graduated from the University of Waikato in 2016, earning a Bachelor of Arts degree and majoring in Writing Studies.

Before graduating, she started her career in the world of community journalism. In 2023, she was named Best Senior News Journalist at the Community Newspaper Association Awards, and Joint Runner-Up for Community Journalist of the Year at the NZ Voyager Media Awards.

The Runaway Man is her debut novel. It is the launch pad for her series about those who choose to leave their lives in place of a new one, and the consequences of that monumental decision.

She has a four-year-old dog called Bagel, an eight-year-old blind rabbit called Skyla, and an ever-supportive husband called Matt.

JUNE 3   DAY 30

Most are still in bed when the man enters Driscoll Street, and though his feet scuff loudly along the tarseal, occupants of the weathered abodes on either side stay tucked underneath marshmallow covers.

They don't hear his heavy breath, the cringing of his lungs as they inhale the cold air, nor do they stir when he trips over his big toe, wrinkled and soggy from wearing damp shoes. They keep their eyes closed and suspicions at bay, and Nick trudges on intently, not wanting to take advantage of their drowsiness.

With every passing minute, the Quince sky above him gets lighter and the stars start to disappear, making way for the morning. He's desperate to get to Number 24 before the sun rises. A cricket rubs its wings as if to urge him onwards, evoking a memory of summer nights, bedroom window wide open and Nick, small then, drowning in navy duvet, begging the black field crickets to come forward. The first would hit his window like a piece of gravel but the second would locate the opening, and one by one, the insects would find their way indoors, using Nick's room like a secret society, convening by the chest of drawers or underneath the bed frame.

The sound would start off deafening, chirps rising and

falling like waves, but it quickly turned into white noise and it soothed Nick and put him to sleep. By morning though, the crickets would be quiet. Some hopped too far down the hall and were eaten by the dog for breakfast. Others lay tipped over on Nick's desk. When the casualties became too great, he stopped inviting the insects indoors and had to learn to fall asleep in silence. The dog didn't live much longer after that.

It's the first week of June. The niceties of autumn have been packed away neatly into a suitcase, and the season has made its way to the other side of the world. Like a parting gift, Nick has been damp for a month. His socks have turned holey and squelch under his feet, and what once were soft hands have now blistered; where once was smooth skin is now layers of dust and bruises.

There are browning newspapers poking from the letterbox outside Number 24 and Nick yanks at them as he saunters up the driveway. He peers through the glass pane of the front door. Intuitively, he runs his hand along the concrete stoop until his gloved fingers reach a garden bed and a rock painted with a rose. Underneath it, a single silver key sits. In a matter of seconds, Nick stands, the key is inserted, and the door is pushed open. Soundless. He steps inside and it shuts behind him. A flick of his wrist and it locks.

He waits to hear raspy breaths coming from underneath a bedspread, a delicate moan or a sudden snore, but there's nothing. The wind brushes through the home and the old floorboards creak, while a fridge hums in the kitchen to the right: ordinary sounds offering up no unordinary action. He looks to the second floor and makes the ascent.

Surveying the rooms as he passes them, Nick notices

nothing but faded bedspreads and dust-covered doilies. Each space is devoid of personality. Each bed is empty. There is another room at the end of the hall, but the door is shut and he doesn't bother going inside. Instead, he locates the master bedroom which has also been left unattended, and when sure that he is well and truly alone, he lifts his arms over his head and stretches until his fingertips touch the ceiling.

The room has a large window that looks down onto the neighbour's yard; blue curtains have already been drawn and a subtle kink of morning's hue pokes out from underneath them. Nick strips and steps out of his mud-stained clothes, abandoning them on the cream carpet, and he marches into the ensuite to hop into the shower. He turns the water to scalding and the force of the pressure hits his forearm like pinpricks. Dirt runs off his body and pools at his scratched toes before it circles the drain. His guilt follows with it, though he thinks now that perhaps guilt is too strong a word.

He scrubs at his arms, legs, and face with a fragrant bar of soap until the water runs clear, and on his return to the bedroom, he uses the bath towel to open drawers and closet doors, locating an old rucksack and stuffing inside it underwear, long johns, and fresh socks. He throws in the towel, too. His old clothes are chucked into the bag's depths and he dresses himself in items found in his search throughout the room; though they are unflattering and large, they'll do.

In the bathroom, he opens the top right-hand drawer of the vanity and locates a toothbrush and paste. He brushes his plaque-ridden teeth before he stuffs those items in the rucksack as well.

Nick stares at his reflection in the mirror; he's in there somewhere, underneath the grit and the bloodshot eyes. He pulls out a pair of scissors and haphazardly chops at the hair on his face and head, brushing off his scalp and watching as the trimmed tresses fall into the porcelain sink like tiny paratroopers. Before departing, he wipes down what his hands touched with a blue sponge that had been left propped on the edge of the bath.

He sidles down into the kitchen, poking his head into pantry cupboards and cutlery drawers. He fries up strips of bacon and an egg that is two days older than the use-by date on the carton. As he waits for the meat to golden and the yolk to turn hard, he turns on the TV in a living room that has been meticulously tidied.

There's a news segment on falling house prices. Another on climbing interest rates. The words become like music in the background until a presenter utters the word 'Quince', and Nick's back arches at the stove.

"Do you know where Quince is?" a woman asks from within the screen.

"Well, I sure know *what* a quince is," a man answers.

Weak laughter follows and Nick, though his ears have pricked and his bacon has turned black, rolls his eyes at the wit.

The two news anchors talk about the disappearance of a man from Quince, a man whom they call a beloved son, brother, and boyfriend. A man who hasn't been seen for a month. They show archival footage from a press conference held not too long after his disappearance, and in the background, the man's mother wails.

"Here's what the leading detective has to offer."

The screen cuts to an ununiformed cop who has wide

eyes deep-set into his sockets and curved wrinkles which extend from them like branches on a tree. The corners of his mouth are downturned, and when he speaks, there's no strength in it.

He tells whoever is listening that he's working hard to find the missing man, and though his segment is short, it feels like it drags on forever. The presenters look between themselves with raised eyebrows, as if they don't quite believe him, and after a beat, they fumble for a dose of lighter news, something that happened on the other side of the country, far away from any town named after a fruit.

Nick washes with great precision the pan he used to fry the bacon, saturating it in soapy bubbles. He does the same with his plate and cutlery, before drying and returning them to their rightful drawers. He turns off the TV set and shoves the remote into the burgeoning rucksack. He empties a bowl of fruit into it as well. Swinging the bag across his shoulder, he moves throughout the kitchen, wiping down every surface. Before he leaves, he takes the sponge for good measure, and locates a thick green jacket and an old pillow in one of the hallway cupboards.

At the door, he listens to the floorboards creak and the fridge hum. He peers through its glass panel and stares outwards, where sound sleepers are still sleeping, and birds are poking their heads out of the privet. He takes one long, last look behind him: the black and white photos on the wall; the clay bowl of keys on the sideboard; the faded spaghetti stain sticking out from underneath the rug. He expects this will be the last time he's here.

Then, a sound so faint he thinks he's dreaming it emanates from an upstairs bedroom. He tilts his head slightly, clutches the key in his hand. It's a recognisable pitch; the familiar rubbing of wings. The locator beacon of a cricket in the upstairs bedroom. Nick smiles to himself. Perhaps it won't be the last time. He keeps hold of the key and it soon joins a raft of random discoverables in his pocket.

*

He carries the pillow behind his neck as the heavy rucksack hangs loosely from his shoulder, hitting the back of his knees with every step. The wind whistles past him and chills his nose, and his legs begin to tire, but Nick can smell the faintest aroma of pine and sap and keeps his eyes fixed straight ahead.

He has no watch to guide him, but he thinks it's nearing 9am when he marches into the forest park, 40 kilometres wide at its broadest point. Usually, he takes the long way around, but there's a low fog hanging about and not a single car has pulled into the parking lot, so Nick cuts through it with confidence. He follows a marked route until he comes to a familiar, sweeping corner. Going left takes trampers through a tunnel before they connect back onto a gravel path, while going right is not advised – there are no markings or signage and it's easy to get lost among the overgrown foliage and rugged terrain.

That's what happened to Nick in the early days of his disappearance. He had no plans to re-emerge from his make-shift camp at the top of the crest, but a soggy morning led to many failed attempts to start a fire, and he made a quick dash back into town for supplies. On his return, he couldn't remember where to go in which location, or what trees he'd already seen and what path he'd already trodden.

The sun had set by the time he stumbled, on hands and knees, across his small tent and half-charred wooden logs.

He discovered how easy it was to go unnoticed when he re-emerged from his burrow a few days later. He walked down to the closest corner store, arms swaying, whistling a tune, and he bought water bottles, a pack of gum, and a can of Pringles. He even said good morning to the shopkeeper. Then, he noticed the local newspaper had a photo of him on the second page, a photo taken last Christmas. He was holding a can of light beer, but the paper had cropped it out. Scanning through the article, it was then he realised his family had only just reported him missing, one week after he had disappeared. Nick raced out of the store and returned to his camp, running so fast the Pringles shook like a rattle clenched in a baby's grasp.

A couple of days after that, he used the park's public toilets and was stopped on the way out by a local fisherman, who grabbed him by the shoulder with such force that Nick thought the jig was up. But then the angler asked if he'd seen a six-year-old with a fishing pole, and Nick shook his head and moved on.

The trips further afield became more frequent and more brazen, and at one point he checked into a two-star motel for the night, using a different name to sign in and paying with cash he kept stored in his backpack. He lay awake watching the door, waiting to be discovered, but the next day he checked out without an issue, realising that to be found, someone had to be looking for him.

The forest park is full of podocarp trees and pine and beech, and houses nothing but possums and rats and mustelids. There is a river that runs through the mountainscape that is wild in stormy weather, but mellow and ideal for swimming on a calm day, and today, it runs smooth, and the rain that escapes from the grey clouds clings to Nick like a film. The forest attracts trout fishermen, travellers, campers, and, in his case, those in need of tranquillity.

He reaches his camp, tosses the pillow into his tent, and hangs his new towel on a tree branch. He pulls a small rock towards his extinguished fire pit and sits on it, removing the change from his pocket and counting the coins like a gambler counting their riches. There is still enough to last for some time – a lifetime of frugal spending has secured him a future as a recluse – and so Nick leans back, tilts his head towards the climbing sun, and tries to forget about Driscoll Street, the empty home, and the morning news.

It's windy in the forest and the canvas of his tent flaps harshly, adding chaos to the gust. He considers spending the day at the fire pit, to wallow in his thoughts, but after finding a moment for perspective, he picks up a small fishing pole from its stoop against a pine tree and heads north.

His camp is located almost two kilometres from the beaten track, but it's a short walk downhill to a small berth of the river. It's here where he washes himself as thoroughly as he can, and where he tries to catch fish to feed himself. He isn't the strongest angler, and he never looks forward to gutting the creatures, but today Nick stands at the river's edge for hours, dropping in his lure, pulling it out, and dropping it in again. When the sun starts to light up the water, the trout begin to appear.

After readjusting his tackle, he nabs one in short time and pulls it from the river, its speckled belly catching the filtered sun. He sits crouched on the water's edge and uses a sharp knife to disembowel the fish. He cuts off its head in a swift movement before running the knife along the back of it, removing the scales before slicing it open. He gets rid of the organs and spine and they slop onto the rocky shore with a sludge. It's not the most precise of surgeries, but once done, Nick delicately places the fillets into a clip-lock container that, despite arduous cleans, has formed a permanent-looking filth.

He tries for one more and it's not long before he reels in another victim. Again, the process is messy, but Nick makes quick work out of gutting the trout and, satisfied, he rinses himself off in the water before marching back up to camp. Here, it's not as easy of a job to light a fire. With the wind increasing each hour, the flames are effortlessly snuffed.

He sits with his back to the direction of the wind and hunches over the small fire pit he's stocked with sticks and logs that were light enough to carry. Darkness has arrived completely before the flames ignite, but once they take hold, they stay for a few hours, long enough to cook the fish and long enough for Nick's body to heat up after a day of battling against the elements.

He spends the rest of the evening like he does every other: lying inside his tent, listening to the trees as they moan and creek and drop branches in the distance, hearing the footsteps of curious possums and hedgehogs emerging from piles of leaves. He imagines it to be past midnight when he finally settles.

Scrunching his body into a ball within his sleeping bag, Nick closes his eyes and breathes in the musty scent of the pillow he stole from Driscoll Street. It fast transforms into a person; the nape of a neck; the arch in a back; the softness of thighs. He flinches as his mind plays home movies of Sunday mornings: coffee kisses and sluggish laughter.

For a moment, he misses his past life and resents the tent and his surroundings. For a moment, the collective of trees and chattering of possums becomes a nuisance and he reaches up to his ears to block it all out. He squeezes the side of his face so hard he can hear inside his head; the sounds of thunder rolling closer or Earth's tectonic plates colliding below. He keeps his eyes shut tight and tries to remember why he's here.

Eventually, the image soothes him, more than any Sunday morning memories ever could, and Nick drifts to sleep; a tiresome routine that will resume when he wakes.

2

As soon as Abbott stands, a waitress trips on his big toe.

Her body lunges forward in a shuddering movement, and her arm extends out in an attempt to rescue the raisin scone that has been flung from its plate. She's not fast enough, it lands with a stale thump on the floor, and Abbott, still a little distracted, takes an uninterested step to his left.

He approaches Rowan, who has walked into the café from the side street. In his pale hand, he holds a sheet of paper, and on his face, he wears a grin. Abbott ignores the grin and snatches the paper.

"What is this?" he asks, hoping for something good.

"Library books," Rowan says proudly.

"Library books?" Abbott is less than enthused. "This is all you got?"

"That's all they could give me. Everything else, we already have."

Abbott clicks his teeth. He moves back over to his table, where nearby, the waitress is busy collecting herself, wiping the dust from her hands onto her apron. He scans the paper's contents and Rowan follows behind, waiting for his superior's reaction.

"This is all you got?" he says again.

"It's something isn't it?"

"*The Rime of the Ancient Mariner*, and *The Hidden Life of Trees*. Sounds like nothing." Abbott puts the list down. "He checked these out?"

"A week before he went missing."

His lips purse and he pauses in thought, clear signs of a man who has tried everything, a man in which library books are all he has left.

It has been a month, a long month in which leaves have fallen off trees, toddlers have learned to walk, and birds have flown the nest. It's seen the cricket team lose another home game, the warrant on his car expire, and the bakery on the corner be converted into a shop for e-cigarettes. So much has happened, but Nick Greene is still missing.

"It doesn't matter," he sighs. "We'll never know where he is."

"That's it? We're giving up?"

"We're not giving up, we're being realistic," he says. "We've got other pressing matters to deal with." Abbott bites his lip to conceal the lie.

The precinct on Lincoln Street hasn't had any serious action for months, if not years. The road cops keep themselves busy writing tickets, but there have been no fatal crashes to investigate, no home invasions or kidnappings. Some might think it's a beautiful thing, a town without any major crime, but Abbott had been waiting anxiously for something big to happen; he felt it approaching in the air. When it landed on his desk in the form of a missing persons report, he almost licked his lips. He sunk his teeth into the case like a carnivore ripping into a piece of meat, leaving no flesh on the bone.

But it's been a long month and so much has happened, and Nick Greene is still missing.

"He didn't skip town. He isn't at home. Sure, he could be lost, which means dead, but we haven't found a trace of him," he says. "We've looked, Rowan."

"I know."

"That's it, then. It's over."

"What will we tell Paula?"

Abbott grimaces. Any whisper of backing away from the case and Paula will rip him apart in a way only a mother could. There'd be nothing left of him, and he's already running low on soul. He rises and rubs his brow with the back of his hand.

In the café window, one of Nick's posters has been stuck on with Sellotape and the ink is fading. He looks at the smiling Nick Greene, at a face he imagines is decomposing and unfamiliar, and his stomach churns at the thought. A flash of a memory rushes behind his retina. He blinks hard to force it away, while from within his pants pocket, his phone vibrates. He recognises the number. It's as if she heard him admit defeat.

"Then again," he says to Rowan, lifting the earpiece to his head with a sigh. "I guess there's no harm in trying again."

*

The family cries every time Abbott sees them and this morning is like any other.

Tissues are squashed into balls and are damp with tears, nostrils quickly become raw and red, and bodies shake as breath escapes lungs; an inflamed, quivering, wet mess. Abbott, not knowing how to respond, attempts to blend into his surroundings, to be as far removed from the scene as possible. He sits low in a plush armchair, his back hunched, as if he's trying to escape beneath the fabric. One arm is wrapped across his chest while the other extends to his face, thumb under his chin, fingers stretched up his cheek. There he waits until the crying stops.

It is Paula who sits with the box of 4-ply tissues infused with aloe vera in her lap. It is she who clutches at them in handfuls, soaking one before swiftly reaching for another. Mollie perches on the arm of the chair, pulling her mother in for an embrace and shedding a few tears herself. Eventually, Paula catches her breath and apologises more than once. Abbott holds his palm in the sky as if to say 'no bother' but a bother, it is.

Paula cried the first time he met her and has done so every subsequent encounter. Whether it's a sniffle across a living room or a full-sized meltdown at a press conference, Abbott has seen all of her stages of grief. She likes to remind him how woeful she is, too, by calling him every morning and night, reminding him that it is his responsibility to complete the puzzle left behind by her son.

"He was Head Boy, you know," she says, catching him looking at a framed image of Nick, dressed in a school uniform embroidered with ironed-on badges. "That is my favourite photo in the entire house." Her voice quavers and she returns her face to the tissue clutched in her hand.

Abbott nods and raises his eyebrows. Surely, he thinks, there have to be better photos than this.

The jug, which had been turned on to boil, clicks, and inside, the swollen bubbles simmer down until the water is still. Mollie stands and moves into the kitchen where she sets four mugs on the counter, scooping dark coffee granules into each one. The girl appears withdrawn, her mind elsewhere, and she hands Abbott the hot drink while her gaze focuses on the view outside the window. He accepts the coffee, though hesitantly. He is anxious to get on with the matter at hand.

"So, tell me what happened exactly?" he says, leaning forward to place the mug on the carpet. "You said over the phone there had been some things taken?"

Paula hears the reservations in Abbott's voice and her mournful demeanour at once shifts to that of a proud woman, not wanting to be made a fool of.

"*Some* things? My house was broken into. My privacy invaded. Somebody is targeting my family." Her voice rises and falls and her words, like they always do, hit their intended target. The woman, late fifties, short in stature with deep wrinkles and greying curls that hang above her shoulders, is hard to ignore when her temper flares.

"There needs to be more done about this. Forensics. People searching for fingerprints. Where are they?"

Edwin stands forward from his position near the bookcase and it is only then Abbott remembers he was here at all. Edwin had greeted him at the door and then retreated, as he usually does, into the background, like a gifted vase that sits undisturbed on a sill, gathering dust.

He's a tall man, a similar height and size to Abbott himself, and a quiet man, who talks not unless spoken to. He wears small glasses and has a mouth that is permanently etched in a straight line, and Abbott, unable to detect a hint of a smile or glint of sorrow, finds him difficult to read.

He's over at Paula's side now, resting a hand on her shoulder. She looks to Abbott for an answer. He stands, careful not to knock the dark coffee across the cream carpet, and dusts himself down. His navy suit, his trademark apparel, is paired with black leather shoes in need of a shine. As he lifts his gaze, his eyes catch another look at Nick Greene, youthful and dignified, trapped in the frame.

"What's been taken?" he asks.

The couple lead the officer upstairs to the master bedroom where there's been no obvious signs of theft. The flat-screen TV mounted on the wall remains firmly in place, and all of Paula's jewellery – emerald rings and pearl necklaces – lay safely unlocked in a box on a chest of drawers.

Edwin and Paula tell Abbott they believed they were going crazy when they noticed a toothbrush, a spare tube of toothpaste, and one of their Egyptian cotton towels were missing when they returned home from visiting their daughter. Then, Ed went to store items in the hall cupboard and realised his favourite green jacket wasn't hanging in its usual position. That led to the discovery of a missing remote control and a call to the police station.

Abbott looks around the clean, white bathroom which also shows no signs of burglary. The couple tell him that no drawers were left open; not a single dust mite was disturbed.

"It's got to be someone experienced." Paula nods as they navigate through the family home.

He is shown the upturned rock at the stoop of the front door and the empty plot where the spare key should be. He is then taken back into the living room, where Edwin and Paula point to the spot where the remote control once sat. He jots down the details in a pocket-sized notepad. Outside, a neighbour reverses down their driveway, arm extended out the window, waving to children calling goodbye.

Further along the street, a young woman walks a large dog, tongue out and hanging, while a contractor mows the berms at the front of an old man's ageing home.

"And no one saw anything?"

Paula rolls her eyes, as if it is a stupid question. She's waiting for him to call in back-up, to kick them out of the house and make it a crime scene. Instead, he does something much different. He closes his notepad.

"I don't think you need to worry too much, Mrs Greene," he says.

"Don't worry too much? I am sick with worry! Someone has hurt my son and now they are coming into our home to taunt us! It has to be connected."

Abbott stands up straight and clicks his teeth. Nick Greene has been missing now for a month, disappeared off the face of the earth. Walked off his med school campus with a backpack, never to be heard from again. Grief-stricken Paula had pleaded with the police to treat her only son's disappearance as a homicide, but after canvassing the campus, rivers, ravines, streets, empty buildings and abandoned houses, there seemed no reason to do so. And yet, Paula's steely determination and deafening influence has convinced the residents of Quince that danger has befallen her young son, and the police have not the consideration or the skill to deal with it.

"They stole a toothbrush," Abbott says, matter-of-factly. "A remote control. They ate food from your fridge. It was likely a homeless person making use of your absence."

Paula's mouth hangs open.

"I'll keep an eye out for the missing items but, in the meantime, my recommendation would be to choose a new spot for the spare key."

Abbott leaves the couple standing bewildered in the kitchen. He knows Paula's face will be red with rage, her eyes throwing daggers into his back, yet his smile is tight, like he's trying to hide it. The pit of his stomach, where earlier there was unease, now stirs with excitement. Every step around the house solidified his conclusion, every minute confirmed his need to press on.

He'll tell the Greenes. Soon. Not quite yet. For now, he'll let them think a homeless person is out somewhere in Quince wearing Edwin's dated green bomber jacket, and that it wasn't their son who crept into Number 24 in the still of the night.

3

Nick has never liked Quince. The fruit, good, the town, not so much. It's as if it is unripe at all times, like someone didn't follow the recipe right. Everything just tastes a little… backwards.

In the town, they plant trees and expand their forests only to use them to build houses in other regions. They erect sporting arenas with grandstands that dwarf neighbouring suburbs but are only ever half-full with screaming fans. They make their students, who spend their days cramming at the purpose-built 1970s community medical school, feel so neglected that they look for jobs elsewhere. Quince is on the edge of nowhere, too, and the hills surrounding it are sharp as if to say: Keep Out.

The name came from the fruit's popularity in the town's glory days. There were quince fairs, quince cooking competitions, ornamental quince displays. There were so many quince trees about the place that market stallholders wouldn't get anything over loose change for a bag. Mums and dads would send kids to school with quince in their lunchboxes, and at barbecues or dinner parties, there would always be a bright, stinky cheese board and a big dollop of quince paste on the side.

Then, like all good things, the famed quince harvest

came to an end, as if all the trees, after years of providing golden-yellow orbs for the thankless community, went into retirement. Autumn came and went with barely any produce and eventually, the fruit became so rare that children would scurry along the garden floor trying to find one that had dropped to the ground in secret; a long-winded game that was never worth the effort.

The fruit now only resides in the quiet back gardens of elderly ladies, who continue to make jams and pastes from its flesh, and like an underground crime ring, they always keep the hoard to themselves.

Nick thinks it's a fitting result for the town that has never felt like the perfect fit. He's always been an outsider looking in. It's not for lack of trying though. He's tried tirelessly to warm up to the town.

He struggles to sleep through the birdsong which plays the loudest at the crack of dawn and wakes early on the 32nd day of his disappearance, staring up at the canvas and recounting the night's dreams. He feels no rush to start the day and instead thinks of things he hasn't thought of in years: the itch of stinging nettle on his thigh as he clambered across to his neighbour's yard; the midnight drive to get ice cream and the streetlights rushing past the car window like streaks; the skeletons of cicadas collected and cared for.

There is a gust of wind and the more delicate trees sway like a boat in rough waters, their leaves a cabasa under the excited hands of a child. The canvas above his head flaps harshly and Nick, though his body begs for further rest, rolls out of bed.

*

The trout stay hidden or perhaps have become wise to his impending arrival, and as he walks down the river's edge, bobbing his rod and pirouetting his fly, the sun burns away nimble clouds to provide much-needed warmth. The water flows contently, down dips and over slick rocks, and Nick joins it on its journey.

He barely had an affiliation with fishing as a child, had no experiences of casting a line or baiting a hook. There was never any banter shared over a packed lunch of sandwiches and chips, or dedicated performances of strength as man heaved back and forward in his battle with fish. He had no knowledge of currents and climates, how to navigate with the stars or make a compass out of cardboard, but still, he was curious about the outdoors. To him, it was a treasure map, a list of endless possibilities. Outside, away from the trimmed lawn and front stoop of suburbia, he felt like anything could happen.

Nick shocks the water when his feet slide off the bank and into its path. He's walked a fair distance, and the opposite side of the river presents a fresh scene: bright ferns and peculiar, looping trees; moss and boulders with what look like eyes and bulbous noses carved into them.

There's a sudden pull on his line and the culprit below the surface isn't messing around. It's feisty, and Nick's arm is yanked and dragged until he stands stiff, feet extended and knees bent, ready to take on the challenge. He's still a rusty angler, but a success compared to his first days hiding in the forest park, where hooks weren't properly attached and attempts were abandoned too quickly. He's learned that without patience, he'll be going without food.

The trout twists underwater and as Nick reels it in, its

body skims the surface. Desperate not to lose his catch, he winds it up in smooth, rhythmic motions, and the trout, though its will to live is strong, is dragged to the water's edge. He reaches into his backpack and pulls out his reliable fish knife, ending the trout's misery with one deep cut behind the eye. He stays crouched as he carves away the outer layer, exposing the fresh pink fillets that he'll cook on his return to camp.

Unashamedly pleased with himself, Nick stores the fish away and begins to reset. He casts his line and continues north, away from his tent and familiar territory. As the trees rustle behind him and the water runs at a gentle speed, he feels the peace he longed for. He knows now that he has made the right decision. That despite the unforgiving nights of damp socks and torturous winds, his escape into nature was the only logical choice.

He makes it to a bend in the river, a crescent moon to those above, and it is here where another fish catches itself on his lure. A tug of war ensues, and this trout proves itself to be a formidable contender. Nick bites his lip, grips the rod until his knuckles turn white, and leans back towards the shore. His line snaps, a bungee cord breaking with the tension, and Nick is launched backwards onto the Tetris of rocks.

All is quiet in the water; the action of the battle has disappeared. Nick looks to his rod, lying sadly in front of him, and to the river, half-expecting to see the trout, fly still in its mouth, giving him the middle finger on his fin. He holds up his rod to inspect the damage; the line has been torn and the lure lost. The nylon hangs like a limp strand of hair and, defeated, he rests his head in his hands. He scoops up a handful of fresh water and uses it to cleanse his face and neck. Choosing to leave his failure behind him, Nick recollects himself and begins the long walk back to camp.

He arrives at the site with an inkling that the time has crept into early afternoon, the noises from his stomach the most obvious indication. When he reaches the top of the slope, he is out of breath and doubles over with his dry hands clutching his knees. He rests in that position until he senses he is not alone.

Impatient feet move in the grass ahead of him, pushing aside loose stones, and there's a sound that resembles a grunt, a clearing of a throat, and the hairs on the back of Nick's neck stand erect.

Sitting on a rock on the other side of the camp is a stranger wearing a heavy blue bush shirt and pants that are tucked into gumboots. A cigarette is perched in his mouth and he sucks on its tip, his lips resembling the trout's when it took its last breaths.

The stranger sits in an accusatory position, knuckles clenched and body hunched. Smoke rising, vanishing. Nick's eyes widen, his saliva runs dry. The man isn't speaking but he's staring across at Nick with an odd smirk. Nick takes a step forward and the dead leaves crunch underfoot.

"I knew there was somebody camping out here," the stranger says, smacking his lips together.

It isn't a question, and so Nick chooses not to answer. Instead, he edges forward more cautiously until he reaches his faded yellow tent, still a safe distance away from the tattered, smirking stranger. He notices a fishing pole, sturdy, trust-worthy, laying at the man's side.

"Are you the one that's been dumping the trout up and down the river, too?"

Nick frowns, and for a moment, he forgets he's living in the depths of the bush, instead envisions he's back home in his mother's living room, being scolded for dragging mud onto the carpet.

He could never lie that well, even then. "I beg your pardon?" he says.

The stranger puts his cigarette out against the rock he's sitting on and stands to his feet, his weary knees wobbling slightly as he does so. He reminds Nick of an old school caretaker, rough around the edges and towering over children as he hands back balls recklessly thrown on the roof.

"Look, I'm not playing, kid," he says.

Nick feels young again but he is determined not to be unmatched by the burly stranger. "I'm not playing either. I may have caught a fish here or there, but I haven't been dumping them."

The stranger is unconvinced and Nick doesn't blame him. There are beheaded trout carcasses scattered along the river's edge, and his fishing pole remains firmly in his hand. Panicked, he peers into the bushes for the signs of a police uniform, the barrel of a gun, the foghorn to yell: 'We got him, boys'.

As he darts his eyes through the trees, the stranger watches him, picking up on his paranoia. He turns around to look through the dense bush, raising his eyebrows towards Nick when he's reassured they are alone.

"Why are you so worried? I'm not gonna hurt you," he says, and though it is a positive affirmation, Nick only becomes more tense. "I just need you to pack up your things and clear out of here."

He shakes his head. "I can't do that."

"You ain't allowed to be camping here, so it's either you leave, or I call the ranger."

Nick doesn't fear the aforementioned ranger, the one in beige who pulls up to the park's entrance in a buggy, swallows coffee from a Thermos, and departs without getting dew on the soles of his boots, but he can feel the stranger quickly becoming an enemy. For the first time in four weeks, he can sense his capture is imminent. He scoffs.

While his jaunts to town certainly put him in the line of fire, the high trout season has long passed, and Nick never considered a possessive fisherman to be his undoing. Still, he raises his hands in a peace-keeping position, and though he has no intention of leaving for long, he'll humour the stranger and return when darkness does its duty.

"Alright, you win, I'll leave," he says. "I'll pack up my things, then leave."

"I'll wait."

"Suit yourself."

The man's smirk unnerves Nick and he's wary of turning his back on him. He walks back and forth over the logs in the fire pit to collect his sad collection of rusted cutlery, knives, and lures.

The men keep watch of one another as the stranger returns to his perch on the rock, his arms folded. Nick's hands are shaking as he tosses his life into his backpack for the second time.

"I've got to pull the tent down now," he says aloud.

"I'm in no hurry," the man answers back. Then, he says, startled: "Hold on a minute".

The angler rises slowly from his stoop. His mouth is gaping open and his eyes are dark and large like a Labrador's. He takes a few heavy steps towards the fire pit, his hands playing with the greying spikes on his chin. It seems as if there's something he wants to say but he just can't get it out.

Nick remains frozen in a crouched position, half of his body inside his tent, half uncomfortably out. He turns around when the silence becomes too suspenseful, pushing his right foot back to join his left.

"I've seen you somewhere before." The stranger has his arm extended, like a blind man reaching out for security, his index finger thrusting in the empty air between them. "You're the kid from the news."

The wind is knocked out of Nick, and he grabs the side of the tent to steady himself. He tries to retain a smile as he peers up to the angler, whose finger is now shaking.

"It is you, isn't it?" The man's voice is quivering; there's a lump in his throat that hasn't dissolved.

"Calm down," Nick tells him, rising slowly, palms outstretched.

With the fisherman's realisation, there comes a shift in power. While his body seems to morph into that of a vulnerable animal, Nick transforms from easy prey to apex predator. There's no point in denying the accusation; the angler has already made up his mind that this is, in fact, the strange face he's been seeing on the evening news before the announcer shifts across to the weather forecast. It is the same face that has been printed in desaturated colour in the local paper. This is the man they've been looking for.

The man in question watches as the fisherman's hand slides gingerly behind his back, his palms dusting the checked print of his bush shirt. Nick's body pricks with heat and his shoulders tense as he follows the stranger's hand as it disappears into a back pocket, and he suddenly recalls the reliable, hard-working fish knife that is packed away in his bag, lying just without reach on the forest floor.

Matching the angler's speed, Nick begins to lower himself back down to the ground, peering out the corner of his eyes and calculating how fast he could move if he had to save himself. But then the stranger's hand reappears not with a Glock or a pocketknife, but with a silver cell phone clutched in his sweaty palm, a weapon more prolonged, more torturous, perhaps, than a bullet to the chest.

"They think you're missing," the stranger says, shaking the phone in the air between them. "They've been looking for you."

Nick sighs. Among all of the confusion and concern rushing through his head, there is also anger. He had given them every opportunity to find him; he paraded in front of them like a man begging for capture. Still, he went unnoticed. Below the forest park, under the ever-constant mist that surrounded Quince, life moved on and eyes stayed closed.

"It's complicated."

"You're a missing person. They think you're dead."

Nick nods now, would be grateful for the angler's company if he wasn't trying to accost him. "I know," he says under his breath.

The man looks straight at him. His Adam's apple bobs as he gulps. "I'm afraid you've left me no choice." He holds up the silver phone and matches Nick's steps when he walks two feet to the left; they both leave footprints on the ground below.

"Please don't do that," Nick pleads, and he lunges towards the angler, extending his arm in an effort to grab the phone.

The stranger pushes him away and successfully dials the digits. Adrenaline courses through Nick's body and his heart beats so rapidly against his chest it starts to hurt. His extremities tingle as the angler lifts the phone to his ear. He doesn't want it to be over.

Nick, not knowing what else to do, returns to the front of his tent and dives for his backpack. He forces his hand inside to retrieve the fish knife, slicing his thumb in the process. He pulls it out and holds it proud and the stranger freezes where he stands. The ringing of the call reverberates around the site. A drop of blood falls silently to the forest floor.

The angler removes the phone from his ear, holding his left hand outstretched. "Easy," he says.

"Hang up the phone."

Nick is not a threatening person, hasn't been, until this moment. The sheer supremacy he has over the stranger makes him feel ill. He holds the knife outright but his hand and insides are shaking. He's not willing to think about the repercussions, he pushes them to the back of his mind, because for now, he needs to deal with what's in front of him: a fisherman and a threat.

"Hang up the phone," he says again.

"Okay. Alright. It's done." The angler puts the phone back into his pocket and begins to retreat towards the fire pit. "I'm sorry I bothered you. I'll, uh, I'll leave."

Nick loosens his grip on the knife as his arm hangs weakly at his side. It feels better this way. He rubs at his brow with the back of his hand and the old fisherman seems to relax, too. Then there's another voice joining them in the forest park and it reignites all fear and tension.

"Hello? Hello?" A female voice tries to escape the fabric

ensconcing the fisherman. "Are you there?"

The calm that was briefly shared by the two men quickly disperses as the stranger reaches for the phone and returns it to his ear. As he begins to speak, the two men tousle and Nick makes another attempt to retrieve the phone. He pushes at the man's right shoulder, but the fisherman, after years of working outdoors, is much stronger and fends him off.

The strangers clash, their angry grunts disturbing the day's ambience. The pigeons that usually survey the forest's scenic dusk from the trees above Nick's head have chosen another spot to bask. The wild rabbits that use the dust puddles to bathe in stay hidden under their burrows.

Nick can still feel his fingers around the handle of the knife; he's holding it so tightly it's as if it's bonding to his skin. He nudges the angler with his shoulder and raises the weapon, but then falters. Nick, who isn't strong but faces the risk of losing everything, instead pushes at the man with both hands and a desperate surge of energy.

The man looks undeterred to begin with and opens his mouth to speak to the woman on the other end of the phone, but he stumbles on his two feet and the fire pit is behind him. One foot rises, then the other, and the man falls so disgracefully, yet so quickly, that Nick doesn't have time to react. His back end lands first onto the forest floor and the earth shudders around him. His head is propelled backwards and it hits a rock with a crunch.

The stranger comes to rest underneath the sharp boulder he was sitting on minutes earlier, his snuffed out cigarette lying a mere inch away.

4

Nick hunches over, panting.

His breath is sharp and ragged and unattractive. His body is hot and sweat sticks to the material of the thermals he's wearing underneath his father's coat. His heart pumps furiously and the emphatic noise ringing in his ears hinders any clear and concise thoughts coming through. One thing is for certain, however: he's alone once again.

He looks at the stranger, lying still with his head hanging to the side. There's a splattering of blood on the rock's sharpest curve and some underneath the angler's head. Nick hovers his hand over the man's mouth but feels no breath. He struggles to find a pulse in his neck and jumps back with a start.

The phone has fallen next to the fire pit and its screen is still bright, the call still connected. Nick picks it up and, with a punch of his thumb, disconnects it. He throws it back to the floor and moves to sit at the fire's edge, its logs spread around the camp like rubble.

The birds restart their chattering: loud, judgemental squawks with a few sympathetic chirps scattered throughout. Nick digs his feet into the soft soil and the soles of his hiking boots leave a jagged indent. He leans forward, a small twig in hand, and traces the lines. He does this for what feels like an age, waiting until he's prepared for what comes next. The clouds above his head move in a time-lapse and the wind picks up, then dies down, and the marks of his boots slowly disappear, their existence overwritten by dirt.

Nick looks around his campsite. The grass in some places has died from his thoroughfare; two towels hang from guide ropes. His iPod, which ran out of battery on the third day, sits abandoned beneath a shrub, headphones lying like noodles. In the time it's taken the sun to sink further west, he's come to the decision that he'll have to depart the forest. He hadn't planned to stay in the park forever, just until he found his feet, just until he was forgotten. Now, all signs point to the exit, even the fisherman, lying by the fire pit like a felled tree. Nick knows it's time to go.

He sighs and dusts his hands off on his knees, gazing towards the angler once more. He is a large man, over six feet and wide, so being taken down by a sharp but slight forest rock is a sinister twist of fate. His feet are splayed out like a penguin's, and in a way, he doesn't look dead, just sleeping, and for that, Nick is thankful.

"I'm sorry," he whispers.

The trees jangle like bracelets on a thin wrist, pointing towards the exit of the park and ushering Nick on his way. He should listen, but he stays standing over the fisherman, his head tilted. Then, as all the moments of the early afternoon flood his mind like a monsoon, his insides flop, his stomach heaves, and over in the bush, Nick rids himself of white flesh, a potent reminder of last night's ill-fated catch.

He collected his things in too much of a hurry, he knows that now. His mind's eye darts around his campsite, pausing at items he forgot to pick up – a pair of shoes he left out in the sun to dry, the pillow from his parent's house – but it's too late, there's no going back. Like a cartoon character who leaves behind a trail of dust at the end of a sequence, so too does Nick as he darts down the mountainside.

The hill is steep and he gains speed a bit too quickly. At the end of the dip, the only way to stop himself is by crashing into an unforgiving pine. He catches the tree with his hands and they scratch along the bark, but his head moves too slow and it hits the centre of the trunk. His nose pulses and pours out blood, and Nick wipes away the droplets on the sleeve of his father's coat. Already, it has seen so much. It was taken from its sheltered home in the hallway cupboard and was forced to witness what no coat should have to; a mistake no man should have had to make.

Nick thinks on this for a moment. An accident, that's what it was. There was no motive behind the angler's demise, no intention to snuff out a life. People will understand that, he thinks, and Nick makes a hasty decision about where to head next.

He arrives at the park's crossroads, where around the bend begins the tunnel. There are no scuffed tracks along the gravel, no remains of litter caught among the ferns. There is no noise bar the sound of wind coursing through leaves, a soft sort of quiet, and Nick's jagged movements destroy the peace. He composes himself here, cleaning up his bloodied nose and readjusting the straps on his rucksack. He holds onto it tightly and trudges along the path. The afternoon is cool, but Nick can't feel its harsh temperature underneath his layers, where, at the very bottom, his heart beats like a steel drum.

He makes it to the park's entrance in good time. Up ahead, there's the council ranger picking up an empty bag of chips, and when he turns to discard it into the rubbish bin, Nick makes a right and remains to be seen. He lifts his body over a short, stone wall which separates the park from the road, and when he lands on the other side, he lets out a sigh, feeling far enough removed from the angler and all that came with him.

People begin to appear as he edges closer towards the centre of town. Bus drivers honk their horns and wave as they pass one another, and Nick jumps with the noise. He's concerned about how he must look, red-faced and flustered, but his emergence is much the same as yesterday's: no one provides him with much notice.

He walks down a back alley that has been painted in vibrant hues of yellow and pink. It's a route he used to take almost daily and one that leads him out onto a cluster of hire shops, cheap bakeries, and uninviting daycare centres. One more street and he's where he needs to be.

*

The Quince Police Station has one of those red and blue neon signs that you typically see outside corner stores that say 'Open'. It flashes in the dimming light of the afternoon.

The station is small and looks like an old villa in the middle of decrepit commercial buildings, blue trim around the windows and a plaque out the front in memory of fallen officers from the past. Its windows are reflective, and Nick watches himself walk up to the station doors. He grabs at the large silver handle and tugs, but the door doesn't open. To his right, there is an intercom on the wall which has a sticker that says: 'press for assistance outside opening hours'.

He stands back and stares at the flashing neon sign before catching another look at himself in the reflection. His feet had brought him here and he obeyed. He had been sure it was the right thing to do, to confess, but now he's not so convinced.

Turning himself in for the death of the fisherman would mean everything he's done has been for nothing. All the preparation wasted, his plans erased, and he doesn't know what's worse: accidentally felling a fisherman or faking his own disappearance. He doubts he can get away with either. He wonders if people really would understand that the fisherman's death was an accident; would they really believe that Nick meant no harm? Is it worth taking that risk?

He stares again at the intercom and at the sign displaying its bright lights. The angler has become an inconvenience, a casualty, but Nick begins to realise he's been provided with a new direction, not a noose.

He stumbles backwards. He watches the station doors, now nervous that they might open, an officer in blue stepping into the scene, but they don't, the doors stay shut. Nick turns with a start and doesn't look back.

5

There's a woman hollering outside the station, yelling at Rowan returning from yet another late-afternoon lunch, donut full of mock cream in his hand. Her feet move like jackhammers on the concrete pavement, her eyes like daggers in the officer's direction.

The station door is locked and she's been waiting outside for an hour under Quince's cool shadow. Her hair is tangled and her cheeks are red and, as she shouts, she stumbles on her words.

Abbott sits inside the station office. He can't decipher the woman's intolerable howls, and, at the moment, he cares not to. He's punching letters into a document on a desktop computer, his thick fingers hitting the keys one by one. His eyes forget to blink. A mug sits next to him and Abbott reaches for it, unaware that the black coffee that once swam inside had been finished off some time ago. He grunts.

He knows it's not a good look for the lock on the station door to be turned, but in Quince, no one is ever really surprised. Officers from neighbouring precincts call it The Backwater, a place where nothing really happens, and if there ever is a case smelly enough to rouse a tired cop from their haze, it's almost never resolved. Burglary victims never get their items returned, trespassers remain at large, and the kids vandalising the back walls of shops are never brought to justice. There just never seems to be much point.

It hasn't always been the case though, and the man sitting forsaken at his desk could attest to it. He has done his duty here for two decades, and started at a time when local cops were held in high regard. There were at least a dozen of them, and praise would flow when they prevented car chases and apprehended crooks, and people would weep on their shoulders after being delivered bad news. But over the years, young officers' dreams took them to bigger cities until only a handful remained, all the worn-out ones. And it was not as if crime came to a complete stop in Quince, it just took a lot for the police to care. Like fruit left to rot on the vine, they became the last ones to reach for.

There is a rush of breeze and then a bang as the station door opens and closes. The woman has made her way inside and Abbott can hear Rowan doing his best to assist her. He rests his head in his hands and lets out a sigh, sitting with his back to the door.

The station is small and cramped and the carpet is yellow. A malfunctioning printer beeps in the far left corner. A few empty desks lie in wait. Rowan enters and Abbott shuts down his computer.

"What is it now?"

"The woman out there says her husband hasn't come home from a fishing trip yesterday morning. Says he went out and never came back."

He clicks his teeth. "That's a classic excuse if I ever heard one."

"I know. She's filed a report. You want to read it?"

36

Rowan shuffles on the balls of his feet, and when he doesn't get a response from Abbott, he steps forward and puts the piece of paper on his desk anyway. "She's afraid that the guy who killed Nick Greene has now killed her husband."

Abbott lets out a snort. "Nobody killed Nick Greene."

"I know. That's what I told her."

He flicks through the handwritten report, though not with much interest. A large yawn shows off the loose skin on his neck. "You think he could have fallen in? Had a stroke or something?"

Rowan nods. "Seems possible."

"Probably the most likely," he says, but for a second, something lingers in the back of his mind – Edwin Greene's bomber jacket. Abbott shakes the vision away. "You deal with it. I have other things to do."

Rowan nods, commits to a silent departure, and spins on his heels. When he's back in the foyer, Abbott faces away, switching his old desktop computer back on. It lights up, then dims as time passes. He spends the day staring at a blank screen.

*

Later, in the station's small dining room, although not tempted by its smell, Abbott fills his mug at the coffee machine. As the dark liquid stumbles out, his eyes catch the headline of the day's newspaper. He blinks twice, hoping to see the words scramble and another, more flattering heading take its place.

'Quince Family Blasts Police Over Missing Son Case'.

Abbott clicks his teeth. He picks the paper up with his thumb and index finger, and as he reads, his tongue slips out of the corner of his mouth.

The parents of a missing man are 'disgusted' police aren't treating their son's disappearance as suspicious.

Edwin and Paula Greene spoke to the Star following reports their 23-year-old son, Nicolas, was in their Driscoll Street home as recently as two days ago.

Police were called to the property yesterday morning on suspicion of a break-in.

The Greenes had returned home from a weekend in Ormiston visiting their daughter to find items in their home missing. That same day, police issued a release stating the missing items included a toothbrush, towel, and remote control.

Nicolas Greene has been missing since May 5. He was last seen leaving his med school student housing around 4.30pm.

Police are still of the opinion Mr Greene has voluntarily disappeared.

"That is the most absurd thing I have ever heard in my life," Paula Greene, Nicolas's mother told the Star. "Nick would never do such a thing. He is a good boy with a lot to live for."

No offer of a reward for information has been made by the family.

Abbott throws the paper down, a recoil, a vampire stepping back from the sun with a hiss.

The Quince Star has become Paula's own personal soapbox, and he finds himself getting angry the editor didn't contact him first, ask for a comment. He'd have probably hung up the phone, told him to fuck off, but it would have been nice to be asked.

Paula's familiar story about her son being met with foul play has been growing a little tired, was pushed to the back pages in recent weeks, but now it's been given new life and seems to warrant a front-page lead. Startling, considering Abbott knows Nick is well and truly alive.

He remembers the day the report found its way to his desk. It was a rather cold morning for May. A low fog was trapped under the pointed hills around Quince and the station's overhead lighting buzzed amidst early silence. There was no note, no indication of what lay in store, just an inconspicuous Manila folder with a case number stamped in the top right corner. He remembers reaching into the file with a rough grasp, pulling the paper out like he was ripping off a bandage. He didn't expect much until he read the word: disappeared.

Missing person cases were a rarity in Quince, and because of who Nick Greene was – young, academic, seemingly happy – the report came with an extra layer of fear: how did it happen? Where has he gone? Its weight was dense. Nick didn't appear to be an average runaway; typically, those who fled their mundane lives were middle-aged and regretful. No, by all impressions, his story felt a little different.

Abbott sips at his hot coffee, gulps down the bitter taste, and revises his plan. As ill-thought-out as it is, his scheme consists of waiting for Nick to mess up, waiting for him to be caught on a store camera or identified by an eagle-eyed commuter. He envisions sitting at his desk like the big cheese as officers haul Nick Greene to the station by the nape of his neck. That can't be too far away from happening, he thinks, not too far away at all.

That night though, after Abbott plonks down in the centre of his old couch – a hand-me-down from a relative – with another cup of coffee cooling on an equally aged piece of furniture in front of him, the same ire that filled him upon reading Paula's babble emerges again, this time in thanks to the TV.

He's already drawn the curtains, he's already shut out the still-lively world outside, which is good, in a way, because no one can hear him groan.

A news bulletin begins and, after a quick minute, the screen switches away from a pretty presenter to Paula's focused face. A live feed. She's in a park, somewhere in Quince, mere kilometres away. She's clutching more missing persons posters in her hands and in the background, people are busy handing them out. The reporter at the scene, who likely lives out of town, asks Paula a question that Abbott doesn't quite hear. It's odd, watching the crowd. A wake for someone not yet dead.

"I am feeling a lot of things," Paula begins. "I am confused, I am angry, I am sad… but most of all, I miss my son."

"Is it true you last spoke to Nick on the morning of April 27?"

"Yes, that's correct, and when I spoke to him he was in high spirits. He did not sound like a boy planning on running away."

"If Nick is out there somewhere, is there anything you'd want to say to him?"

Paula takes a long breath. Her deep-set eyes and thin lips are both downturned, and she moves her head to stare directly down the lens of the camera. "Well, I'd say to him... Nick, come home, we miss you." Abbott notices how her voice comes out clear, her words crisp and stern like a mother disciplining a child. As if realising this, she speaks softer. "We love you."

The reporter starts to pull the microphone back but Paula snatches at it with both hands. The camera wobbles but regains steadiness and focuses again on her face.

"Now, to the person who has harmed my son, for I think that is what has really happened here... please turn yourself in. Give us closure," she says. "And to the Quince police, who have done nothing but mess around and push aside my son's case... shame on you!"

Abbott feels as if she is talking directly to him, eye to eye. Through the television set, he can feel her piercing gaze staring at him as he sits perched on the dusty couch cushions. He grabs the remote and hurriedly switches off the channel, throwing the control to the ground once the screen turns black. He reaches forward to take a sip of his drink; too hot. He clicks his teeth and waits. He taps his hands on his suit pants, listens to the hum of the fridge, leans forward to burn his lips on his mug once more, then stands.

His home is small but cosy and has everything Abbott needs: a quaint kitchen with enough cutlery and dishes for one; a single bathroom with a single set of towels; and a bedroom with a wardrobe full with only his clothes. There's a spare room, too, but behind the hardwood door it is full of curios and junk; items collected effortlessly through the years but not as easily discarded.

He moves to the kitchen and pulls out a leftover pasta dish to defrost in the microwave. He's never been a good cook, wasn't a skill he'd ever thought he'd need, but pasta dishes, or dishes he could easily make by throwing a handful of items in a saucepan, were enough to satiate what little appetite Abbott had.

When the beeping stops, he pulls the dish from the microwave and, with a fork, napkin, and his black coffee nicely cooled, settles back down on the couch for supper

6

Ironically, Nick is given keys to Number 24.

It could likely be the worst room on offer, but the rate is cheap and he is in no position to negotiate. He hardly looks at the manager as she hands him the keys, hardly makes conversation when she asks what brought him to Abercrombie. He tells her he's there for a wedding, the first thing that comes to his mind. She gushes at the thought.

The room is dark with very little natural light and he has to turn on every lamp to rifle through the notes from his rucksack. He's booked in here for a few nights, might stay a little longer, depending on his funds, depending on the aftermath.

He steps into the small shower and washes away all traces of forest, all dirt, all lingering blades of grass. He almost feels despair as he watches the particles float down the drain; they leave him so easily. There are dark rings underneath his eyes now and his lips are cracked. He runs his fingers across them and holds the bottom one between two fingers: a desperate cling onto reality. He lets them go with a snap. There's a dead fly, black and grey carcass, on the vanity.

He decides not to get dressed in the same clothes he left Quince in, and instead sits on the edge of his single bed with the short towel provided by the motel around his waist. He buries his head in his hands and, using the balls of his fingers, he massages deep into his skin. Though his surroundings are not the most calming – there's a couple in the room next door with raised voices – for the first time since he killed the fisherman, he starts to relax.

Nick caught the late-afternoon bus to Abercrombie, a city with the unfortunate feature of being close to Quince. There's only about 90 minutes separating the two towns, but they represent two different worlds and Nick found himself living in the wrong one. Because while Quince doesn't want to progress, Abercrombie dances into the present, and while one remains dull and grey, the other is enigmatic and vibrant. One is the perfect place to start a new life, and the other is where one could be left behind.

He watched as the bus ascended up and away from Quince. The town looked like shit from above, all brick and smoke and abandoned bush. He was born in its small hospital and he was expected to die in it too, but he was only studying medicine to cater to his parents' wishes, because truthfully, Nick was a lousy practitioner.

He completed minor surgeries like removing benign skin lesions and haemorrhoids well enough, and the patients would smile and say what a bright young man he was, but when it came to the real stuff, Nick couldn't keep down his lunch.

One summer, when he was shadowing the experienced doctors at Quince's community hospital, a man was rushed in with dripping flesh. It was hot that day, high-twenties, and the man had been tending to a barbecue. The contraption exploded and he was set alight. When Nick took one look at him, deep red with oozing, open sores, he knew. He knew he didn't have the stomach to help. Four years of theory, passed and wasted. Yet, Nick persevered until May.

The bus had its first stop at a town called East Chapel; nothing but an isolated school and old Presbyterian Church. Then it arrived at Albertan, another town surrounded in trees. With thick bush ideal to hide in, but with a small population that doesn't take well to strangers, Nick thought it best to persist on to Abercrombie, a city he's visited only twice before.

Its main street, in vast contrast to Quince, contains buskers and street performers and dog walkers, and the shops are livelier, with pop music blaring out from speakers and waiters and waitresses from ethnic restaurants dressed in flamboyant garb. Everyone greets one another with air kisses or coy looks, and as winter's early curfew covers the city in darkness, the city responds by turning on hanging lights and neon signs and tiki torches. It refuses to be put to bed.

Nick's first visit to the city had been with Victoria, but he didn't take a shine to it then. He felt the town was too gaudy, too rambunctious, but Victoria was infatuated. They walked arm in arm, peering through shop windows at jewellery with emerald pendants and leather bags with rhinestone clasps, and laughed at all the wacky and wonderful characters they passed.

Victoria had bought him a watch for his birthday, one of those classic chronographs with a stainless steel face, and Nick walked with his shirt sleeves rolled up, enjoying his reflection each time it came into view. He wasn't usually so ostentatious, and had actually rejected the watch at first, thinking it was too grand a gift, but it grew on him. He liked the way it made him feel, and liked the way *she* made him feel, like he was worth all the time and effort in the world.

That trip had been a good one for them, as a twosome. They stayed in a cheap motel in the city centre, one with walls so thin you could hear the sidewalk hollers and hallway ramblings, but they didn't care. Every time Victoria stirred, she reached over to run her palm across Nick's chest, breathing deeply and slipping back into the first stages of sleep. Nick stayed awake, knowing that he'd never tire of the closeness; never again would he want to wake up alone.

On the second night, they went for dinner at a converted church and sat out in its courtyard, the evening sun setting behind her supple shoulders. With a glass of merlot in her hand, Victoria blatantly blurted out that they didn't belong in Quince. They belonged here, among the bright lights and enigmatic personalities. She said they deserved to make up the moving parts of Abercrombie. She said she was too good for Quince, and so was he.

After arriving in the city, Nick ventured up and down its side streets, subconsciously retracing his steps. The only difference now was that he was alone. There was no Victoria tugging at his arm, no ear to whisper into, no watch on his wrist to help him feel smug. Instead he felt small, isolated, and the city still made him uneasy. He passed the motel they stayed at together, and he briefly stared up at its brick exterior, trying to pick out what room they were in. Deciding it'd be too painful to return, too pathetic to sleep in the same bed with nothing but empty sheets at his side, he pressed on.

He walked until he was away from the main drag and the music emanating from the restaurants was nothing but a murmur at the back of an eardrum. The weight of his rucksack was wearing on him, and when he stopped outside one motel, Sub Rosa, despite the litter stuffed in the curb and the blare of a police siren one street over, he decided it was as good a place as any to reside.

The couple on the other side of the wall sound as if they've made up now, and Nick worries he'll begin to hear other, more awkward, noises, and so reaches for the motel's remote control to flick on the news. He gets a fright, almost falls backwards on the bed, when he sees his mother's face fill the screen.

Paula is wearing a pin he knows she keeps locked away for special occasions, while his father, loitering in the background, wears the same suit-and-tie combination he wore to Mollie's graduation. The visual then briefly flicks to Victoria, who is dressed in yellow. It pains Nick to see her; there's a physical tug beneath his chest and he averts his eyes. But then foolishly, he misses her, and looks up to try and detect whether she misses him, too.

There's a public gathering in Quince's Jamboree Park, where the Scout Club sits on the edge. A few people have shown up, but Nick wonders if the majority is made up of lost troops and cubs, caught up in the fracas on their way to their weekly meet. There are a few faces Nick recognises though, his flatmates Lars and Fish (real name unknown), a couple of guys from his classes, even a boy Nick hardly knows whom he met on a work placement, all standing like dominos, anxious to hang around but hesitant to leave.

It embarrasses Nick, having an event like this on his behalf, and he can't help but smirk coyly. He tries to withdraw himself, to watch the news segment like an innocent bystander with the right amount of nosiness and

47

sympathy. It helps not to think that it's him they are searching for.

Paula takes up the shot again and he listens as his mother says she misses him, and, when she says she loves him, Nick grimaces. His heart twists into a knot and it's painful. As a child, he thought his mum was like all the rest; cut from the same cloth as all the other mothers, but he soon came to learn there was always something off, something unmaternal about the way she acted around him. She was… cordial, like she and Nick were nothing more than two work colleagues who got on most of the time but didn't particularly enjoy each other's company.

He started noticing it at about age 10, when Mollie, two years older, would skip through the door and ramble off the stories from her school day to eager ears. She'd get thrilled responses and additional questions, which she'd answer with enthusiastic glee. It seemed, by the time his parents were done listening, they couldn't tolerate any more and Nick, who waited patiently at the foot of his mother's chair, was given a tired flick of the wrist and was stepped over on Paula's way into the kitchen.

Thinking about it now, he likely never heard his mum say she loved him, not when getting tucked into bed, not after winning the 100-metre sprint on athletics day, and not when he was walking out the door, the contents of his bedroom packed into canvas bags, heading for his new home at his med school flat.

His father had much the same discontent.

So, upon hearing those words for the first time in at least 10 years, Nick feels fury rattle his bones. There is no longer time for embarrassment. In fact, he hopes the public gathering has cost Paula a fair bit of money, all those pamphlets and flyers and fake attempts at being the perfect family.

His palms are sweaty and he rubs them down on the towel. The camera switches away from his mother and pauses at Victoria again, as if the operator appreciates the look of a pretty girl whose face is forlorn with the thought of her missing boyfriend. Nick sits on the edge of the bed. He hopes she says something, anything, maybe even her own confession of love, but Victoria's lips stay sealed shut, her eyes looking into the distance behind the lens.

The bulletin ends and Nick sighs, switching off the set. How could things change so damn quickly? One fleeting moment of his life was made up of happiness and merlot-induced tipsiness, and the next was consumed with guilt and stained motel bed sheets.

There had been a point when he was so happy it hurt, and he sees now he had taken it for granted. If only he could relive those days when he didn't worry what his mother thought of him, and he could cruise around Abercrombie without a care in the world and a nice girl at his side.

Nick touches the back of his neck and realises he is dripping with sweat there, too. He discards the motel towel and steps lazily into his own clothes which make him feel dirty, like the shower was all for nothing. He opens the door to the world outside his matchbox room and is hit with a breeze more delicate than what he was used to in the park, but it does the job. He can feel the sweat slowly seep back into his skin. He stares out at his new change of scene: an empty, quiet car park now replacing the earthy canopy of green and brown, but he's pleased to see a midnight blue sky remains, identical to the one he's grown accustomed to.

He drags an old plastic chair from inside his room across

the car park, its legs rattling as they are pulled through the gravel. He stops and sits, leaning back ever so slightly so that his face is naturally pointing to the sky.

He never looked at the stars before he disappeared, saw them, but never really looked. It wasn't until his first night in the forest, when the wild wind tugged at his tent and he felt, for the first time, afraid, that he turned to the stars for comfort. He wrapped himself tighter in his sleeping bag and pulled the tent door open a crack so that the night sky shone through. As the wind brushed madly across his face, chilling the tip of his nose, the stars remained calm and steady up above.

He could tell winter was drawing near and he feared that he was no match to the elements. He wasn't strong enough, had been told that before, but in the forest park, there was no other option. Strong was what he needed to be.

The stars were constant throughout his tenure in the wood. He came up with his own constellations and found the brightest star that he'd stare at until his eyes glazed over, sometimes talking to it when boredom took hold. It seemed to blink back in response, communication across lightyears, and the simple belief made Nick feel like he was less alone.

He stares up at the night sky and tries to spot his old companion but sees only clones. All of the stars seem dimmer from Abercrombie, and he's forgotten where his constellations lie, so he lowers his eyes to the stretch of road in front of him. It is quiet in this part of the city, and if they find him here, he'd be at peace with that. He leans back further and rests his hands on his stomach. Yes, if they come now, that'd be best.

He decides then that he doesn't want the police to bother

the motel manager, demanding she divulge any information about her recently arrived guest. And, if they come now, there needn't be a commotion, no dreaded knock on the door of Number 24, no onlookers in cotton pyjamas standing around with mouths gaping open. He envisions the cops driving up the road slowly, red and blue lights flashing around Sub Rosa's parking lot. He imagines the door of the police car opening and the lead detective, Abbott, stepping out, a smile curled up at the corners like a cat who got the cream. There would be a crunching of gravel beneath his feet and he'd stride towards Nick, leisurely unwinding a set of handcuffs from the clip on his pants. Nick would sit there, the ruby glow of the motel's neon sign shining onto his face, then there'd be a pause, and Abbott would humour him with a minute or two before taking hold of the runaway and bringing him home.

There's a sudden crash and he jumps with a start, his foot slipping on the gravel and the chair launching him forward. To his left, by the motel's reception, is a figure standing at a vending machine. A can of Coke lies on the ground.

"Shit. Stupid thing."

Nick watches as the woman bends down to pick up the soft drink, loose hair falling forward over her face. When she stands, she looks at him, and Nick quickly turns away. When he gazes back, ever so gingerly, she is gone. He sighs and again leans back in his chair, neck craned, returning his view to the night sky.

"What are you doing out here?"

Nick collapses forward. He spins around to see the woman standing behind him, smirking, with unkempt eyebrows raised. Her long hair looks frayed at the ends and mascara has rubbed from her lashes onto the skin underneath her eyes. The slippers on her feet are dirty and discoloured. The can of Coke looks out of place in her hand, glossy and new.

Nick stammers a moment. "I'm getting some fresh air."

The woman lifts the drink to her lips and takes a swig. She nods her head slowly. "Sounds normal enough."

He looks away, back towards the road. He's mindful not to stare too long, drag out a conversation, or linger in a moment when another person is involved. He fears he'll slip up. The woman notices this and takes two steps away. Then, she pauses.

"I thought you might have been waiting for someone."

Nick sits stiff, the curve of the plastic chair poking into his back. He considers looking at her, seeing that smirk again, that wild mess of hair. He considers keeping the conversation going, to have banter with something that isn't a star. But he doesn't. He stares at the ground while the motel's neon sign buzzes, its red glow a ghoulish spotlight.

"No," he says, and the woman finally departs with an unsatisfied scoff. He looks up in time to see her close the door to the room next to his own.

An hour passes. There are no further interruptions. No police car, no cuffs, no long ride home to Quince. Nick has not only cooled down but is beginning to shiver. He solemnly trudges back to his motel room, dragging the chair behind him.

Before entering, he takes one last, long look at the parking lot and the navy blue sky above it. There's a star, brighter than the rest, moving at a great speed across the azure. Nick holds his breath. His long-awaited friend has arrived. Its presence again makes him feel a little less alone. But as the star gets closer, he starts to see the subtle blink of lights shine upon a moving silhouette and realises it's not a star, or a friend, after all.

1

Abbott sits in a poky café down Quince's main street. He likes it here because no one else does.

He has chosen a table by the window but the room is still too dark to see any of its uninviting features with clarity. He's alone, with only the distracted staff meandering to and from the storeroom, and he savours the seclusion. It gives him time to think.

Nick Greene's photo isn't in the paper today and, after last night's news segment, Abbott is a little relieved. Though he wants it in every newsprint, in every shop window, on billboards and pamphlets and posters, it is nice that Nick, for once, hasn't followed him here.

He tries to recall his life before Nick Greene but the memory is like a painting without colour. There are shapes and lines and shadows but nothing concrete, no image to grasp hold of. Each day as monotonous as the next, as if he slept through them all.

He sighs emphatically and slurps back his coffee. He ordered black but it arrived with the milk already poured.

He knows he doesn't have to be here, do any of this. Each night, he vows that the morning will see the end of his efforts, but then he wakes, from a nightmare or a memory, and he can't bring himself to let the case go.

Because when the Greenes filed the report, Abbott's curiosity was immediate, his interest was piqued, not for the horrors that could be waiting for him, but for its similarities to a case that fell on his desk years ago. It was a selfish interest, one that took hold like flames to kindling.

He shakes away the thought and instead projects the last known footage of Nick to the back of his mind. He wishes he could know what he was thinking when he walked out the tall gates of his school, for those closest to him didn't have the slightest clue to impart. As far as Abbott is aware, Nick attended a lecture, laughed with his classmates, and, when the whole world stopped watching, he vanished. His family's delay in filing the missing person's report didn't help the matter either, and there are now very few roads left for Abbott to take. He sits awake at night trolling through CCTV footage, rereading reports and drawing maps of likely routes and trails, and although he has searched every conceivable spot and Nick's body hasn't been found, the Greenes don't want to hear it.

"Why would my child run away?" Paula had asked him. "Look harder. You're not looking hard enough."

Abbott stares down at his watch. It's a quarter to 10, a time when most people head to the shops or a spin class, or pop to their neighbours for a cuppa. A time when even those hard at work still escape into the streets for fresh air. He sighs and makes a deal with himself. Forget the past. Forget Paula. Find Nick Greene – today.

*

Abbott leaves his car idling as he watches the couple depart, checking the inside of the letterbox for bank statements and home furnishing catalogues before they go. They fall into the front seats of their beige sedan and reverse down the driveway, their heads like figurines through the foggy windows. He waits another moment before unclipping his seatbelt, switching off the ignition, and letting out a great heave that carries him up to the front door of the weatherboard abode. He knocks twice.

Mollie looks surprised to see him. She tucks loose strands of long blonde hair behind her ears and stands defensive, clutching the door frame like a soldier wielding a shield.

"My parents aren't home," she says bluntly.

"I'm actually here to see you." Abbott stands on the edge of the doorframe, half inside, half out. He knows he could get turned away, could cop some abuse – wouldn't be the first time – but Mollie doesn't seem like that kind of girl. She hesitates and frowns with what Abbott suspects is fear, but lets him inside, nonetheless.

She directs him to the kitchen, though he knows his way around by now, and offers him a cup of tea. He'd rather not, but he accepts the drink anyway. "Shouldn't you be in Ormiston?" he asks.

"Oh." She flicks her hand in front of her face. "Mum and Dad are a little worried since the burglary. I'm going to stay here a while."

Abbott looks down at his tea and lets out a low hum. The sound comes out more sceptical than he intended.

"Is there something I can help you with?" she asks freely, though a little standoffish.

"Not particularly."

The young woman cocks her head, confused, but Abbott clicks his teeth and draws her back in.

"What was your relationship like with your brother? If you don't mind me asking."

For a moment, Mollie's face lights up with a tender smile, as if the question evokes some sort of memory; an impish summer playing backyard cricket and her brother mending her bloodied knee when she fell.

She leans on the kitchen counter. "It was good. We were close for brother and sister; we rarely fought."

"Did he talk to you about stuff?" Abbott asks, sipping his tea.

"Well, we talked about *stuff*. But he didn't really have any complications growing up. He was always the one looking out for me, even though I'm the oldest." Mollie rolls her eyes and again, Abbott can read more into these subtle gestures than she realises. With a glimpse, he sees an unassuming little brother, and with a sigh, a big sister with regrets.

He lets her rest inside her trance for a few seconds. Her eyes flicker when his voice picks up again. "What about your parents? Did he get along with them?"

"Oh, of course," she says. "We're just your standard, happy, normal family."

Abbott rests his mug on the countertop gently. On the fridge he sees a photo of the four of them, wholesome, just as she described. He moves towards it, lips puckered. The photo is being held up with a purple plastic fridge magnet, and Abbott lifts the image free from its clutches. The photo must be at least 10 years old. Inadvertently, his teeth click.

"I'm going to be honest with you, Mollie," he says. "That's what every family says after someone goes missing." He returns the photo to the fridge with a slap. It slides an inch down the stainless steel.

She folds her arms. "What do you want?" she asks, less free, more standoffish.

"I need to talk to you about your brother."

"I've already told you everything I know."

Abbott takes one last slurp of his tea and pushes the rest aside. "There's just one thing I need clarity on," he says clearly. "Just one thing."

"What is it?"

"You say your brother did not run away?"

She pauses. "Is that a question?"

"Is it?"

There's become a frosty tension around the kitchen island. Whatever cordial relationship there was left between the two, Abbott feels he has quickly erased, but the month has worn on and his patience is wearing thin like the stitching in his jacket.

Abbott knows it was Nick who stumbled into Driscoll Street in the early hours barely a week ago. Call it an inkling, a hunch, whatever, but the day he got the call about the break-in was the day Abbott knew wholeheartedly that Nick Greene wasn't dead.

Mollie's voice stammers. "I don't know what you're asking me."

The fridge hums and the clock ticks, but other than that the house is silent. Abbott prepares to soften the tone of his voice, like how a man does when coaxing a cat down a tree or encouraging his kids to get in the bath.

"Mollie, I think you know nothing happened to your brother. I think your mum knows that, too. Nick ran away, didn't he?"

Her face looks pained and Abbott knows he is getting through to her, but then she says: "You should go."

"I don't want to pressure you, Mollie," he lies, "but the longer your family puts this off, the longer you refuse to believe Nick ran away on his own accord, the worse it's going to be for you all."

His voice is hurried, he wants to get his point across before she kicks him out of the house. She's tugging at her hair and biting her lip.

"Nick ran away, didn't he?" he asks again. "Why?"

"I don't know," she says. "If he did, I don't know where he went."

"But he's your brother, Mollie. How could you not know?"

Abbott has already learned that Mollie hadn't spoken to her brother for almost four months at the time of his disappearance, but when pressed, she denied there was any malicious intent, they had just grown apart. He hopes that any guilt she's felt since Nick's departure overwhelms her, and that for once, big sister will come to the aid of little brother.

"Has he done something like this before?" he continues, walking around the kitchen counter so that he stands just a few feet away from her. "You have to tell me if he has."

The firstborn Greene child starts to cry, not heavy, ugly tears like the ones that come from her mother, but soft, delicate tears that just can't be held back any longer. "Yes," she whispers. "He's run away before."

Abbott slaps his hands together, and the sudden movement makes Mollie jump. He rebounds and comes back to her side with a desire to know more. "When? Why?" he questions impatiently.

"A few times as a kid and then once when he was in high school."

"Where did he go?"

"What?"

"Where did he go, Mollie? When he ran away, where did he go?"

She shakes her head. Tears fall. "I don't remember. I think, once, we found him at the school. The other time, I don't know. He was in a park somewhere?"

Abbott leans in closer; he grits his teeth. "What park?"

"I'm not sure. He was hiding out in the bush. I don't know where."

Abbott stands erect. His brain flicks through information like it's rifling through a file cabinet, documents flying until he grabs hold of the correct one. He turns sharply on his heels, leaves Mollie in the kitchen, and hastily departs.

*

The two men pull up into the forest car park, which, nearing dark, is close to abandoned. Abbott enlisted the help of Rowan and he'd searched the records for any mentions of Nick Greene, any mentions that he'd run away as a child. There was nothing.

"Weird," Rowan had said. "Who wouldn't call the police if they knew their son was missing?"

The slam of their doors echo up the mountainside. Rowan scans the skyline, daunted by the task ahead. "You really think he'll be here?"

"I'm not sure."

"And what will you do if he is?"

The men cross a large swing bridge that hangs over running water. It trickles past boulders and fallen trees.

"I'm not sure."

He makes a sharp right and descends the path but doesn't follow its route to the river's edge. He continues under the canopy of trees that rest softly among one another. Breeze brushes past them as if to drag them in the right direction, bringing with it smells of dew and pine. Eventually, the two men come to a clearing, and the smooth dirt path makes way for a rocky shoreline. They balance on top of boulders, edging closer to the water.

"Where are we going?" Rowan asks.

Abbott clicks his teeth.

They walk along the river's edge, peering into the water, a murky green colour with desaturated leaves floating on its surface. They poke their heads through gaps in the woods and navigate so far down the course of the river that they can no longer see the clearing where they entered. Rowan's boots are wet and his legs are tired. He suggests they turn back.

Abbott disregards this idea and bends over to collect the skeleton of a fish that ceased wriggling some time ago.

Following the hunch of his, he continues down the river, balancing on his two old, unreliable feet. Along the way he amasses more trout bodies, bones, and tails, knowing that the forest park isn't home to any animals, big or small, capable of leaving this odd, haphazard destruction. He scans his eyes across the bank, long grass sticking up tall in most places, bar one, as if a path had been cleared to make for an easier route from the water. With a heave, Abbott makes his way up.

He huffs his way through the dense bush, his heavy breath noticeable among the silence. Further along the short incline, a different odour climbs up his nostrils, not one of cedar or forest air, and not one of dead fish or animal droppings. It's largely unfamiliar but he has smelt it before.

It doesn't take long until he makes out objects beyond the low-hanging branches: the top of a tent, the remains of a fire. Officers don't carry guns in Quince but Abbott reaches for his holster like a bad habit; he clutches nothing but material. The smell is more enveloping at the top of the crest and his nose wrinkles.

"Nick Greene?" he calls.

Twigs snap under his feet as he moves slowly towards the centre of the camp. He can't make out any shadows in the tent so he walks cautiously around it with his back hunched.

"Whew! Something stinks up here!" Rowan reaches the site and waves his hand in front of his face, trying to brush away the stench. "What the hell is that?"

Abbott ignores him. "Nick Greene?" he calls again. "I only want to talk."

He clutches the material of the tent and pulls open the flap to see an empty interior. It looks as if it was abandoned in a hurry.

"Sir?" Rowan takes a step closer to his sergeant and Abbott stands up straight to look at him. Rowan is nodding towards a shape lying opposite the tent, a shape that, even in the dark, looks terrifying.

A man is lying on his back a few feet away. Flies have already found him. Rowan turns rigid and doesn't move but Abbott steps over the fire pit and leans down to the corpse. Peering to the side, he finds red marks like spilt sauce on the forest floor and on the rock the dead man lies under.

"What do you see?" Rowan calls from behind. "Is it Nick Greene?"

"No," he answers.

"How can you tell?"

Abbott steps over the fisherman and quickly inspects his surroundings: the burnt out logs splayed out around the makeshift fire, the fishing pole lying next to it. There are a few loose spoons thrown around.

"Because this man isn't 23," he calls to Rowan, who is standing back with careful earnest. After a moment, he hears a response: "Who the hell is he then?"

Abbott groans as he bends back down in front of the tent, his knees clicking under his weight. There are random items spewed everywhere: batteries, an upturned book with wrinkled spine, a blue sponge, toothbrush, broken matches, and a box of plasters. Then, in the far corner, his hand reaches out to grab something white, soft, still clean. A towel. Underneath it is a remote control. He clicks his teeth.

"What have you found?" Rowan calls.

Abbott holds the toothbrush in one hand and the remote in the other, bringing the objects to his eyes and twisting them in circles. He puts them down and instead picks up the book, reading the laminated sticker on its spine: Property of Quince School of Medicine, 424 Allen Street.

He smacks his lips and the book's cover. "Recognise this?" he asks.

Rowan takes a tentative step forward. His eyes squint to read the title. "*The Hidden Life of Trees*. Hey!"

"And what about this?"

"A toothbrush?"

"Not just any toothbrush," Abbott says sharply. There's a beat of elation in his chest, reaffirming an idea he had so hoped to be true. "This is the toothbrush stolen from Driscoll Street."

He waits for the officer to connect the dots and sighs when he's left waiting.

"This is Nick Greene's."

*

The next night, Rowan alerts Abbott to a piece in the paper. Third page, two columns, no image.

Police have released the name of the man found dead on June 7 in Quince Forest Park. He was 62-year-old Hugh Douglas Fir, of Quince.

Witnesses described the scene at the park as "chaotic" and said the man's body was escorted down an unmarked path on the park's eastern border. Officers from neighbouring precincts have been called in to help assess the scene.

"It's bizarre," local woman Margaret Wright said. "I was just walking through the park last week."

Police at the scene said they were pursuing a line of inquiry but would not comment on the matter further. They did, however, state they were looking at the case as a homicide.

"I just hope there's a resolution soon. The public is starting to worry," Ms Wright said. "These things don't happen here in Quince. For everyone's sake, I hope they catch the bastard who did this – and soon. It's keeping me awake."

Abbott slept soundly that night.

8

JUNE 9   DAY 36

Over the next few days, the Quince police department transforms from a barren land into a hive of activity. The officers in blue are the bees.

The coffee machine is pushed to its limit and continuously splutters out lukewarm cups of joe, and the printer in the corner has been fixed and now coughs out reams and reams of shiny paper.

There are cops lining every surface of the small room and Abbott doesn't know what half of them do. Some stand with their fingers behind their vests, pursing their lips and gazing up at the ceiling, while others wear suits and saunter through the building like 80s mobsters, complete with gall.

When Abbott alerted his wider colleagues to the fisherman's body – shaking fingers pressing the keys of his cell – they were all routed here. Like the main attraction at a carnival, the cops rushed into Quince with tickets in hand, all eager to hear about the fisherman; the first (alleged) murder in the town in more than ten years.

At first Abbott liked the fact his station was alive again. It reminded him of the days when he first started walking the beat, young, late-20s, good-looking. Everyone wanted to be a police officer then, and in the early 90s, Quince was the place to be. Over in the city, in Abercrombie, there had been a spate of attacks on authority, a bunch of insubordinates using their fists, feet, and teeth to fight back against arrest warrants and speeding tickets, but in Quince, it wasn't like that. It was an easy shift, colleagues were friends, and Abbott, who already stood at six feet, didn't feel so small back then.

Now, he walks through the station like he's shrunk. The voices are louder than his and the mug he favours has been swiped. There are discussions of half-baked hypotheses surrounding the fisherman's body and its connection to Nick Greene, the most outrageous being that Nick and Hugh Fir were involved in an organised crime ring and were slain by a member of their inner circle. Others enjoy insinuating that Hugh Fir and Nick Greene had planned to run away together but then the old man died and the kid had to think on his feet.

It's pathetic, so Abbott keeps to himself. He holds case files tighter to his chest and sits alone.

"Morning!" Rowan speaks in a little singsong, but his face doesn't look so cheery. He rubs the fringe above his eyes flat to his forehead and pokes his chapped lip out at the bottom like an upset child. He yawns a big bear yawn.

"You alright?"

"I'm fine," he says meekly, taking a step towards Abbott. "Just a little tired, is all."

"You didn't get much sleep?"

"Well, I fall asleep alright. It's in the middle when I wake up and stay up."

Rowan pulls out the chair from the desk adjacent to Abbott's and falls into its cushioned seat. Abbott, not realising his question would turn into a conversation, turns away but Rowan takes no notice and wriggles forward slightly, so that the two are crowded together like friends at a lunch table.

"It's the fisherman. I can't get him out of my mind," he says.

Abbott tries to shoo him away by explaining that it is perfectly normal to have trouble sleeping after stumbling across a dead body. He wouldn't be human if he didn't, he tells him. Rowan sighs and lifts his elbow onto Abbott's desk.

"It's just how he was found. I can't shake it," he says. "Did you hear Cole is looking into it as an accident? I mean, when I first saw the wife's report I thought, sure, an accident seems plausible, but now I'm not so convinced."

Abbott taps away at buttons on his computer, heavy fingers hitting keys to construct one line of babble.

"What do you reckon?" Rowan asks.

The detective, Cole, had arrived with one of the first squadrons and, after one look at the rural waste of space that was Quince, he came to the hasty conclusion that he would be calling the shots. He was the kind of man who could drink black coffee at midnight, who enjoyed using his dark eyebrows in the art of intimidation and, Abbott could tell, had a hidden penchant for classic rock music. He had a bumper sticker on his Commodore which said: Welcome to the Rat Race.

The first time Abbott met him, Cole didn't make a good impression. He marched over with a file in his hand and slapped it hard on Abbott's desk.

"So, Abbott, is it? You say this kid went missing a month ago? What makes you think he up and killed this man?"

The noise inside the small station was shrill as each cop

rattled off their list of achievements, like peacocks showing off their plumage, and Abbott had to try hard to keep his focus on Cole. He spotted a wedding ring on his finger.

"There were some items found with the fisherman that belonged to Greene."

"So?" Cole stood with legs spread. He took a slurp of coffee and flinched when it scalded his tongue. "What if this kid left his campsite weeks ago? The old man found it, tripped on his feet and fell on his ass? Accident. Case closed."

"That's one possibility, but…"

"Or what if Fir killed Greene?" Cole continued. "Why would Greene kill Fir? It sounds like Greene was a hard-working kid and this Fir guy was a bit of a nut."

"I have a hunch," Abbott said.

"Oh, a hunch? Why didn't you say so?" Cole laughed and looked around the station for added espousal. "I'm gonna go ahead and look into this Fir guy's background. For all we know, there's a dead Nick Greene lying somewhere in Quince."

Abbott tugs at a loose thread on his jacket. He's wearing it inside because the sun has moved into its late-afternoon position behind the clouds and the station has a chill. He disagrees with Cole, doesn't think it's as straight-forward as Fir clumsily falling over firewood. But then if it wasn't an accident, if Fir and Nick are connected, what is the link? Where does the trail end? The only thing a little curious, a little odd, is the fact the fisherman's wallet wasn't found with him, and the wife was sure he took it that morning.

Abbott tries to connect dots that aren't quite there. "What would you do?" he asks, leaning forward with his elbows on his knees.

Rowan stops looking around the precinct, stops biting his puckered lip. "What would I do when?"

"You're Nick Greene. A man is dead at your camp. What would you do?"

Rowan moves his mouth from side to side to display his thinking. He shrugs. "I dunno. I think I'd call the cops."

"But you can't," Abbott says. "You've faked your disappearance and there's got to be a reason for that. If you call in now, your cover is blown."

"Oh. Well, then I guess I'd leave a note."

"A note?"

"Yeah. It Was Not Me. Sorry," Rowan says, matter-of-factly, like transcribing a simple document. "Or – It Was Me. Sorry".

Abbott laughs a little. He didn't think of that.

In their small circle there's silence, yet around them, the officers are still jeering at one another and making unsophisticated jokes. Abbott continues to type nonsense on his computer, hoping his diversion from Rowan will be clue enough to leave him be, but he doesn't get the hint.

Instead, he says: "I guess I'd keep running."

"What do you mean?"

"He's already dug himself a pretty big hole. If there's already no way out, I guess I'd keep digging."

Abbott looks at his companion, wise beyond his years in an oblivious, absent-minded kind of way. Rowan sees the world a little differently than he does, a fresh pair of eyes and an unpolluted perspective. It's refreshing, like drinking a cold sip of water straight from the tap.

"That's a good point," Abbott admits. "Thanks."

He goes back to typing away babble on an otherwise empty document and eventually, Rowan stands to leave.

Before he departs, he lets out another loud yawn and stares down at Abbott with a careful curiosity.

"I've never seen a dead body before," he whispers. After a beat, there's a snigger. Rowan seems to recall the stench in the forest park that had him recoiling. He takes in a deep breath like he is breathing in fresh air for the first time since. "Have you seen a dead body before, sir?"

Abbott stops typing. He sighs. "Just once."

"What was it like?"

Abbott turns to Rowan, whose eyes are wide and whose mouth is curled into an inquisitive line. It's not a memory he draws upon often. With it comes a stomach ache. His belly flops just with the thought. He can't bring himself to mention it, not one fragment, not one shred, and thankfully, he doesn't have to.

"We need to have a little chat."

Cole has sauntered over to his side. He is half Abbott's age but has double the confidence, and Abbott surmises that maybe Cole hasn't had a set-back yet, one that breaks him down and makes him second-guess his career. It's bound to happen soon enough, he thinks.

"Sure," he says, though it comes out with a little chide.

Rowan hastily departs and Abbott lifts himself from his chair as the wheels squeak.

The men walk to the back of the station and into a small office, where Abbott is instructed to sit in a cold metal chair that he can feel pressing into his spine. His feet are crossed at the ankles and he holds his hands together in his lap. For a man about to be given the third degree, he is surprisingly calm.

Cole begins pacing the room in front of him. He is shaking his head in a way a father does towards a child and he's wearing a suit with bullseye cufflinks. He is part of the CIB in the busy precinct of Abercrombie, and Abbott can see how a large personality can secure even the most conceited of men a high rank.

"I understand you've been comfortable here," he begins. "Keeping an eye on things."

There's a pause, like he expects Abbott to say something. When he doesn't, he continues. "Must have been difficult for you after '97."

This time, Cole allows the room to stay silent. It's a boxy room full of junk and all of the crap stations like these tend to accumulate, not important enough for proper storage, yet not immaterial enough to discard. Cole weaves around the boxes, craning his ears to hear Abbott's stomach flip; straining his eyes to see the sweat on Abbott's neck start to fall.

It is the year from his memories, his nightmares, and Abbott feels like running back out to Rowan, grabbing him by the shoulders and confessing: *yes, I have seen a dead body and this is what it was like*. Instead, he's stuck reliving it with Cole, a man he's just met and already isn't fond of.

"Yeah… that kid was my friend," Cole says, crouching down so that his eyes line up with Abbott's. "It was because of him that I became a cop, you know, so I could do the job you were meant to do."

Abbott lifts himself from the chair, muttering curses under his breath. Cole, who prefers loud, vocal disputes, spins Abbott around by his jacket and looks him straight in the face.

"I think we've met before, actually. Yeah, I came into the station, wanted to offer my suggestions but… you weren't interested." Cole shrugs. "I guess I was only a kid back then."

The memory Abbott had buried away, the one he tries desperately to keep hidden, begins to break out of its once-impenetrable shell. He can hear the cracking. In the small room, there is nowhere to hide.

"I need to get back to work," he hisses.

"Ha!" Cole lets him reach the exit, but when Abbott's hand clutches the doorknob, he offers up one final statement. "You did good finding the fisherman, but there's another kid still out there. Are you gonna let this one down too?"

Abbott closes the door with a slam. A stacked box tips its contents onto the floor.

9

The rain hits hard on the motel's roof; heavy droplets that fall from the watering can in the sky and pool in Sub Rosa's parking lot. It is a night Nick is thankful to be spending out of the forest.

Yesterday, he wandered up to the motel's lobby, wrapping his father's thick green coat around him and hunching into himself. It's an old coat, one he saw his dad wear in pictures from the 80s, with large shoulders and deep pockets. He hides loose coins and notes down in the compartments within the material; impenetrable by pickpockets and no-gooders.

"How're you doing, honey?" the motel manager asked when he sauntered into the lobby, shaking raindrops off himself. "You checking out?"

"Actually, I'm wondering if I could stay a few more nights."

The manager smiled tightly. Nick had already come in to extend his stay once before and she seemed happy to extend it again.

"Sure you can, sweetie. What room are you in?"

"Number 24."

She nodded and tapped delicately on the motel's computer keyboard, humming a tune and brushing her

73

short, dark curls away from the frame of her face.

She wasn't what Nick was expecting when he arrived at Sub Rosa. He was anticipating an ill-tempered man with a moustache who spent his days and nights glued to the TV in the back room, who asked nosy questions and complained about the dust from the gravel outside. Nora, in stark contrast, remembered her tenants' names and helped them drag luggage across the parking lot. She tended to broken appliances and unwelcome insects and, when she was nestled inside her small lobby, she listened to golden oldies radio and wrote down the titles of songs she enjoyed.

"Did you want to stay another three nights?" she asked him. "That'll be 'til the 13th."

"Sure."

The old motel was cosier with bad weather but the darkness did it no favours. The light dangling from the ceiling was flickering, casting shadows like eerie portraits on the foyer's red wallpaper, and in the distance, Nick could hear droplets hitting a plastic bucket. There were flyers on a pin board by the window: spa retreats, helicopter excursions, a guide to Abercrombie's ultimate food destinations, a missing parakeet but no missing men or dead anglers. He was grateful that Sub Rosa appeared to have no fascination for the world outside the city.

"Do you want me to arrange a day out for you on a high ropes course?" Nora asked, surveying the brochure Nick held in his hand.

"In this weather?" He laughed. "I'd be a dead man."

He walked back over to the counter and pulled out a small amount of cash from his coat pocket.

"That's all sorted for you, sweetie," Nora said. "Check

out's still at 10 o'clock, but let me know if you need a later one, alright honey?"

Nick nodded and prepared to head out into the thickening rain.

"Oh, hey," she called to him, leaning forward across the counter inquisitively. "How was the wedding?"

"Huh?"

"The wedding you came here for?"

Nick looked at her curiously, just as she did to him. There was an uncomfortably long silence before he remembered the supposed reason he arrived in Abercrombie and let out a shameless snigger.

"Oh, that wedding. They called it off."

He walked out the door into the rain, while behind him, Nora was noticeably deflated, saddened by the news.

*

He leans back on the motel bedspread, raising his arms above his head and staring up at the ceiling, for the first time noticing the fly shit spots and leak stains.

The previous days have been damp and miserable, and there have been fewer comings and goings from the motel. Still, every car that skids through the surface water of the parking lot has Nick, a hermit in Number 24, preparing himself for questioning.

As a child, he always worried about getting caught: getting caught with the wrapper of the chocolate bar he bought from the school tuckshop still in his lunchbox; getting caught coming home in the early hours of the morning with Mollie, comatose and stinking of vodka, tucked under his arm; getting caught testing the boundaries, seeing how far he could go before people started to notice his absence.

Each time he ran off, his jaunts took him a little further and his hiding places became more concealed. He was frightened at first, but his feet always knew where to take him.

The first time, he walked to the bottom of Driscoll Street and sat underneath the shade of a transformer box. He watched his mother run past him twice before she spotted him.

The second time, he hid at school, heading out early Saturday morning. He wasn't found until later that night by his dad, who didn't say a word as he dragged him back home.

The third time, Nick packed a bag and was gone for two days. He was found when Paula's friend, who worked at the local steakhouse, called her, telling her that her son had just walked in and ordered a 200-gram eye fillet, duck fat chips and a baked potato, paying for it with loose change.

The last time he ran away, as a 15-year-old, he paid a couple of bucks for the bus to take him to the forest park which, as a scrawny kid, epitomised the ultimate in runaway adventures.

It was summer and he hid in plain sight, barely hiding at all. He pitched a small tent in the same area where the tourists liked to stay. He smiled and waved at the people passing by, he used the public restrooms, and ate nothing but junk food for four days.

Nick remembers sitting at the water's edge, the smile that had been stuck on his face since he departed suddenly morphing into a thin line. Where were his parents? Where were the police? He waited and he waited but no one ever showed up.

It was by chance that he was found. A mate of his, Gary Gray, had been out fishing with his grandpa and spotted Nick skimming stones. Nick lied and said he was out camping with his dad, but Gary's grandpa, suspicious of the boy's skittish behaviour, called the Greenes.

When sitting in the back seat of his parents' car, Mollie leaned over to him and warned him not to go missing again.

"You'll be dead next time," she whispered.

Only later did Nick learn his parents hadn't called the police, hadn't even started searching. For four nights they had eaten dinner with only three plates at the table.

There is a sudden knock on the door and Nick springs upwards, the speed of which he does so making him feel dizzy. He sits still, quiet, his eyes on the door. He waits for the footsteps to move on but the person outside knocks again. The rain continues to hit the roof of Sub Rosa.

Nick rolls off the bed, landing on his knees on the carpet below. He stays on the floor, curled up in a balled position, biting his lip. He stares at the clock at the side of his bed; it's a quarter to 10. It must be the cops.

"Dude, I know you're in there, open the door," the voice calls from outside.

Nick raises his ear to the sky like a pup listening to distant howls. Not the typical call for an officer about to bust an angler-killer.

"Who is it?" he cries back.

"Marina. I'm from the room next door."

Nick hesitantly crawls across the carpet, the frayed nylon itching his skin. When he reaches the door, he stares up at it, the rusted brass handle gleaming back down at him. He rises and tries on a few nonchalant poses in the mirror:

hands shoved into pockets, lips slightly pursed. He doesn't want to open the door but he's curious, so he does.

"What's up?"

Outside is the woman who approached him that night under the stars. There's no can of Coke in her hand tonight, but her hair, still a mess, gives her away. She is standing with arms folded on the patio, wearing denim shorts despite the cold. On her feet are her faded slippers. She looks surprised by Nick's awkward manner and raises her eyebrows, smirks. "You wanna go get a drink?"

Nick's mouth falls out of its casually puckered position. The request is unusual in normal circumstances, but tonight it is nothing short of crazy. He turns to look at the clock, then back up at the dark clouds filled with rain.

"Now? In this?" he stammers.

The woman shrugs and smiles gently. "I've been stuck inside for two days," she says. "And besides, it's only rain."

Nick peers behind her, trying to make out any ominous shadows in the darkness. He's suspicious and his hackles are raised.

There's a voice inside his head, his voice, screaming at him to say no, to shut the door and only open it again when he's sure there's no one on the other side. He begins to listen, if only for a second.

"Sure," he says, and Marina smiles.

She collects a different, more appropriate, pair of shoes from her room while Nick runs around inside his own, cursing at himself for his weakness, and yet, there is a strange feeling akin to anticipation bubbling in his stomach. His breathing is heavier for some reason, as if he is at the top of a diving board preparing to jump.

It's not normal for Nick to be at the receiving end of any

late night invitation, especially one involving a girl he'd just met. The only way he managed to get a date with Victoria was thanks to a confidence fuelled by whiskey sours and a throbbing determination not to spend one more night alone. The same feeling presents itself tonight.

By the time Marina returns to his door, a gentle but direct rapping of knuckles on wood, Nick is out of breath, dressed in a pair of jeans that are now too baggy, and a black shirt hidden underneath his father's coat. Marina peers behind his shoulder at the mess he's left behind and Nick can smell the cheap motel shampoo in her hair.

"Not a fan of unpacking?" she asks with a nosy grin.

Nick pulls the door shut. "I'm only passing through. Look, I don't think…"

"Come on, there's a bar just around the corner."

Nick glances up at the rain with a worried look. Marina sidesteps a few tender drops. "We're walking?"

She scoffs. "Does it look like I own a car?"

Nick smiles and tries not to look too presumptuous. No, the girl doesn't look like she owns a car, maybe she never has. She's wearing a university leavers sweatshirt but Nick doubts she's ever studied. She's a little rough around the edges, a little bit worse for wear, like a bar of soap that has been used too many times.

She is antithetical to Victoria, but standing next to her feels surprisingly comfortable, as if meeting Marina was always part of the plan. Allowing that to sink in, Nick pulls the door the rest of the way and it closes with a click. The pair step out from the walls of the motel and into the rain's torrent and Nick holds his father's coat above his shoulders, trying to shield himself. Up ahead, Marina stops suddenly, unconcerned about the current downpour, letting the rain hammer at her head.

"Hey," she calls out. "What's your name?"

Nick pauses a moment. He thinks back to his first day at Sub Rosa; Nora's innocent expression when she asked him the same question.

"Rick," he answers over the noise of the rain. "Rick Brown."

10

JUNE 12   DAY 39

Cole wades through the water like a digger clearing debris after a storm. He walks up the embankment and, arriving at the top of the crest, he kicks through piles of leaves and bends the branches of trees like a man with a death to avenge.

The officers packing away items into plastic containers give him a brief look before returning to their mundane task of collecting tent pegs and dead batteries. This is the last of it. Within the hour, the campsite will be desolate. All empty cans and rain-soaked socks will have been carted off to spend life inside cardboard boxes at the Quince Police Station. They'll fill an empty shelf, at least.

There's no longer any indication that Nick Greene had spent time here. The forest floor has been scuffed with the soles of officers' shoes too many times to count, and the air, if anyone took notice, no longer smelled of sap and soil but of cologne and another man's breath.

Cole walks around the site with his hands stuffed inside his pockets. He plays with a loose thread poking up by his thigh and mumbles a little to himself. Preliminary results from the fisherman's autopsy didn't give too much away. He fell, that was clear, sometime between midday and 5pm on the 5th. Blunt force trauma to the head. What the report couldn't tell them was whether or not the man was pushed.

"Uh, sir?"

Rowan stands with one of the plastic boxes. He juggles between feet a little, as if the weight inside the box is unbalanced.

"Yes?"

"That's the last of it."

"I can see that."

Cole watches Rowan hesitate before turning on those unsure feet. He's almost under the shadow of the canopy but then Cole calls him back, changing the tone of his voice to sound less bitter, less twisted. "You were there when he found him, weren't you?"

"Uh, yes, sir, I was."

"Describe it to me."

Rowan puts the box down. "It stunk."

"Mmm. How was he?"

"He was… not well, sir. He was lying over there, not breathing."

"Not the fisherman," Cole spits. "Abbott."

"Abbott?"

"Did he seem… concerned?" Cole paces around the patch of dirt where the fire pit used to be. He looks intensely at Rowan and buries his fingertips in his palm for warmth.

"I'd say he was pretty concerned, sir."

He scoffs and shakes his head, continues to play with the thread inside his pants.

The day Harvey Price was found, or Happy Harvey, as the kids knew him, was a day much like this one: overcast, with rain hanging over them like mist from a sprinkler. His name sounded like a childrenswear line, Cole knew that, but the kid never went without one of those ear-to-ear smiles, that's just how happy he was, so the name, it just stuck.

Cole knew him as Happy, knew him as the kid who'd ride around the streets on his bike with cute girls sitting on the handlebars. He'd weave left and right and the girls would laugh and that grin he wore would be stretched to its limit. Cole would watch on from behind the windows of his house or, sometimes, when he was brave enough, he'd wave to Happy when he passed him on the street. Happy would always tilt his head and flash that smile. He was the kid everyone liked.

Cole was a year younger than him, but Happy was the kind of guy who'd accept anyone into his circle, even the ones with lisps or stutters. Cole remembers one night, when he was 13 and Happy was 14, how everyone gathered down the end of the cul-de-sac on Fox Crescent to watch Happy do a wheelie on his bike from one end of the street to the other.

The kids lined the road, standing shoulder to shoulder; kids from all walks of life, brought together by one affable teen. They cheered when Happy began his one-wheeled journey down the street, with the cheers turning into roars the closer he got to the finish line. He did it, of course, he conquered the coolest wheelie any of them had ever seen, and he waved to the crowd like a rockstar.

Cole wandered over to him, speechless, in utter admiration of him. Happy stuck out his hand and he shook it. They talked for only a few minutes, and Cole can't even remember what they spoke about, but that night, with Happy's face smiling against a backdrop of a burnt orange sunset, has been ingrained in Cole's memory. As has what followed.

"Cole?"

He is snapped from his trance. He's pulled the thread clean from its seam. He stares down at it between his fingers before letting it fall, watching as it delicately floats to the forest floor. As soon as it lands, it is lost.

Rowan bends down to pick the plastic container back up. "You alright?"

"I need you to do something for me," Cole says, his voice quiet, still torn from the memory. "I need you to keep an eye on him."

"On Abbott?"

"Mmm."

The box bangs against Rowan's body and its innards rattle and shake. The officer bites at his lip. "How come?"

Cole thinks back to Happy. Young, charismatic, lovable. He thinks of Abbott. Rusty, untrustworthy, unreliable. Why do all the good ones go so soon?

"Because," he says, "something stinks." He whispers the next part under his breath: "And it's not the angler."

II

Nick dreams of her again. A simple dream but in black and white.

They're sitting in the outside patio of a bar they've been to before, but all characteristics other than the brick wall behind them and the tall bar leaners they're sitting around are veiled. They're with friends of theirs, figures he can't see the faces of, but he knows they are smiling because loud, unapologetic laughter fills the dream and they all reach for their drinks to quench a thirst.

Then, Victoria's simple gesture: her lean into Nick's shoulder, her face buried in the nape of his neck, her smile wide and a stitch at her side. She uses Nick for support as she laughs.

The picture is in monochrome but he knows his face is flushing pink with glee. Blue eyes close as he leans in towards her and feels blonde hair on his cheek. The dirty red of the brick wall behind them. The yellow of a lemon slice bubbling in a glass. The pumping of his heart beneath his green shirt.

He wakes.

*

The bar Marina has dragged him to for the second night in a row is nothing like the dream. The colours here are too bright and it makes him squint, makes him want to close his eyes completely.

The room is mostly wooden and is covered in a deep red light, like a seedy nightclub. There's no live band but music escapes from a speaker barely attached to the far wall. There's a stag's head at the entrance and its dead eyes stare across the punters, while the punters' eyes stare at Nick.

Marina waltzes in and leans forward to shake her head wildly, drops of water from the outside deluge falling onto the wooden floors. It's still raining, but it's that annoying kind of rain, the kind that eases as soon as you get comfortable with the sogginess, the grey clouds, the rough winds. Then, when the air is calm, and the rain subsides, it comes back again, soggier, greyer, rougher. The bar, it seems, is as good a place as any to wait until its temper wanes.

Marina flops herself down on a stool at the bar and starts spinning. "Two bourbon and Cokes, please. It feels like a bourbon and Coke kinda night."

The bartender nods and begins pouring the liquor. Yesterday, it was a gin and tonic kind of night. He asks Marina if she is okay and the stool stops with a squeak.

"Yeah. It's just been another long day."

They give each other a knowing look and Nick wonders what it was about the day that had them both withdrawn, begging for a clean break. His day was anticlimactic. He sat in front of the TV and read *Rime of the Ancient Mariner* for what felt like the 17th time, but still, he wouldn't say his day felt long. No, long were the days in the forest park. Long were the nights that dragged.

Sometimes, when it was too stormy to head to the river, and the wind was blowing like a jet turbine through the trees, and the sky was too grey to see anything with perfect clarity, Nick would huddle down inside his tent and use the drop of the leaves to count the hours that ticked away from him.

He'd rewrite his history for the hell of it, concocting a back story that made him a top surgeon, or better yet, a commercial airline pilot. There's nowhere further from Quince than the sky. He'd imagine a future with Victoria and, maybe one day, they'd have kids of their own with her beauty and his brains. It was a fun game to play, one that would distract him when his body ached from the cold, but Nick had to remember not to get lost in it, not to get addicted with the dream. He couldn't grab hold of false hope.

"So? Are you gonna say anything or what?"

Marina is staring at him with her chin jutting outwards. Nick isn't used to such brassiness. In his world there's been no one as brash as Marina. Everyone he knows of speaks in soft tones and uses big words and never invites a stranger for a drink. They never order a bourbon on a weeknight, either. He stammers when he attempts to clear his throat.

The best he can come up with is: "Does he know you?" His eyes flit across to the bartender and Marina's eyes follow.

"Yeah. Let's just say I come here too often."

Nick smiles tightly before he takes his first swig of the drink. Strong. "How come?" he asks her.

"I get bored in the motel by myself. I hate it."

Marina frowns and her dark eyes get lost. The corners of her mouth are drooping down and it's a look Nick resonates with. He's seen it somewhere before. Last night, he tried to ask for her backstory. He dropped the question casually into their weak conversation but she caught grip of it with a deft hand and threw it away.

He tries again. "Why are you there?"

Marina sighs. The song blasting out from the speaker comes to a quiet stop and in the silence, the rain's growing wrath can be heard. She takes another swig before looking at Nick. For the first time, he notices the scar on the bridge of her nose.

"I kinda live there," she says.

"You live at the motel?"

"Yeah. Lotsa people do. You didn't know that before you checked in?"

Nick shakes his head, thinks back to the motel's disarming signage and vacant parking lot.

"Oh, well, yeah. My boyfriend and I have been there for months."

"Your boyfriend?"

"Yeah, he works long hours. A truck driver. He goes all over the place. Hardly ever see him now."

Marina takes another sip of her drink and lets her lips linger at the edge of the glass. When she pulls it away, she slams it down onto the top of the bar.

"It's okay, though," she says. "I don't know why I'm complaining. He's the best damn thing that has ever happened to me."

There are a few other punters scattered around the bar and Nick can hear the whirring of a slot machine in the distance, but other than that, the room is empty. He never knew a place like this existed when he moseyed around Abercrombie with Victoria. She wanted to avoid the side streets and back then, he didn't complain. He wouldn't have ventured into a bar of this calibre without her, and he definitely wouldn't have ordered a drink.

He tells himself now that he's not the same man he used to be. He's adventurous, a risk-taker, and isn't that what she always wanted?

"You ever felt like that?" Marina is looking up at him earnestly. "Felt like you owed someone the world?"

He gulps. He wants to tell her about Victoria, hell, he just wants to feel her name escape from his lips. He wants to construct the tapestry that is her and lay it out on the bar in front of them, analysing each seam, but he knows he wouldn't do her any justice, and he knows any sense of mystery he has over Marina would quickly fade. She doesn't know him yet and that's a powerful thing, but still, maybe a little history could be divulged over a concoction of bourbon and melted ice cubes?

When he doesn't answer, she says: "Seriously? No one? I highly doubt that."

Nick takes another sip of his drink. After a month of no alcohol, its strength grows on him quickly. He was never a big drinker; he'd watched Mollie gulp down enough vodka shots for the two of them. When she was out partying or hanging her head out of taxis or vomiting into a drain, he was at home, waiting for the mistyped text or slurred phone call, the ones that begged him to pick her up from an isolated street corner or a house down a road they never ventured to in daylight. The ones that begged him not to tell his parents. Each and every time, he obliged.

It wasn't until Nick moved out of home and into his med school's crummy student housing that he properly tasted alcohol, the bitter mental injection he'd missed out on. It was through a game of beer pong or Edward Fortyhands that he came out of his shell, became the Nick Greene that wasn't so uptight, so anxious, and instead transformed into a good man, gregarious, one to joke around with or confide in. He'd be the one to talk up a mate if he was close to scoring with a girl from down the hall, or the one to sober drive when everyone else was faced. He'd bring a friend home and tuck him into bed, all in the hopes that if he needed it, one day, someone might do the same for him.

"Okay, maybe once," he says to Marina. "But I don't feel like that anymore."

"What happened?"

Nick shakes his head and the images of Victoria wobble around from side to side. He could stay watching the tilted pictures for hours. He opens his mouth to speak, but then, a pause. "I'm sorry but… I don't know you."

Marina rolls her eyes. "Why are you being so secretive? I mean, what's the harm in bitching to a stranger about your life?"

Nick's afraid of what he'll say. He loved Victoria but she was like a vile of poison. She looked harmless, vibrant, and beautiful, but she killed him in the end, didn't she? That's why he's here, isn't it?

He gulps down the entire black and amber drink.

*

It was a Wednesday night in autumn. Leaves had long since turned red and orange and had fallen to the ground, leaving the trees bare like brown skeletons. There was a party Saturday night, a costume party, and although Nick had declined the invitation, said he'd rather wake up on Mars than with a pounding hangover, Victoria had insisted he go and he was powerless to resist her.

He rented a costume that smelt like piss and he carried it back to school at arm's length. After throwing it to the floor of his small unit, he made a call to a restaurant in Abercrombie, the renovated church he and Victoria ate at the last time they were there. He booked a table for two for that night and asked them to have it ready with a bottle of merlot in an ice bucket. He got dressed in his only suit. It was the same one he wore to his high school ball so it was a bit snug, but it did the trick. He wore a cologne he only brought out on special occasions.

Nick's stomach was in knots as he walked from the campus to Victoria's flat. He stopped to look at himself in store windows along the way, and like a treasure hunter admiring a jewel, the reflection shone back to him and even Nick felt attractive that night. His face was looking nice; his usually pale skin had an olive complexion and his blue eyes glinted with the perfect blend of harmless and wholesome. He had a bouquet of gardenias in his hand, Victoria's favourite, and the watch she gave him was clasped on his wrist.

He took in a deep breath, the cool air tunnelling through his windpipe, and felt pleased with himself. He was glad he'd finally found a girl who chipped away at him like a sculptor working on a masterpiece, knowing that the beauty lay beyond the surface of the imperfect stone.

He had checked with one of Victoria's flatmates that she would be in that night, that she didn't have any late classes or other people to see. Nick also knew that the girls hardly ever ate dinner before 7, and that if he got there by 6.30, he could quite easily whisk her away. Usually lousy at keeping secrets, he had well and truly kept his arrival a surprise.

The small house was within sight when Nick saw Victoria walking up the street in the opposite direction. She looked beautiful. Black jeans, tall boots, red lipstick. The lamplight was shining down on her and when Nick took a moment to take in her beauty, he noticed there was a man at her side, one he didn't recognise.

Nick assumed the guy was from one of her boring BPharm classes. He stopped walking, though, still hesitant, and lingered back to watch the pair together from a distance. They were laughing – innocent enough – but they were comfortable in each other's presence, Nick could tell. It was the way the man was looking at Victoria that made his stomach flip.

*

Marina stops to order another round of bourbon. She drinks half the glass before she leans in close again to listen.

*

They arrived at the front of the house and Victoria pointed to the door. Nick urged her to go inside from behind his sidewalk shadow. She did, but before she walked up the steps leading to her front door, she leapt at the man and they dove into a kiss.

Nick turned away, unable to watch the scene. For a second, he thought that if he didn't admit to seeing it, he could go on believing in Victoria's fidelity and her love for him. For a second, he thought if he erased from his mind the picture that was causing him so much pain, he'd be able to go on living with her, and being in love with her, and planning a future with her.

All of those options disintegrated when he finally had the courage to turn back.

When he saw the man slowly wipe Victoria's red lipstick from his smirking mouth, the hurt became so much worse. A dagger straight through the heart. Nick's hands shook with a violent rage and his brain felt like it was on fire, and perhaps it was, literally burning every happy memory and foolish dream that lay within the cells.

Throwing down the gardenias, Nick watched as the man left Victoria to enter her flat and walk back the way they had come. He followed him with the pace of a lion, determined to track down its prey.

The man was more attractive than he was, in an athletically charming kind of way, and Nick hated that; hated Victoria for what she had done and hated this man for his role in abruptly ripping his life apart. He stared at the back of his skull through furious eyes, eyes that wanted to crinkle and shed tears but were too occupied by the mousey-blond oval in front of them. He bit his lip to stop from yelling out. Then, when the man made a turn down a path that weaved through a dense piece of parkland, often used as a short-cut, Nick followed.

It was dark down there; the road's streetlights had not the strength to cut through the untrimmed and overhanging branches of the macrocarpa and oak. Still, the stranger in front of Nick took the walk like a leisurely stroll, whistling and humming to himself. The sound of it obscured Nick's heavy footsteps, though the pounding of his heartbeat was like a door slamming shut, over and over. He bent down, felt something connect with his fingers. He stared at the back of the man's skull like it was a target on a dartboard and envisioned it bursting like a balloon.

*

The drinks are empty again. It feels like they've been here for hours. Nick doesn't know how long he's been talking but he decides to end the story there before he says too much.

Marina isn't happy with his sudden silence. She had been listening intensely, never once interrupting to ask a question or request clarification. She urges him to continue.

"There's nothing more to tell," Nick says.

"Oh, come on. You didn't speak to her? Call her a bitch?"

"I did speak to her."

"And what did she say?"

Nick twirls the empty glass around in his hand, staring at the design's intricacies. Marina snatches it off him.

"She said it was my fault," Nick tells her. "And maybe it was."

"Fuck that!" she yells. A couple of punters look up from their beers while others don't flinch. Nick smiles again at her bold choice of speech. "God, if Trevaughn ever cheated on me and then told me it was *my* fault, I'd kill him. I'm surprised you didn't kill her."

Nick looks down at his hands and they look back up at him; the lines in his soft palm like a frown. A mournful country song plays in the background. His eyes have adjusted to the strange red light.

Beside him, Marina orders another round and appears to be in a great mood despite the sombre atmosphere. She laughs at something the bartender has told her and her smile is wide and, in a way, manic. A type of manic Nick adores. It makes him feel less like a loner, a freak, and more like a piece of stone waiting to be sculpted.

He decides then that her random request for a drink the night before had so far been the highlight of his hiding out, and that, in many ways, she could be even better than Victoria. She could be the muse that carries him into the soul of Rick Brown, living and breathing. He doesn't know why, but he knows they were destined to meet.

*

The pair and new comrades depart the bar not long after the third round is finished. Marina walks a little wobblier on the way home but she still has her wits about her. When a carload full of rowdy men call out to her, she yells back, middle finger in the air, and when Nick's shoelace comes undone, she's the one who crouches down to retie it.

They walk side by side back into Sub Rosa and stand outside their neighbouring motel room doors.

"This was fun. You're good company," she tells Nick as she pulls out her key. "Hey, Rick? Let's make this a regular thing, yes?"

For a second, Nick forgets he's hiding out and that he's not a normal man drinking with a normal woman, but then his mind sees that yellow dress and his mother's brooch and he's reminded of the man he really is, and what the real Nick Greene has done. He tells Marina he'll think about it, like an answer to an impossible test, and hurries inside his room.

He lies in bed that night feeling a little tipsy from the

first drink of decent conversation he's had in a month. The rain continues to pour, although it's tamer now and soothes him. He hasn't thought about that fateful Wednesday night for a long time, doesn't know if it heals him or deepens the wound by talking about it. Sometimes, it comes back to him as a nightmare. Other times, he feels vindicated.

Perhaps he should have known then that it was the beginning of the end for Nick Greene. Perhaps he should have kissed his life as he knew it goodbye. Because, as far as he was concerned, from that night, Nick Greene no longer existed.

12

JUNE 12   DAY 39

There's a cup of Earl Grey sitting on a yellow coaster on a glass coffee table. A young mother's son screams for a gingerbread cookie from a jar on the counter. In the courtyard, an elderly woman's dog barks at every falling leaf and nips at waitresses' ankles. It's not the solitude Abbott craves, but his change in scenery is necessary, if not crucial.

He sits on a brown leather chair that has been pulled at and scratched and jumped on; his rear end sags a little too close to the ground. He frowns towards the mother who, frazzled, quickly grabs a gingerbread man from the jar and forces it into her son's mouth. She collects her coffee from the barista and throws him the amount owing in loose change. A bell chimes as she departs.

Abbott rubs at the bags under his eyes which he suspects will only get bigger and darker with time. He's not typically a sweet tooth but this morning he scoops three teaspoons of sugar into his mug of tea, stirring it just once before taking a swig.

He spent last night in bed with his laptop perched in the folds of his stomach, his striped cotton pyjamas rubbing at his skin each time the computer slid down the sheets. He's never been fond of computers in general, but ones that have been shrunken down with gaudy blue lights behind the keys bother him quite profusely. His fingers are too large and too slow to type the words as fast as his brain concocts them, and his eyes are too degraded to see past the brightly lit screen.

Still, he tried his hardest to note down his thoughts as they came to him, and peered at the timetables and titbits he's been collecting since Nick Greene's disappearance more than a month ago.

Abbott clicks his teeth. In spite of Cole's taunts, his desire to solve the case has grown in strength, to really, truly solve it, not simply dub it an accident and call it a day.

Last night he collected all of his files from the office, jammed them inside the beat-up rustbucket he uses on his rare jaunts out of town, and spent the evening in a sorry heap. Cole's words lingered around him: *Are you gonna let this one down too?* No, Abbott thinks, he's not going to let that happen again.

Another young lady, wearing a jacket with a faux fur trim on top of purple scrubs, enters the coffee house. Abbott watches her as she orders a latte to go and a piece of biscotti. She's wearing a lanyard around her neck and Abbott cranes his head to read what's been printed on it, but the woman moves too fast in a jittery sense and the lanyard jangles and twists and turns all too quickly to inspect. Abbott withdraws his eyes from the woman and instead turns his attention outside. She is not the reason he's here.

The coffee house is one of the highest quality joints in Quince – in contrast to his favoured disconsolate café along the main strip – and due to its close proximity to both the small community hospital and adjoining medical school, it is frequented by overworked doctors, obedient nurse practitioners, and restless and disengaged students. Its location also makes it the ideal spot for Abbott to lie in wait.

He's already been here an hour and in that time, he has gazed out the window at a flurry of ordinary people. An old lady took two steps out the doors of the hospital, sneezed thrice without covering her mouth, and wandered off, leaving her germs to ravage someone else's immunity. A young man, tall with glasses, unknowingly walked through the particles. Now the waiter from behind the counter is sashaying across to the table behind Abbott, slapping a soggy tea towel across its surface. He cranes to look at him with a nosy curiosity and Abbott frowns, pulling his papers closer into his chest. He hates being watched.

He looks down at his notes but he quickly gets annoyed by them. Like a child unhappy with his Christmas present, so too does Abbott push the papers away with a grunt. No matter what happened, whether he was executioner or victim, Nick Greene has to be spoken to. There will not be another case on Abbott's record marked as a failure, he is sure of that.

He stares back outside the window, growing impatient though he's been involved in stakeouts much longer than this. He knows her routine, was told where to find her, and yet he's been left waiting. A concern starts to grow in his stomach but as soon as it takes hold, it disappears.

Across the road, the woman walks out of one of the medical school's old buildings, her face towards the ground. She's wearing a light blue coat over a grey dress and her delicate hands are stuffed inside woollen gloves. There's never a mark, never a crease, never a strand of blonde hair out of place when it comes to her.

Abbott gulps down the last of his tea and collects the papers splashed across the table. He shoves them into a briefcase as he marches in great strides across the concrete quad towards the girl.

"Miss Day?"

Victoria looks up with a start and her heels make a sudden scrape along the hard ground. Abbott is used to people greeting him less than enthusiastically, and Nick Greene's girlfriend does just that when she's interrupted from her thoughts.

"What are you doing here?" she snaps.

"I just want to talk."

"What is it? Have you found him?"

Abbott shakes his head. "No. But I will."

Victoria looks as if she doesn't believe him but she nods anyway. She's trying to move herself away from him, to continue on the line she had been following, but Abbott stalks her steps like a ghost. When she spins back around he is just a foot from her.

"When was the last time you spoke to Nick?"

"I've already told you that."

"Can you tell me again?"

She sighs. It's a nice day but a cool morning, and the sun beams down on them relentlessly. Steam rises from damp tiles.

"Two…three nights before he went missing? Am I being interrogated?"

"No, you're helping me with something," Abbott assures her. "He didn't say anything to you? Anything at all that indicated he was planning on running away?"

"Like I told you," she says, "no."

A couple of students wander past, raucous laughter

escaping their mouths. Abbott softens his voice. "He hasn't reached out to you? No phone calls, text messages?"

She shakes her head.

"What about phone calls in which the caller hung up before you could speak to them? Any of those?"

Victoria sounds frustrated. "No!"

"And are you still convinced something bad happened to him?"

Much like Mollie, the young woman seems easily worn out by his questions: cheeks turning red, eyes starting to water. He has sympathy for her, sure, but he also thinks it's odd.

He knows Victoria met Nick during their first year at med school, at a party where they both dressed as Smurfs. They had a good laugh about it, apparently. After that, they dated for four years. But Abbott had to admit he judged Victoria's character based on her decision in choosing a man like Nick Greene, a man who could run away at the drop of a hat. If she was so smart, he thought, why couldn't she see through him? How did she not know this was coming?

She balances on the balls of her feet and rubs at her forehead. She stares at Abbott with bright blue eyes.

"Something has happened to him though, hasn't it? Either way, if he ran away or if he was killed, something bad has happened."

Abbott lifts his chin, clicking his teeth. "What do you mean?"

"Well, something bad had to have happened to him if he decided to up and leave without telling anyone. Don't you think?"

"Like what?"

"I don't know. But for the past month I've been trying to put myself in his shoes. What would make me run away?"

"What *would* make you run away?" Abbott presses, genuinely curious.

Victoria thinks on it for a moment. Her pretty face begins to look pained. After a while, her mouth is pushed to the side and her eyes dart from her feet to the sky, then back down to Abbott.

"I guess it's pretty simple," she says. "I'd run away if I didn't want my life anymore."

Silence grows between the detective and the student. The morning sun casts shadows on the pavement, and the medical school looks ancient under its glaring light. It was only built in the '70s. Abbott guessed someone figured Quince needed to be known for something, not just trees and fog and dust and a fruit nobody admitted to hating.

"You seem sure that he ran away. Why?"

Her eyes flicker. "What do you mean?"

"I just thought he would've left you note or something."

"Well, he didn't."

"And you weren't worried? The costume party, Victoria." Abbott steps forward. "He was meant to be there, wasn't he? There was a costume in his room."

She shrugs. "Nick used to say one thing and mean another."

Abbott's eyes narrow. He's never been good at reading people because he's never taken the time to do it properly. He practises on Victoria but she remains a closed book.

"There isn't anything you want to tell me, is there?" he asks.

She's quick in her answer. "No."

Abbott clicks his teeth. He nods. He turns away from her and takes a few large strides in the opposite direction, not back to the coffee house and not back towards the station. In truth, he doesn't know where he'll go from here.

"Abbott?" Victoria calls, a touch inaudible. "I read the paper. That man's body in the bush. Nick's not involved is he?"

He thinks, tries to figure out what sounds best. A lie? Or the truth? Part of him wants to say 'absolutely, yes, 100 per cent', but as he looks at the girl, her face drooping under the sun's light, he figures those things can wait. He goes for the second best choice: "I'm not sure yet."

He takes a few more bold steps, feigning purpose, before he turns back, catching Victoria before she steps out of the quad.

"It was a Smurf," he says.

"Excuse me?"

"The costume at Nick's flat. It was a Smurf."

Her eyebrows raise, her mouth is ajar. She emits a small 'huh' and stands there, unblinking. Abbott isn't a good reader of people but he does know guilt when he sees it.

*

A few hours later, he's sitting on his couch, a cup of coffee too hot to drink on the table in front of him and a leftover mince dish defrosting in the microwave. The television hums out the weather broadcast: clear skies on the way. He scratches slowly at his chin and wonders where'd he be if he left Quince all those years ago.

He could be married, with a wife who cooks fresh meals rather than the mush he makes for himself. He could have a couple of kids, young adults by now, submitting university applications or starting apprenticeships. He could have a son eager to follow in the footsteps of his police officer father but to that, he would disapprove and instead push him in the direction of something simpler that allowed more time for weekend sports and travel. He could have a couple of mates around for the big game on Saturday nights, rather than falling asleep on the couch before the final whistle blows. He could have a house big enough to play Hide and Seek in, and a closet that bore more than just a set of men's clothes.

Abbott shakes his head, the fantasy falling away, and reaches for his coffee. He sips at the edge cautiously, a tang of whiskey mingling with Arabica beans, then downs the whole mug.

13

She hurries back to her flat as if hot on the heels of a sordid piece of gossip, a tantalising titbit that she knew she wouldn't be able to keep close to her chest the second she heard the words.

She cares not for the strands of hair stuck in her lipstick or the concrete scraping away the perfection from the tips of her heels. She's too distracted to notice the familiar flurry of faces as she passes them, and she doesn't take in the traffic as it meanders nosily alongside her, hairy arms hanging from open windows.

Usually, she arrives home like a burst balloon, bouncing from one room to the next until she's run out of air and her enthusiasm has deflated. But today, Victoria slinks into the house like a thief surveying a store, preparing for an evening heist. She doesn't walk to and from bedrooms to draw attention to herself or raise her voice above its usual tenor. Today, there is nothing she wishes to share.

She tosses her handbag down onto the carpet as she enters her room, the one at the front with wide, ornate windows staring out towards the road. The flat is old, grungy, with mould on the bathroom ceiling and crumbs stuck down the side of the fridge. She turned her nose up when they came through to have a first look at it, but those windows, those large and lavish windows in the room which she could make hers, won her over and she happily signed her name on the lease.

It's when she's secure inside with the bedroom door closed that Victoria starts to wallow. Her bottom lip quivers and her hands begin to shake. She doesn't like crying, doesn't like the way it makes her face look, and so, despite being alone, she takes a deep breath, holds the air in her lungs for a moment, and the tears, in some miraculous feat, creep silently back into the ducts.

She flops herself down on her bed, wrapping herself in the duvet as if it were a cocoon. She used to jump into bed at the end of each night with a smile on her face, excited for what the next day may bring. She used to lie on her back, stare up at the night patterns on her ceiling, and think of him with the giddiness that she only felt during the early stages of her romances. Now, she just lies awake, yearning for sleep.

Once so unconcerned, she is now so uptight. Maybe she learned that from him.

Victoria's arm emerges from underneath the bedspread as she gingerly pulls open the top drawer of her side table. She rummages around until her hand clasps hold of something hard and cool. She brings it into bed with her.

Inside her makeshift nest, she peers at the watch she gave Nick, still ticking, still shiny. It could pass as being brand new. It's the same watch he hadn't taken off since the day she handed it to him but now, it seems, he had.

He refused the watch at first, told her it was too expensive. He placed it inside the box it came in, forcing her hands to take it back.

"No," she said, "I want you to have it."

Nick looked at her, his smile was crooked, thoughtful, and she pulled the watch back out and clasped it around his wrist. "I know you don't have one. Well, now you do."

Nick leaned forward to embrace her and she remembers running her hand along the back of his head.

"This is…" He wanted to say something but didn't. "Thank you."

Victoria rolls the watch in her hand and stares at its engraving: "Love always, V."

It had shown up unexpectedly on the morning of June 3. A pretty little package, all done up in a red ribbon. She was giddy when she carted it back to her bedroom, thinking it was from an admirer. She delicately lifted off the Sellotape, piece by piece. When she opened the lid of the box, however, her body tensed and the wrapping paper she tried so hard not to damage fell to the floor in a heap.

Tears try to escape from the corners of her eyes again and this time, Victoria lets one slip. It slides down her cheek and lands quietly on her pillow.

The last night she saw Nick, he was wearing that watch. She told the police about it, told them that if they find his body, look for the watch. He'd be wearing the watch, she told them. But now the watch is with her and there is no sign of a body, no sign of Nick. She didn't think it possible at first, but now she knows that he has been toying with her, an act of revenge for how she treated him. He wants her to know that he is out there and that although he is gone, he is around. He is watching.

The night Nick ran into her bedroom, panting and sweating profusely like a farmer working in the outback's heat, the night he confronted her about kissing Liam Whittaker on the sidewalk, was the last night she saw him.

"What's the matter?" she asked, noticing the ragged and rushed demeanour that was uncommon in Nick, who was usually so brooding, so calm. She walked across to his side but he pushed her away.

"I saw you!" he cried. "I saw you kissing him!" His voice was shaky as if a helicopter was whirring in his ribcage.

Victoria placed her hand over her mouth. She recounted her kiss with Liam only moments ago. A loving, tender kiss that was now ruined upon knowing her boyfriend had been watching from the darkness, his heart shattering from the ill-timed embrace.

She sat on her bed, atop the same duvet she is now cocooned under, and shook her head. "I'm sorry, Nick. I should have told you."

"No!" Nick answered, baffled, searching for the words. "You shouldn't have been with him at all!"

He paced back and forward, and it was then Victoria noticed how he was dressed: smart, and handsome, if not for the vicious look on his face. She felt a pang of sadness for him then, his safe face, his demure eyes, but she could only ask him where he had been.

"Where have I been?" Nick replied, exasperated. "I've been outside, watching you cheat on me! How could you?"

There was desperation in his voice, a man fighting for a diminishing love, but Victoria felt like a child, told off for putting a foot out of line. What love she had left faded and a suppressed anger rushed out of her like a wave.

"I was so bored, Nick!" she yelled. "Our relationship, it was just so… boring."

Nick frowned and took a step back as if he was wounded. "Our relationship was boring?" He rebounded and moved his face closer towards Victoria and she could see sweat on the nape of his neck. She loved being loved, but Nick's love could no longer cut it.

"Come on, Nick. Sometimes I didn't even know if you were in the room with me. Whatever I liked, you liked, too. Whatever I wanted, you let me have it. Whenever I started an argument just for something challenging, something different, you told me I was right because you couldn't be bothered discussing it."

Nick paced the room, scoffing to himself and shaking his head. He rubbed at his forehead furiously before he returned to face Victoria, putting his hands on her knees. She pushed him off her.

"You cheated on me because I gave you everything you wanted? Because we had things in- in *common*? Because I loved you?"

"You don't get it!" Victoria cried. "I want excitement. I want someone to challenge me!"

"I supported you!"

Victoria looked up at Nick. That damn watch was clasped on his wrist. The gleam of it shone in her eyes. Exhausted, he sat on the edge of the bed but Victoria stood up and out of his way.

"I thought you wanted to move to the city?" he asked her, staring down at his hands entwined in his lap. "I thought that's what you wanted?"

"Are you serious?" The room was quiet. "I didn't want that for me. I said *you* should go to the city. I said it so that you would do something, anything. Then all of a sudden it was *us* going to the city."

She paced the room as Nick listened to her ramble on about life goals and aspirations. His body stayed stiff, his eyes unblinking. She talked about the dreams he must have assumed were mutual. She told him Liam was adventurous and exciting and she told Nick she no longer loved him, and then, after a few seconds of mournful silence, he stood up, put his hand in the pocket of his suit pants, and left.

Of course, the story she told Abbott was different. Sure, she saw Nick, but it was only for a cup of tea and a goodnight kiss. She had an early class in the morning, she said. She told the cops that the last time she saw him, he was happy, there was no inkling that he would run away; they were in love. But then why hadn't she called them when he didn't show up at the costume party that first week of May? Why, after days of no contact, was she not concerned?

There was guilt in her stomach then and there is guilt in her stomach now. She knows Abbott can see straight through her.

She clutches her abdomen, begging the pain to stop. She tosses the watch underneath her pillow where she can no longer see it and presses her eyes firmly shut. A short distance away, she hears the front door of the old flat fling open. A voice calls out to the figures lounging in the living room and they respond in their own high-pitched squabble. There are footsteps along the wooden floor of the hallway and Victoria, nestled within her nest, waits.

A man lightly taps on her wooden door before pulling it open to reveal a large, toothy grin. He's a stocky man and his wide appearance makes it seem like getting through the dated entranceway is a struggle. After the grin, comes a muscular shoulder, a toned bicep and then an arm encased in a sling.

"Ta-da!" he cries. He proudly waves his left arm in the

air, its movement restricted by the fabric cradling his skin and tied around his neck. "Finally got the bloody thing off."

He walks towards Victoria who lifts her head from the bed, and gives her a peck on the lips. He doesn't notice the streak of salt down her cheek.

"How does it look?" he asks her.

"It looks like you've got your arm back."

Liam stands in front of the full-length mirror Victoria has tacked to her wardrobe. He checks himself out unabashedly.

They had met in the most serendipitous of ways: she was rushing down the street, a few minutes away from being late dropping in an assignment, when a lick of wind caught the loose pieces of paper in her hands and scattered them along the sidewalk. Liam, in his brutish way, clamoured after them all, catching each piece under his size 10 sports shoes.

He was so enamoured by her, the blonde hair, the pointed nose, the way she so gracefully ran down the street in a bid to catch the runaway homework, that he asked her on a date. She didn't say no. On a night when she knew Nick was cramming for a mid-week test, she was sitting in a low-key Quince restaurant, flicking her hair and falling in love with the man opposite her.

At the end of the date, they kissed, and it was only afterward, when Liam had gone from view, that she thought of Nick. She thought of their first kiss, awkward but endearing, something innocent that soon turned passionate. With Liam, the passion was already there, she couldn't deny it, and Victoria, who at that moment had already started on a months-long period of deceit and excuses, knew she would see him again.

Unlike Nick, Liam was always in good spirits. He was a man who got high off the simple things around him: the brightness of the sun in the sky, the perfectly crisp bacon delivered to his plate, the look of his girlfriend when she rolled out of bed in the morning. Nick, on the other hand, always had something on his mind, a thought bouncing around in his brain, and whenever Victoria asked him about it, he'd pretend it wasn't there.

Even when Liam was attacked, sent to the hospital with a concussion, broken ribs, a fractured arm, split lip and bruised eye socket, his positivity didn't falter. While Victoria was fretting, his charm earned him extra dessert from the nurses, and while she was being told that a mugger had pummelled him unconscious with a tree branch, he was cracking jokes with other patients.

The cops didn't find who did it, though the mugger population in Quince was said to be small. It was an unfortunate incident they needed to move on from, they told her, but how could she do that when deep in her bones, she knew Nick was responsible?

There was no proof, of course, no witnesses, and even if there was, now that Nick was missing, she wouldn't be able to say a word. If she told the police that she was the reason he ran away, how would they treat her? What would the papers say? *Woman's Infidelity Caused Loyal Med Student to Flee*. Because that's all they knew of Nick. They'd see him as hard-working and dedicated and trusting, a man not even capable of hurting a fly, let alone a stranger with a tree branch.

But now this fisherman is involved, and worse, he is dead. Victoria thinks back to Abbott's face when she asked if Nick had anything to do with it. She knows that he knows, and she knows that the answer is yes.

She recalls the watch. Its mysterious reappearance. The fear she felt then rising in her stomach now. It's a taunt, one left by Nick one month after his vanishing, a message to her and only her that he is alive and out there somewhere.

Her fingers gently play with the watch's strap underneath her pillow. Her face must show her thoughtful pain.

"You okay?" Liam wanders over and gently rests his good hand on the top of her head.

"Yeah," she sighs, "just thinking."

Liam's flesh wounds have healed, his ribs are bruised but recovering, and the arm, once wrapped in plaster, is hanging from the less obstructive sling. The smile that was there throughout the process persists.

"Well, snap out of it," he jibes playfully. "I'm hungry. You hungry?"

Exhausted from being confronted by Abbott, sick from reminiscing, and confused about what step to take next, Victoria nods in quiet submission. She lifts herself from the bed, where the watch remains unwanted.

"I feel like sushi," she tells Liam, who has already bounded back towards the door.

"Na," he responds. "Sushi sucks. We'll go get pizza."

Victoria frowns to herself as she fixes her hair in the mirror but slowly, a smile forms.

She welcomes a challenge.

14

She's some distance ahead, walking, no, floating along the sidewalk, avoiding any cracks in the concrete and having a difficult time staying balanced.

The pompom on the beanie on top of her head bobs and as she wavers, her gloved hands stretch out like a baby bird preparing to take flight. She's stepping in large strides, then small paces, exaggerating her movements in order to make the game more fun. She curses every time she falters.

Nick is watching her, a few feet behind. His breath comes out like fog and, up ahead, Marina's does the same. It stays with them for a while before evaporating into the cold air. By the next breath, though, it's back again.

She leads him down a side street, thinks twice, then turns back; rounds the corner behind a butcher shop, pinches the bridge of her nose to block out the smell, then picks a different direction. All the while Nick watches, eyebrows raised but saying nothing, and he lets her drag him through Abercrombie like they're school kids, split from the rest of the group on a field trip.

Finally, when another misdirection takes them to an abandoned upholsterers, where there's a colourful poster advertising a drag show that was on the weekend before, Nick offers help.

"What are you looking for?"

Marina turns. She's biting her lip, there's a frown on her face, and she looks around with hands in the air as if to say: it was right here, I swear. "I… it's a… it's a shop," she stammers.

Nick nods. "What kind of shop?"

Marina floats past him without answering and he sighs, his feet becoming heavy.

When they pull back out onto the main street, his lumbered gait makes him lose her and he starts to panic, but then he sees the pompom squashed between a red beanie and dreadlocks and he relaxes. When he catches up to her a few beats later, she's smiling, pointing at the sign above an old, paint-chipped door.

"It's right here!" she exclaims, hot breath coming out in puffs.

Nick turns to inspect the building. There's a long window at the front but half of it has been covered in faded newspaper. There's no advertisements or posters or photographs. Nothing that would give away the building's intention. Except its name.

"A pawn shop?" Nick thinks she must have made another wrong turn. He begins to laugh at her, but then she turns to face the shop's entrance and his smile drops.

"I'll meet you later, 'kay?" she says.

There's a bell that chimes as she enters, and all at once, Nick is left out in the cold. He claps his hands, looks around. Strange faces pay no notice of him. They all talk to each other or to their cell phones or their dogs. He walks back the way he came, to the left, away from the butcher shop and to an internet café he spotted when they wandered past the first time, tucked between a lime-green coloured bank and a beige nail salon.

The café is really more a small room with a coffee machine that's out-of-order and a couple of heavy computers pushed against a back wall. The business targets tourists, and there are guidebooks and translated brochures tossed across the desks, and the only person using the space is a German with a tramping pack.

Nick wanders up to the counter. A tired-looking clerk flicks through a magazine and greets him with a dull bob of his head. He charges him $10 for 10 minutes of usage and Nick, cringing with the price, digs into the pocket of his father's coat. He pulls out a wallet. Puts it back. Rummages around some more until the $10 sits in front of the worker in loose change. The clerk looks at him critically, like Nick's dragged in a bad smell, but he nonetheless gives him the code needed to access the ancient machine, before returning his focus to the magazine.

Nick pulls up a chair and punches in the code. The internet takes a long time to start up but once he's in, he taps away until he finds the national Police website and a list of the country's missing persons. It's long.

Listed alphabetically are names of old men and young men, old women and young women, fathers, mothers, grandads, and nanas. Each with an image and a bio that details their basic characteristics and the circumstances surrounding their disappearance. One woman, Nick reads, had been gardening in her front yard, barefoot, before she vanished without a trace. Another had told family she was meeting up with friends but never arrived. One man really did go out for a packet of cigarettes and never came back.

Nick gulps. There are just so many of them.

He scans through the list of names before finding his

own, midway through the page under 'N'. The picture from the posters has been used again and the details of his disappearance are eerie when he reads them on the fluorescent screen: Nicolas Greene. Age: 23. Location: Quince. Circumstances: Last seen leaving Quince School of Medicine. Police and family have concerns for his welfare and are appealing to the public for any sightings.

He feels sick seeing himself on the page, tucked between a teenager and a former teacher. It makes him feel dead already, as if the heavy beating of his heart and the erect hairs on his arms are nothing but a mirage, a memory of how life used to be.

Nick rests his elbow on the white melamine desk, the top of which has been graffitied with scrawled names and misshapen love hearts. There's a picture drawn in blue pen of a headstone and inside it, someone has written R.I.P. Using his fingers, he rubs at his forehead until crinkles form and roll like waves crashing onto a shore.

He closes the tab and digs back inside his coat pocket. He empties it out until he finds the piece of paper with the address on it, the one he's been carrying around since the day he disappeared. The destination isn't far from Quince, isn't far from Abercrombie, but it is far enough away for him to become someone else. Pursing his lips, he opens another tab on the computer and finds a bus schedule. There's one that leaves in the morning. He'd be there by early-afternoon.

Nick sighs and rubs at his brow again. He hovers the mouse over a bright blue 'purchase' button, but then he yanks his hand back. They'd find him. Everything leaves a trace, nowadays. Quickly, he shuts the computer down with 50 seconds of time to spare and hurries out of the café.

He careens down the main street, his breath hotter, heavier. As he walks, he thinks he sees the woman who went missing while gardening, the man who went out for a packet of smokes. He focuses harder, desperately wants them to be here. With him. All alive, but with new lives.

Marina's waiting outside the pawn shop. Nick searches for a new purchase in her hands but sees nothing.

"Get what you came for?" he asks her.

"Sure did."

She's smiling, but today Nick is finding her difficult to read. Why has she searched so intently for a dusty old pawn shop? Was she buying or selling? Why was it so important? There are so many questions inside his head but he thinks it's best not to prod her with them. It's sort of an unspoken arrangement they have. She doesn't ask him questions, and he doesn't ask her. Everything he knows about her he can count on one hand: she isn't close with her family, her boyfriend Trevaughn carts logging trucks to and from the city, and she likes that one *Mental is Anything* song from the '80s.

She starts to hum it as she jumps into a puddle that has formed next to a drain clogged with fallen leaves. Some of the splashes get on Nick's shoe. By the time they get back to Sub Rosa, they're both hungry, and Marina slinks through the carpark imitating a starved stray cat. She clutches at her stomach.

"What should I have tonight, instant ramen or chocolate from the vending machine?" she asks mournfully. "I'm leaning towards the chocolate."

Nick looks down at his feet. Money is tight. That's something she needn't tell him. He can tell by her clothes, either too small or too baggy, and by the way she longingly stares into shop windows as she passes them, as if dreaming up a reality in which she can wander inside, grabbing items off the shelves at leisure. She also wears the same look he wears, one only a person who gets ecstatic about finding coins under couch cushions can have.

"Hey, why don't we go out for a real meal?"

Marina's eyes narrow.

"At, like, a place that sells actual food," Nick says. "My shout."

"What?"

She looks at him as if he's crazy. And maybe he is. But Nick thinks to the money stuffed inside his rucksack and concludes there's more than enough there for a treat, and nods to Marina enthusiastically.

"Yeah, I know a place. We'll go there tonight."

Marina stares at Nick dubiously. Her eyes dart across to Number 23 and back. Finally, she settles on saying: "You're gonna have to give me time to prepare. I haven't showered in, like, two days."

Nick smiles at the honesty. "Sure."

He watches as Marina races, no, again she floats, to her motel room, the pompom gliding along with the rest of her. For the first time in a long time, when Nick returns to Number 24, he finds himself floating too.

15

JUNE 14   DAY 41

The wait staff at the renovated church are glad to see them.

It's a Wednesday, so it's been a quiet night, with only an elderly couple at one table and a party of six at another. They're led to a spot inside, in front of a large stone fireplace which crackles and sends sparks in the air. Marina gets a fright the first time it happens and Nick smiles, appreciates her tender naivety.

From where he sits, he can see the table in the courtyard he and Victoria dined at some months ago, when she told him they belonged here. Now, he is here, and she isn't. The waitress, a younger girl with a dark bob, hands them each a menu and points out the specials on a chalkboard in the far corner. She pours them a glass of ice water and both Nick and Marina gulp the drink down fast. Its taste is heavenly compared to the stuff that comes out of Sub Rosa's taps.

When the waitress departs, Marina opens her menu and gasps at the prices. Nick takes a look and cringes too. He can't remember things being so expensive the last time he was here but then again, he had money to spend back then.

"Don't worry about it," he tells her with a flick of his hand, but she shakes her head, slams the menu down onto the shiny wooden table.

"Let's go someplace else."

She starts to rise but Nick leans across the table to clutch at her shoulder. Gently, he presses her down until she's seated again. This time, it is he who shakes his head.

There's jazz music coming from somewhere within the restaurant, and the diners are all talking subdued. The elderly pair are being served another glass of red wine and a dessert, a dark chocolate rectangle with honeycomb on top and a dollop of vanilla bean ice cream to the side. Marina's eyes widen.

"There's chocolate for ya," Nick says.

The waitress returns a short time later and takes their drink order – Nick asks for a beer on tap and Marina, still anxious about the pricing, orders a Sprite.

"I don't know what half of these ingredients even are," she says, returning her attention to the menu.

"Which?"

She doesn't answer him. It's as if she's embarrassed. Nick instead scans through the list himself. He skims over the fish, pretends he doesn't see it, and when the waitress returns, planting the bubbling drinks in front of them, he orders the steak. With a big helping of garlic butter. Marina smiles and looks relieved.

"I'll have the same," she says.

She's pulled her hair up into a ponytail but a few loose curls remain hanging down by her cheeks. One strand is so long it sits at her collarbone. She's wearing the same black jeans she had on this morning, a pair of black boots with dried dirt on the sides, and a navy-blue jumper that has a dark red line knitted across the centre. Nick has on jeans of his own and a long-sleeved shirt that isn't thick enough for this kind of weather, which is why he keeps stretching his back to feel the heat of the fire. Together, the two of them look out of place. Nice, but out of place.

After a couple of minutes pass without either of them speaking, Marina says: "This isn't weird, is it?"

Nick takes a swig of his drink, plays with the napkin underneath the glass. "No?" he says, unconvincingly. He can see a wave of worry wash across her face and he clears his throat. "What's weird about it?"

"Well, the fact that I'm letting a stranger buy me an expensive dinner."

"We're not strangers anymore," he says. "And come on, we both deserve this."

Marina's dark eyes flash across to him. "Why do I deserve it?"

There's a loud crash as one of the diners from the group drops their phone onto the restaurant's wooden floor. Nick flinches, shrugs. "You've been cooped up inside that motel. It's... it must be hard."

She ponders on that for a moment. "And why do you deserve it?"

"I'm... it's the same for me," he says.

Marina reaches for her Sprite. Nick can see it bubbling under her nose. "But that's your choice, isn't it?"

"What do you mean?"

"You can leave anytime you want to, can't you?"

"Yeah, so?" he says, defiantly. "You can too."

"No, I can't."

"How come?"

"Because I have nowhere to go."

"Yeah. Well. Maybe that's the same for me."

There's silence around them bar the crackling of the fire and Marina plays with her nails underneath the table. Then, she sits up straighter in her seat and looks across at Nick with a new thought. Her tone is flat, direct.

"Why are you even there?"

"I told you," he says, his voice slow and rough. "I was invited to a wedding."

"Right."

"Yeah, right."

"And, what? You decided to stick around because it's such a beautiful place?"

Nick becomes hot. He turns to face the exit but sees the fisherman instead. "Why the third degree?" he asks, chuckling anxiously.

"Because you don't get it."

Marina folds the serviette over and over. She looks as if she is about to cry. When Nick says: "What don't I get?" the serviette is thrown back onto the table.

"None of us want to be there," she says. "Do you think Suze does? Rico?"

Nick blinks twice. Rico is a guy who stays in the room two doors down. He doesn't have a job. Nick has never seen him leave. Suze is the woman responsible for all the cigarette butts in the parking lot. She walks around with her face to the ground, self-conscious about her appearance since her ex threw her false teeth in the trash.

"I... I don't know why they're there."

"Because they have nowhere else. Sub Rosa isn't a choice for them."

"I get that."

"It's a choice for you."

The waitress returns carrying their steaks at the most awkward of times, a large, ignorant smile on her face. She asks if they want another round and Nick says yes, desperate to stay calm, to act normal, and in dire need of a refreshment. Marina draws the waitress in and asks for a different drink this time. A cocktail. The most expensive one on the menu. Nick purses his lips and she picks up on his annoyance.

"How rich are you, anyway?"

He almost spits out his steak. "What?"

"I've seen your wads of cash, Rick. I'm not an idiot."

He picks up the sharp carving knife from the side of his plate and flicks it around, the shine of the blade sparkling under the restaurant's orange lights. He forces out a pleasant laugh as he cuts his meat with precision, recalling his days in the med school lab.

"I'm hardly rich," he insists.

Marina slices her steak more timidly. The knife's handle wobbles underneath her grasp. The incisions she makes are uneven because she's keeping her eyes fixed on him, her head cocked.

"But you have money?"

"I don't."

"You're lying."

"I'm not."

Nick jabs his fork into his side of beans and their watery innards squirt onto the plate. Service is quick, and the waitress comes around another time with their drinks, noticing the change in atmosphere. She clears away the old glasses and scarpers.

"Why would it matter anyway?" he asks, mouth full. "What do you want?"

"What do I want?"

"Clearly, there's something."

"You invited *me* here."

"I know," he says. "It was a stupid idea."

Marina drops her cutlery and the steel crashes against the porcelain of her plate. She pushes herself away from the table and stands, giving him a lasting glare before storming into the toilets at the far end of the church.

Nick tries to look normal, though the nape of his neck is hot. In the corner of his eye, he sees that damn table again. Victoria laughing, smiling, lying. He hoped Marina would be the one to heal him from his barbed memories but now he resents ever telling her anything. She knows about his money. She knows too much. He scoffs and feels a familiar rage starting to brew.

He continues with his steak. The elderly couple finish their dessert and leave, hand in hand. When the waitress comes over, clearing only Nick's plate, she asks if everything is okay and Nick says: yes, of course, his date will be right back.

"I meant with the meal," the woman replies.

His glass is empty by the time Marina returns, and he wants to stay pissed off at her but as soon as she sits, an apology shoots out of his mouth so fast it's almost undecipherable.

Her shoulders are staunch, but like the soft cascade of the jazz music that surrounds them, they begin to ease. "Look, I'm sorry," she says. "I feel all sorry for myself. I feel like nobody has it as hard as Trev and I do."

Nick waits for more but realises he isn't going to get it. He rests his chin in his hands and says: "It's okay," though he doesn't really mean it. He looks at her with a newfound suspicion.

"It really isn't. None of this is," she tells him. "And who am I to say you don't deserve Sub Rosa?"

He squints. "You didn't say that."

"Oh, well, I thought it." Her manic smile returns. "For all I know, you could be having a hard time, too."

"I am."

"Running from the law?"

He chokes on spit. She laughs.

As they walk back to the motel he tries to ask her again why she's living at Sub Rosa, tries to get her to tell him her story, but all she says is: "It's complicated" and by that stage, it's pitch black. The warmth of the fireplace is no longer with them and they shiver as they trudge along the lamplit streets. Nick pulls the sleeves of his shirt down and holds the fabric in the palm of his hands, then reaches up to his mouth to blow warm air into them. As he stares at the back of Marina's head, he tells himself that dinner had been a bad idea. It's not that he doesn't want to be around her, it's not that he doesn't enjoy her company, and it's not that he doesn't like her, he does. He does. He does.

He is enamoured by her as much as he is terrified of her, and as he watches her walk, he can imagine wrapping his arm around her, keeping her warm, just as he can imagine smothering her with the inside of his elbow.

"We're almost there," she calls. "I can see the sign."

He thinks about the address he typed into the internet café's computer. He thinks about the journey. Could he make it? He saw what time the bus departed in the morning, he could pay cash for a ticket and go undetected. It would be the wise thing to do, he thinks. Marina knows something, she recognises him, and like she said, she isn't an idiot, and despite all her naivety, all her flaws, Nick doesn't doubt her that.

They come to a stop outside their motel rooms and Nick

quickly turns to head inside, but Marina touches his back between his shoulder blades and the gentle graze returns him to the stoop. It's dark, with only a dim light overhead, but Nick can see she's rubbing at the scar on the bridge of her nose.

"I appreciate what you did tonight, and I enjoyed myself, I did."

"Yeah, you seem ecstatic," Nick mumbles.

She touches him again, this time, it's more of a punch to the shoulder, but then she feels guilty and she strokes him at the spot instead. "I just… get a bit moody." She laughs and Nick is happy to hear it. "But I'm really glad you're here, if that means anything to you."

She smiles softly and waves good night to Rico who's hauling a bag of clothes from the laundry room. She disappears inside Number 23 and Nick unlocks his own weathered door. He turns on his room's electric heater and the air starts to stink of burning dust. Through the wall, he can hear Marina kick off her shoes, throw her bag to the ground, and run the shower.

He sits on the edge of his bed. He wonders if her being glad he's here means anything to him, because typically, it wouldn't. In an ordinary life, he'd act smarter than how he's acting now. He'd keep the woman at arm's reach and ignore the fact that she is a lost soul like he is. But he imagines moving forward alone, continuing on to another new town and leaving Marina behind like she's luggage not worth taking, and the picture finds a way to break his heart.

As he unfolds the sheets from their loose tuck under the mattress, he discards his plans for the following morning, because as it turns out, Marina being glad Nick's around does mean something to him, whether he wants it to or not.

16

JUNE 15   DAY 42

Abbott drives mindlessly through the suburbs. He passes a row of introduced cypress trees which stand tall like totem poles along a quiet avenue. He passes a spaniel and a poodle circling one another down a side road. He passes the intersection which leads him down Driscoll Street and spies the dead end at its base.

His foot lingers above the brake. Thoughts come to him like a carousel, and around they go until he decides he doesn't want to see the Greenes after all, and so flicks his indicator on and returns the way he came.

He pulls into the forest park and once stationary, he reclines his seat all the way back. He leans across to the passenger side and collects the papers that have accumulated there. Through strained eyes, he flicks through the contents for the two dozenth time. The initial report, the library books, the witness statements, the angler's autopsy, it all sits on his lap as the most valuable information of the case and yet it means nothing to him. It's nothing without Nick Greene himself.

Among the sheets of paper collected is Abbott's tattered diary. He pulls it open to today's date and sees nothing but blank pages. He flicks ahead. Under tomorrow's heading he's written: 'Fir funeral' but now the words act more like a taunt than an invitation. He'd have felt better going if Nick Greene had been caught and he could show up feeling proud rather than defeated.

He moves the car's visor out of the way and stares out into the ruggedness of the forest, wondering if Nick still hides somewhere within its depth. Pursing his lips, he grabs another item from the passenger seat: his pocket-sized notepad. He turns each page over and it's as if he's getting another tour of the Greene residence, like that morning on June 4.

His scribbled writing starts in the master bedroom, it locates the untouched jewellery and luxury items left behind by the burglar. Moving to the bathroom, it makes note of a missing towel and sponge. The writing begins to glide down the carpeted stairwell but then Abbott, as if he has been transported there, looks across the hallway to the bedroom at the far end. The door is shut.

The ghost of Abbott walks into the room. He can see dust particles floating in the sunlight leaking through pulled curtains. The earth-green sheets of the bed have been tucked in, hospital corners, but the burnt orange pillows are for some reason stacked at the end, as if someone forgot to place them nicely against the headboard. The room is clean but dust has settled and has created a layer of soot on the surfaces so it feels neglected. Photos hang on the wall and they show somewhat sporadic images: a dog with only its collar in focus; the shadow of a person at a beach; and what looks like the forest park, only identifiable now that Abbott has been there so many times.

This is the room he was led to after the Greenes reported their son missing. This is Nick's room, as it was when he disappeared.

It's eerie to reflect on it, knowing now that the bed would remain empty for more than a month, that the curtains would stay closed. With his own eyes shutting out the forest park in front of him, Abbott surveys the empty room for a little longer, making sure there is nothing there he missed. He lingers at one of the photos, this one tacked to a mirror against the far wall. Edwin stands at the back, a figure of authority. His hand rests on Paula's shoulder. Mollie poses on the left. Sitting on the floor, legs crossed, grinning widely into the lens, is Nick.

Abbott can't put his finger on it but there's something not quite right with the image, and it's as if Nick noticed it, too. Why else would it be stuck so deliberately in the centre of the mirror? Why, out of all the other photographs, did this one take pride of place?

The notepad closes with a pop. Abbott pulls the car's visor back down and swings his arm over the passenger seat, reversing out of the forest park with a rev of his engine and a dry taste in his mouth.

17

JUNE 15   DAY 42

He sits on the porch outside his room sucking on a piece of chocolate, a perfect blend of sweet and bitter consorting on his tongue and on his cheeks. Once swallowed, the taste lingers but never for long enough, and he finds himself reaching for another piece from the block Marina has balanced on her knees.

"Oi!" She swats him away. Then, she relents.

It's close to 6 and this feels like their dinner for the evening, but this time, neither complain. This seems a better fit than the renovated church. They won't be going back.

Trev's been asleep in the room behind them but now Nick can hear the clinking of glasses and the pounding of tired footsteps on the carpet, and as his warm mouth melts the chocolate, soaking it into his tongue, he savours the time he has left with her here, alone.

The sun has set but darkness hasn't yet consumed the view. There are still birds floating in the sky, stretching their wings for a final time before they tuck themselves into their nests for the night, and there's still movement on the parking lot in front of them; a late arrival nervously pulling an orange suitcase through the gravel. The wind isn't ready for its slumber and it too feels wide awake, whooshing through Sub Rosa and leaving goosebumps on their skin.

Marina discards the chocolate block to the wooden patio in order to wrap her arms around her bare legs.

"You have a scar... on your nose." Nick says the statement quietly, like a man pointing out discoveries under a microscope. Marina flinches and rubs where he's looking. When she finally lifts her fingers up, the mark looks more profound.

"Yeah. So?"

"How'd you get it?"

Marina scoffs a little, clears her throat, and looks out to the sky, like she's searching for something. Maybe the words. When she returns, she shrugs her shoulders. "I can't remember."

Nick groans. Her walls are up, so thick and high, and all he wants to do is get over them. He's tried a rope, a ladder, a trampoline. What hasn't he tried? Brute force.

"Fine." He stands.

"Where are you going?" Marina calls after him.

"Inside."

"No, stay. Sit." She pats the floorboards but Nick already has his hand wrapped around the doorknob. The wind picks up his hair and chills his face.

"Inside," he says again.

The breeze can't reach them in Number 24 and both of their bodies relax. Nick pulls the curtains shut and turns on the heater, keeping the temperature at a comfortable 21. Marina walks slowly through the room as if mentally comparing the space with her own. She hears Trev cough clearly through the walls and pauses to raise her eyebrows. Nick looks away.

The copy of his library book sits on the small dining

table and Marina picks it up, opening the novel to its centre. She scans her eyes over its contents until Nick rushes at her, yanking the book away, his hand covering the spine. He tosses it into his rucksack and the bag and the book land back on the carpet with a thump.

"It's really old," he explains.

He cleans two glasses and fills them with tap water from the kitchen sink, and the pair sit on the bed taking sips and swapping chocolate. Eventually, their conversation resumes.

"How'd you get it?"

Marina sighs. "Does it matter?"

"I guess not," he says, though not knowing kills him. To him, it looks like she was hit with an object with a sharp curve, like a pan. Or maybe someone bit her, their top row of teeth hitting the upper cartilage of her nose. Or maybe she just fell. Or was pushed.

There's another sound from behind the wall and Nick thinks he sees Marina's body stiffen. He thinks he sees something change in her. He thinks she looks scared but he can't be sure. He flops down onto his back and the bed's weak springs wobble under his weight. He looks up at the fly shit stains and for a second he hopes Marina lays down too so he can point them out to her, but she doesn't. She sits upright with her back hunched, her faded slippers knocking at the heels.

"I broke my nose once," Nick says, cutting through the quiet.

Her head turns slightly. "How?"

"I ran into a wall."

She scoffs. "You're an idiot."

Nick puts both cold palms on his forehead. He

remembers that day, all the blood, and Paula screaming for Ed to get a damp cloth from the kitchen. Luckily, it was only a minor fracture, nothing too serious, and when they got home from the doctors some hours later, Nick's nose swollen and throbbing, he was allowed to trudge up to his room and spend the rest of the day watching TV in bed.

"I saw you," Mollie said when he arrived at the top of the landing. "And I'm going to tell mum."

"Tell her what?"

"I saw you," she repeated.

"Saw me what?"

His older sister took an accusatory step forward. "I saw you take four steps back and then run straight into the wall. I know you did it on purpose."

Marina rises from the bed and Nick jolts upwards, watching her, making sure she doesn't touch anything too incriminating. Her fingers caress nondescript items casually brought into the motel and Nick doesn't worry too much, but then she somehow locates a single brass key on a thin carabiner and his back straightens. She lifts it up to her eyes and squints.

"What's this?"

"A key," he says offhandedly.

"For what?"

Nick considers lying but doesn't see the point. "My house."

"Your house?" Marina puts her hand on her hip.

"Well, not my house. My parents' house."

"Oh." She looks at the key with more disinterest now. Eventually, she slaps it back onto the surface of the dresser. "You gonna go back?"

"Hmm?"

"Home?"

Nick shakes his head. "Na."

"How come?"

He opens his mouth to give a blasé explanation but then he realises he doesn't have to. "Does it matter?"

He holds the door open for Marina and she steps back out into the early evening's stubborn gust. Her arms are folded tightly across her chest. They smile a goodbye, but before Nick can walk back into his room, the door of Number 23 opens, and out comes Trevaughn.

"I thought I heard voices," he says.

Trev is wearing a white singlet and grey track pants. His feet are dressed in thick woollen socks with a hole at one of the heels. He has tan skin and brown hair and dark eyes that have dark circles underneath. He leans against the doorframe, rubbing at his forehead.

"I've been wonderin' where you've been."

He's not quite what Nick expected, although, in his mind, Trevaughn has been a silhouette, with no facial features or quirks. When Marina said his name, Nick pictured a monochrome figure, talking in the same gruff voice he heard behind the walls. Now that he's in front of him, he tries to imagine the two together. He knows they met in high school and that Trevaughn drives logging trucks for a big corporation. He knows that Marina speaks of him fondly but still, Nick can't help but think she suits someone else, someone who doesn't have holes in his socks.

Trevaughn suddenly looks across at Nick, as if reading his mind. He runs his eyes up and down and finally, extends his arm. The two men shake hands while taking in each other for the first time.

"What's your name again?" Trevaughn asks, to which Nick replies: "Rick."

"The wedding guest, right?"

He nods.

Trevaughn is slightly shorter than Nick but he's stockier, and Nick can tell that when Trev isn't sitting behind the wheel of a logging truck for ten hours a day, he's at the old, cheap gym down the end of the street, lifting weights the same mass of the trees on his haul.

"Where are you from?"

"Ormiston," Nick says. It's been a long time post-normality and his backstory has been well developed.

"Huh." Trevaughn folds his arms. "Never been."

The breeze picks up again and Nick slams his palm into the centre of Number 24 and kicks the door open. Trevaughn ushers him back.

"You got a job?"

"No."

"A girlfriend?"

"No."

Marina pushes past them both and disappears into the darkness of her studio room. Trevaughn stays outside, holding the door open with his foot. He's staring at Nick in a way that makes him uncomfortable, a look which has Nick recalling the fisherman's eyes before the scuffle.

Trev stands in an odd pose, his shoulders and upper torso are pushed back, like on a lean, while his sock-covered feet remain firmly planted on the floor, in line with his hips. The way he purses his lips is strange too, the bottom thicker and more noticeable than the top. These are minute details that make Trev so distinguishable; things that differentiate him from another man; things only good

136

friends and loved ones and observant types, like Nick, could notice.

"I don't know if Marina told you, but I have a couple days off. We're getting some drinks tonight, if you wanna come?"

Nick longs to say no. Really, truly, with every element making up his existence, he wants to refuse Trevaughn's offer. Not only is he uncomfortable by his neighbour's intimidation, but there is only so much company Nick can keep. Marina is one thing, her questionable boyfriend, a whole other obstacle. An obstacle with a furrowing brow and hands that could break a neck like a twig.

"Sure," Nick hears himself respond.

Trev smacks his lips together and sticks a thumb in the air, an innocent gesture but a battle cry to someone like Nick.

*

He's alone when he arrives at the bar at 10, their usual drinking hour. The same bartender from his first few nights out with Marina is working and offers Nick a drink, and though he'd rather wait, it feels weird sitting hunched on a stool in a bar without something to sip on, so he asks for the cheapest thing on tap – a beer that barely foams and tastes watered down.

There are the usual punters scattered about the place and it makes Nick wary as tonight he can see the fisherman in every one of them. He's forced to do a double take when he sees a man wearing the same colour bush shirt, and another with similar tufts of greying hair.

There's been no news for too long. For the fifth night in

a row, Nick's name is not mentioned in any television report, and the people he encounters around the motel have become a lot friendlier, too. Rick Brown is transforming into a real persona, a cool guy who waves hello to anyone he crosses. The kind who helps out a neighbour. The kind no one could say a bad word about. It seems like Quince agrees. The town that he hated for so long appears to finally be letting him go.

He scans the dark bar, red glow. *Wagon Wheel* plays around the sound system and a slot machine whirls in the distance. The gambler's hand reaches up for another wistful pull. Nick takes a swig of his drink, then another, and another. He gets close to finishing it off and there's still no sign of Marina or Trevaughn.

The bartender gazes towards him occasionally, and when he starts to feel more than one pair of eyes staring at the back of his skull, Nick decides to go.

"Oi, you leaving?"

Trevaughn enters first while Marina trails behind him, her long hair covering her face. He slaps Nick on his shoulder and swaggers past, sitting at the stool where Nick had been sitting just seconds ago. He orders three bourbons with no ice. Marina hesitates at the door and Nick notices the redness of her nose and eyes, only exaggerated by the bar's seedy glow. He can tell she's been crying.

He doesn't ask what happened and he doesn't ask if she is okay, and so Marina walks on without saying a word. Nick follows slowly and before long, the bartender has all three drinks in front of them.

"We got held up," Trevaughn says. "You been waiting here a while?"

"No," Nick lies, and he and the bartender share another

knowing look.

On the other side of Trevaughn, Marina rests her elbow on the countertop and into some sticky residue left behind by a previous patron. She doesn't seem to notice. The usually chatty woman is dominated tonight by her partner, who rattles off questions to Nick like he's conducting an interview. He wants to know his age, his birthplace, his family tree, his likes, his dislikes, and when Nick fires the same questions back, Trevaughn's responses are so offhand, Nick doubts they were ever asked.

He hears again how Trev met Marina in their first year of high school, long before they both dropped out. The words he uses to describe her are encouraging – words like sassy and breath-taking – and he could pass for loving if it weren't for the clenched fists that hit hard on top of the bar throughout the night. When Nick answers a question, there's a bang; after Trevaughn takes a swig, another bang; before he leaves to take a piss; another bang. Nick grows more uncomfortable with every passing minute.

Marina still hasn't made eye contact with him, and she keeps her eyes firmly on her drink or on the bar when Trev sidles to the toilet. When Nick clears his throat, she still doesn't lift her gaze.

The woman from earlier in the week has all but disappeared. The puddle-stomping, pompom wearing force of nature, gone. Replacing her is a withdrawn, red-eyed loner, staring through malt-coloured bourbon to the bottom of her glass. Though Nick hardly knows her, he's come to be protective of her, and he knows Trevaughn is the cause of her unhappiness. He is a bad guy, he fits the bill, he looks the part. Of all the depressed punters, no matter their flaws or their ailments, Trevaughn is the one to look out for, he knows it.

"Marina," Nick whispers. "What's wrong?"

She lets out a deep sigh. "I'm just not feeling well, that's all."

He knows it's a lie and he hates it; hates being lied to. He stands up from his bar stool and heads to the restrooms.

He can hear Trev taking a leak as soon as he enters, sees him hunched over the urinal with his palm on the adjacent wall. He turns back and sees Nick and sniffs harshly, nose wrinkling.

"Oh, hey," he says.

Nick doesn't respond. He walks to the urinal next to him, looks at his surroundings. A mirror with smudges is stuck to the far wall. The sinks are made from porcelain and the paper hand towels slide out of stainless-steel dispensers. He could rip one off the wall, he thinks, but then he abandons the idea. Who is he kidding? He doesn't have the strength.

"What's up with Marina tonight?" he asks.

"Huh?' Trevaughn has finished up and spits into the john. He walks past Nick and washes his hands at the basin.

"She's quiet."

"She's always quiet."

Nick pictures the woman from the first night at the bar: rowdy, boisterous, intimidatingly happy. Trev shakes his hands twice but water still clings to them. He takes two steps forward so that he's face-to-face with Nick. He puts his hands on his shoulders and Nick can feel them soaking through to his skin.

"Look. Mind your own business, okay? We've got our problems, sure, everyone at the fucking motel has some sort of problem."

Sure, he thinks.

"But if you don't mind your business, I won't mind mine."

Trev sniffs again and Nick looks down at his fingers, so close to his face. He hopes he used soap. He can hear the music steadily pumping from the speaker out in the bar. He imagines punters refilling their drinks and he hopes one of them walks in to empty their bladder, to interrupt the scene. There's no such luck.

After a while, Trev lifts his hands from Nick's damp shoulders.

"Nice jacket, by the way," he says with a smirk, and when he exits the bathroom, a deep exhale escapes Nick's lungs.

When the two settle back at the bar, Trevaughn, all smiles, drinks away what little money he has left. He fills the time talking with the other bar goers, and though the angler's doppelgangers continue to run their eyes over Nick, Nick keeps his attention on the truck driver as the words of his threat tumble around his head like a car crash.

18

The call comes through about 1am. Abbott, in no state to drive, does his best to keep his glazed eyes fixed on the road ahead. The headlights of an oncoming car shine bright and force him to look away, but then he starts rolling a little to the left and has to quickly correct himself before he ends up a poor old man in a ditch.

He's one of the last ones to arrive at the station, though he doesn't know how that's possible. He flung himself out of bed as soon as he got the call, dove into a fresh outfit, unironed, and reached his car before he could even wipe the sleep from his eyes. Still, a gaggle of other cops have already poured themselves a pick-me-up and stand gathered around a circular table in the middle of the station. They all look at him when he enters. Abbott thinks he can see Cole roll his eyes. They continue where they left off with their discussion.

"They're bringing the kid to us. Should be here in about 40... 50 minutes."

"And they're sure it's him?"

"That hasn't been confirmed yet. Kid won't tell them his name, but he fits the description: early 20s, 6ft, blue eyes."

Abbott's own blue eyes want to close, but he pries them

142

open as he walks over to the coffee machine. When he presses the 'pour' button, the system whirrs like a jet engine, and the other officers turn to look towards the noise.

"We'll reconvene when they arrive."

They all disperse except Rowan, who takes his place by Abbott, sipping his own hot drink. He sniffs a few times but doesn't say anything about the smell of alcohol on Abbott's breath.

"Do you think it's him?"

"How'd they say they found him?"

"He messed up." Rowan sniffs again, then clears his throat. "Got into a fight at a bar. Apparently tried to smash a pint over some other guy's head."

They both take a sip of their drinks.

"Bartender called the cops, our guy stole a car, fled. Found him at East Chapel, I think."

"Huh."

Abbott hoped this would happen, that Nick Greene would mess up somewhere along the way and he'd be dragged back home with his tail between his legs. He did envision it a little differently, though; he certainly wouldn't have been the last to find out. Instead, he'd be standing at the front of the station, its red and blue 'open' sign flashing down on him like a strobe. He'd be clapping his hands and doing a victory dance, all the while chanting a little song – *nobody can out-run me*.

"I'm gonna go listen to music." Rowan yawns as he departs, dragging himself over to one of the corner desks and popping his headphones into his ears. When 30 minutes has passed, Abbott can still see him gently bobbing his head as it droops closer and closer to the top of the table.

The rest of the precinct act like zombies too, all preferring they were back home in bed, next to their husbands or wives. Eventually, when the coffee machine has been used to breaking point, and when it looks as if all, including Cole, are beginning to drift off to sleep, there is a knock on the station door. Cole rises first – he's fast – and races towards the foyer. Abbott follows – still quick, still agile for his age – close behind.

"Where the hell is he?" Cole asks the constable, who is used to late nights and looks more awake.

"He's in the car."

Cole and Abbott exchange glances. The other cops are still making their way to the front of the station, while some have lost interest and stay idling in the far corners. Cole sighs, but accepts that he and Abbott, together, would be the ones to collect Nick Greene.

As they make their way to the car, the constable from Abercrombie leading the charge, it begins to feel as if the end is near. Abbott can see the dark silhouette of the man in the back seat, staring straight ahead. His heart starts to beat faster and his hands tremble from excitement. He's back inside his head, picturing himself pulling open the door of the police car, yanking Nick Greene to the floor and yelling: Gotcha! They are only a few steps away.

"Want to question him here or bring him inside?"

Abbott begins to say "inside", but Cole's voice is louder and it's the one the constable listens to.

"Here is fine."

The man nods and pulls open the car door, and like the paparazzi dying to get the first shot, Cole and Abbott try to step in front of one another, a game of who beats who. Cole wins, of course, but Abbott can see from behind his broad shoulder, and the kid, although he does resemble the man from the missing persons posters, isn't Nick Greene.

Abbott wobbles backwards as if the wind has been knocked out of him. Cole doesn't notice, and he bends down to the man's eye level and begins his questioning: who are you, where have you been, what have you done? The detainee is no help: no one, nowhere, nothing.

"Are you Nick Greene?"

"Who the fuck is Nick Greene?"

Abbott taps Cole on the shoulder. "It isn't him," he says flatly.

"And how the hell would you know?"

There's a simple answer. The kid in the back of the police car talks with a noticeable lisp. Paula never mentioned Nick had one. There's also a small tattoo on the side of his right hand.

He raises these observations to Cole, who looks at the man quizzingly. Eventually, he too has to face the truth: that the man in the back seat, the one who got into a bar brawl and stole a car, is not the man involved with the angler at the forest park. He slams the car door and curses, and the sound bounces off the sharp angles of the surrounding buildings, echoing through the still of the night.

19

JUNE 16   DAY 43

Nick walks two paces behind. Marina, who has perked up after a few drinks, has her arm thrown around Trev's neck and her head resting sleepily on his shoulders.

It's about 1am, and there's a cop car screeching through the streets less than a kilometre or so ahead; they can hear the car's tyres and the whining of its siren. The noise used to frighten Nick in Quince. It always meant something bad was happening to someone he knew, and he always pictured the worst: a mangled car wreck, a fire gutting a house, or, like that summer's day, a barbecue explosion and a hole left in a lawn like a crater. Here though, the siren can mean anything: a burglary, a domestic incident, a car-jacking, and it never involves anyone Nick knows. The noise is just an annoyance, a reminder that bad people are walking around the city getting busted for their crimes. He always forgets that the noise could soon be the same one coming for him.

After those initial drinks, Nick opted for water, which Trevaughn teased him about but he knew it was wise. He wanted to keep his wits about him. If things turned sour, like he feared they would, he wanted to have a clear head, to be able to out-run whatever misfortune came his way. But nothing happened. All Nick was left with was a full bladder and a sorry look on his face, while the people he was with ignored him the whole night and he felt like the new kid at school they were told to be kind to.

"You still with us?" Trev calls back.

There aren't many more steps until Sub Rosa, and so Nick answers with a loud scuff of his shoe. A small stone skids from under the sole and rattles across the seal of the road like a button that's popped off a shirt. Trev turns around and raises one eyebrow while Nick buries himself further inside his father's coat.

It smells stale in here, he thinks. Earthy, like rotting wood. He wonders when the last time the jacket's sleeves covered his father's arms; can he picture it? Can he remember his dad reaching for the coat from the downstairs cupboard before going to work or to the doctors or to the shops? Did he ever wash it? Hang it on the line to dry? Did his dad even leave the house at all?

While some memories flash in front of Nick's eyes as if they're trying to cause a scene, others are harder to bring forward, and memories of his dad lay concealed under the fibres of his brain. He can form a picture in his mind, an image he thinks is real, of him and his dad on Christmas morning, only for it to disperse like dust particles, like it didn't happen at all, like it was a dream. Nick's spent so much time in his head he begins to doubt his own hippocampus. Why is he here? What happened tonight? Who is he – Nick Greene or Rick Brown?

"Hey Rick, hurry up, will you?"

His head shakes and his feet keep moving but Nick is still caught up in thought. "You go ahead," he says. "I'll catch up with you later."

Trev and Marina both purse their lips and shrug. Their

147

steps become elongated and their laughter grows louder. It isn't long until they step onto the gravel of Sub Rosa's parking lot and pass underneath its sign's neon glow. Mosquitoes are attracted to the light. They hop onto the balcony outside their room and pull open the door. Trev walks inside first, followed by Marina, and neither turn back to make sure Nick makes it home.

20

"Phew." Trev sighs when the door is shut and locked behind them, while Marina heads straight to the bathroom, searching inside the vanity drawers for a hairbrush that has lost bristles. When she finds it, she uses it to comb through her wild hair, tugging at the knots each time they catch.

"Are you happy?" Trev asks her, but she hardly hears him as the brush catches on her tangled strands.

He clicks on the TV set and mutes the picture before chucking the remote control onto the motel's double bed. He has his hands on his hips, and Marina watches as his face pauses in thought. They think they hear the door to the neighbouring room open and close.

"You got what you wanted. You got me to hang out with the guy. So, are you happy?"

Marina tilts her head to the side. "Do you see what I mean?"

"I see the guy's a freak."

"He's not a freak," she insists. "He's… different. He's like us."

"In no way is that freak like us."

Marina walks back into the small bathroom. She looks at herself in the mirror and doesn't like what she sees. Her hair has gone fuzzy from the brushing, and there are dark rings under her eyes, and her nose is still chapped from the tears and the tissues. She throws the brush back in its drawer and slams it shut.

"He could help us."

Trevaughn moves to join her, moving his body in that staunch yet heavy-footed, lumbering way. He wraps his arms around her waist and the two stare at their reflections through the smudges and the grease. They're both a sight, and, like the kids at school that no one is kind to, they've become attached to one another; an exclusive group of just the two of them. Trevaughn's hot breath dances on the nape of her neck.

"I know you want to think that," he says, his voice low, "but he can't help us. We're on our own."

"Why do we have to be on our own?"

"Because." Trev pulls away. "That's how it's always been."

He's right. They had met so young, technically still children in a school parking lot, and his loyalty is just as unwavering now as it was back then. He could have left her one hundred times, easily, but he hasn't; it seems the thought hasn't even crossed his mind.

She was so small then, when they met, with bony elbows pointing out from skinny arms. Legs like spaghetti. Big brown eyes that would curve up at the corners whenever she smiled. Bruises the colour of squashed grapes on her shoulders, her knees, her face. Still, she was beautiful. He told her she was his baby bird and that she needed to be taken under his wing.

"He was worried about you tonight," he says, clutching hold of the bathroom door.

"Who?"

"Rick. He said you were acting quiet."

She looks to her feet, still inside wedge heels that only make her legs look more knobbly. "What'd you say?"

"I told him not to worry about it."

She nods. A tight smile. "So what do you reckon?"

Trev walks into the main living area of the motel room and turns the volume up on the TV. He throws himself onto the bed and rests his hands behind his head.

"I still don't like it," he says.

"But we could really use him."

His face turns to the wall behind his head and he's silent for a moment. Rick is definitely in the next room; he's dragging his plastic chair around again.

"And you're sure he has money?"

"I've seen it," she insists. "In his room. And at the restaurant, the prices… the mains were, like, $35 a pop."

Trev lets out a long breath. He's almost convinced, she knows it. "I just don't like the idea of him hanging 'round you while he's got the hots for you," he tells her. "That's all."

She scoffs. Brushes it aside. "So… are you in?"

Marina has her fingers linked, ready to beg, but Trev glances at her and submits. He is bigger now than he was when they met. He had a funny haircut and a tattoo drawn in pen on his forearm. He was wearing shoes too big for his small feet and they slapped a little too loudly with every step he took. He used to show up to school hungry and so he'd steal food from the canteen. Still, he was admirable. A hero Marina never asked for but needed. A hero that was rough around the edges, vulgar and unkempt, but hardworking and faithful and a fighter.

"Fine," he says, rolling his eyes.

She realises now that she doesn't say thank you enough.

*

She dangles her legs from the porch outside her room. She can see Rick out in the middle of the parking lot, knows it's him because his silhouette sits on a white plastic chair and his head is tilted towards the stars.

She rubs at the bridge of her nose and wonders why he cared so much about the scar. She hardly notices it now, some days she forgets it's even there, but every time she feels the bump in her skin she remembers what she's done, and it makes her chest go all tight.

It wasn't planned, it just happened, and she likes to remind herself of that, to remember that she isn't an awful person, just one who made a mistake. Of all people, she thinks Rick would be the one to understand if only she'd tell him.

She checks behind her, makes sure the door to their room is still shut. It's almost 2am now and Trev told her to go to sleep but she couldn't. Not yet. She walks towards Rick and stands silently behind him now, staring at the back of his head. He's looking up at the sky as if he's waiting for a shooting star to appear. Marina's never seen a shooting star; isn't even sure they really exist.

"Hey, you." Her voice comes out in a whisper but still Rick lunges forward in front. He turns around quickly to see her standing a few feet behind and she laughs at the fear on his face.

"Shit!" he says. "You scared me."

"I see that."

She walks over to his side, and, without checking to see

if it's okay first, she sits on the thin arm of the chair. It's not very comfortable, and she feels like the seat could tip at any second, but she stays there and looks up at the sky, wondering what all the fuss is about. Rick leans further to the right, as if trying not to let any part of him touch her.

"What are you doing out here? Is there something I should be looking for?"

He looks back up. The sky is a picturesque midnight blue, with bright white stars blinking down at them like diamonds. She follows his gaze. It is perfect, she thinks, and she wonders if he stares up at the sky for its beauty alone. Maybe that's why he's out here most nights.

"It's peaceful," he tells her. "What are you doing?"

Marina exhales a long breath. It sounds like a wave crashing onto the shore. "I've had a bad week," she admits.

"Is it Trevaughn?"

Marina pulls her eyes from the darkness and stares across at him, a frown creating wrinkles on her forehead. "What? No, of course not. Why would you think that?"

He shrugs. "I just had to ask."

"You think Trevaughn's the reason why I'm upset? That is…" She thinks for a second. "The stupidest thing I have ever heard."

Rick turns to her but his left arm touches her right thigh and he flinches, withdrawing further back. "Good. I just, I just needed to check, okay?"

Marina laughs, rolling her eyes to insinuate that Rick's an idiot. She knows Trev's right about him, about his growing fondness for her. That had been her intention all along. Ever since that night she saw him sitting as he sits right now. "You worry a lot, huh?"

"What? No, I don't worry at all." Rick tries to play it

cool, kicking his foot up to cross his legs, but the move is too hasty and the chair skids a little, almost sends them both flying into the dirt.

Marina can't help but laugh a little louder and she spots Rick smiling at the sound. They regather themselves and look up at the stars again. This time, he lets her arm touch his shoulder and, when she slinks down to use his body as support, he doesn't push her away.

"Can I tell you something, Rick?" She drops her voice to a whisper, barely louder than the crickets chirping within earshot.

"Sure."

"I've... I've done something I regret."

Rick almost looks at her but doesn't. He instead stares to the left, up at Sub Rosa's sign.

"I don't know what to do about it," she continues.

The parking lot is empty, abandoned. The air is cold and there's that kind of wind that indicates a storm is coming and it has sent everyone else into their rooms, under cover. They must look mad for being out here, two acquaintances perched on a plastic chair like two birds on a power line.

Rick coughs a little to clear his throat. "What are your options?"

"I have a few," she replies, "and that's kind of what I want to talk to you about."

He looks at her now, confused. He waits for her to go on.

"If I do what I think I need to do, can I come to you for help?"

Rick is shaking his head, laughing a little at the question, but then he catches a glimpse of her and she's wrapped her arms tightly across her chest as if to hold herself together. She knows there's something about her pain that he can't resist. She knows that she's pulling him in, little by little, and she knows that he wants to throw his arms around her, cradle her in the way men do to feel powerful and protective.

"Okay," he says quietly. "I'll help. I mean, I don't know how I can help, but I can try."

Marina smiles now, nods her head slowly. She pulls one arm away from her body and rests it lightly on his shoulder.

"Trust me," she tells him. "You'll be able to help."

21

JUNE 16   DAY 43

The funeral for the fisherman is held on a Friday, nine days after his body was found. A little delayed, sure, but that is to be expected here. Everyone seems to be slowed down by something, a pull that Cole can't see. They take their time moving into parking spaces, squeezing themselves down supermarket aisles, and finishing sentences that should've ended minutes earlier. It's the same at the station, and it's the same at the fisherman's funeral.

Cole stands back like a sentinel guarding the proceedings, and from here he gets a better look at the thin crowd. The men and women are dressed casually, following a dress code Cole didn't get, and move slowly towards the pine coffin that holds the angler. Closed casket. A baby's breath and daisy wreath. Behind dark sunglasses, the guests trudge along to pay their respects, bending their heads ever so slightly as they pass. The fisherman's wife, raggedy on the best of days, looks withdrawn and keeps to herself. One hand clutches the opposite wrist.

The cemetery is built on a slight hill, and the fisherman's plot has a good view of the northern end of Quince. He'll be facing towards the forest park that claimed his life, and Cole doesn't know how he feels about that yet. It'd be better if there were answers before the dirt, but eventually, the dirt comes and the answers don't.

He looks around as a breeze whips through his hair. There are about two dozen of the fisherman's acquaintances staying close to the casket, while two more handfuls linger a few metres away. There's a woman with black hair jotting things down into a notepad under the shade of a tree. A wind collects leaves and drops them to her feet.

Either side of her, there are more people wearing sunglasses. Cole peers at their faces, trying to see if any of them look like Nick Greene. He doesn't expect to see him here, and yet not seeing him makes his heart sink a little. How good would that be, he thinks. That he'd be the one to accost Nick Greene while Abbott mopes about someplace. That'd teach him.

A thought comes to him then. Happy's funeral. Abbott was there that day, Cole remembers. Standing by the treeline just as he is now. He hated seeing him, thought it was an insult to Happy's memory. Abbott hadn't even tried to find him and yet he'd shown up to his funeral. In typical Quince fashion, it was too little, too late.

The funeral director, dressed in a black suit with a red pocket square, clears his throat to mark the end of the proceedings. Cole's eyes flit back over to the casket, which is being lowered into the earth. The men stand stoic but the fisherman's wife lets out a loud holler. The noise makes the hairs on the back of Cole's neck stand erect. He hates grief – knows it, has felt it, and still, he hates it.

The crowd begins to disperse and Cole kicks dirt with the point of his boot as he turns. He's the one that moves slowly this time, letting the others pass him. He doesn't want to look like he's in a rush to escape. No, this time, each measured step is his way of showing the dead angler he cares.

"Detective?"

Behind him is the woman with dark hair. She still has her notebook out. She's wearing a blazer that looks more blue than black and Cole can see a thermal shirt poking out from under its too-short sleeves. "Yes?"

"I'm Pippa Dobson, from *The Quince Star*."

Cole grunts and turns his back to her. His pace quickens.

The woman is not deterred. "I just wanted to ask for an update on the case."

"Is that why you're here?" He wants to call her a vulture, a shark. He bites his tongue.

"No, actually," she says. "I was invited to attend by the family."

Cole stops, raises one eyebrow. "Really?"

"Really. I'm writing an obituary."

He forgets this is how small towns work. "Still, I can't help you," he says.

Pippa keeps up with his pace. "Maybe not this second but... here." She reaches for something deep within her blazer pocket. "Here's my card."

Cole takes it but flicks it around between his fingers like it means nothing to him.

In Abercrombie, the relationship between reporters and cops is best described as polite resentment. Every morning, Cole or another one of his colleagues has to sit in a low-lit staff room with a reporter from the daily paper, who asks questions about the armed-robbery-they-definitely-didn't-hear-on-the-police-scanner-they're-not-supposed-to-have, and Cole has to answer as vaguely as he can. It's always: 'I can't comment further' or 'It's under investigation', and the reporter sighs, takes it or leaves it, and they each go back to their respective offices, bitching about one another under their breath.

Cole begins to give Pippa the same laissez-faire response, but she cuts in before he can speak. "My editor is thrilled you're on the case," she says.

Cole's shoulders arch back a little. "Why's that?"

She giggles to herself. "It's the other guy, the other cop. My boss hates him."

"Abbott?"

"That's the one."

Cole tries hard not to let a smile slip but one falls out anyway. He clears his throat. "Why does she hate him?" he asks, as if he hasn't got the slightest clue.

"Something happened here. I was a baby, so I don't remember it, but he does. The whole town does, apparently."

Cole's steely eyes urge her to go on.

"That Abbott guy screwed up a case and a kid was found dead. Everyone blames him for it. I'm not sure if I do, but like I said, I don't remember it."

Cole licks his lips and nods, says thank you for the information. He turns his back again and this time the woman doesn't follow.

That night, alone in the precinct, Cole picks up Pippa's card from where it had been sitting on his desk, staring up at him. He bends the sharp corners until they are not sharp anymore.

At home, he only ever thought about Happy occasionally. Here, in Quince, he comes to mind often. Maybe it's because Fox Crescent is only four roads back from the station. Maybe it's because Drury Road is only five. He wanders there in his mind sometimes. Replays the day Happy went missing, only, it happens differently. In his new version, a young Cole waits outside Happy's house for him to appear, pulling his bike alongside him. Instead of going left, towards Quince's outskirts, Cole would convince him to go right, towards the bustle of the town centre. Happy would listen. His life would go on unchanged. He would be alive today.

Cole ignores a phone call from his wife and makes a mental note to ring her back soon. They usually talk at this time of night, and she'll know he'll be toying with something in his mind, a game of tug-of-war between two versions of himself.

Clearing his throat and rubbing his brow, he picks up his phone and punches the numbers in. It rings a half dozen times.

"Hello?" a strained voice answers.

"Pippa. This is Chris Cole."

"Oh, thanks for calling. Hold on a sec, let me just get my notes..." There's a shuffling of papers, a drop of something onto the floor.

"No need," Cole interjects. "I want to speak to your editor."

22

JUNE 19   DAY 46

Steam rises from the mug on the coffee table, on which a ring of dew begins to form. The fridge rattles, indicating a fault in the system, and there's static coming off the digital clock on the kitchen counter. Abbott sits alone among it all, in a dark room, hunched over so far forward he's become a gargoyle, a solitary statue on a sofa.

He sits with his hands covering his weathered face; hasn't moved from that position for hours. If anyone saw him, they'd be concerned, alarmed, perhaps they'd even call the cops for help, but Abbott knows there'd be no use in that. The police, well, they just don't care anymore.

The morning's newspaper is lying on the floor in a heap. It wasn't always like that, had been thrown there after its reader couldn't bear to look at the contents any longer. It had been thrown with such force its delicate pages bent. It remained there when the neighbours' children waddled off to school and was still there when they returned seven hours later.

The Quince Star *can now report that the disappearance of Nicolas Greene and the body of Hugh Fir, found in the town's forest park on June 7, are linked.*

To what extent, Police have not yet revealed.

According to a statement from leading detective Chris Cole, Fir was found at an abandoned "makeshift campground" they have determined was visited by Greene.

Greene vanished from his medical school campus on May 5.

"We have deduced that the campsite, located roughly 2km from the park's main entrance, was used to accommodate Mr Greene sometime after his disappearance on May 5.

"When he vacated the site, we don't yet know."

Greene's mother, Paula Greene, who has been vocal in the search for her son, expressed shock at the news.

"I don't believe it," she said. "I simply do not believe that Nick knew this man. If anything, this man has something to do with Nick's disappearance. Maybe that should be the real question."

The Nick Greene mystery has eerie similarities to Quince's last missing persons case involving a young person, Harvey Price, in 1997. The officer in charge of that case is the same one overseeing Mr Greene's vanishing, senior detective Duncan Abbott, of the Quince CIB.

Cole was adamant the outcome would not be the same.

"We'll find Nick, one way or the other. What happened in '97 does not reflect our ability to solve this case now. For Hugh, for Nick, for Quince, we'll solve it."

Harvey Price was 14 when he vanished from his home in Drury Road. He was found –

Abbott stopped reading then.

Now, like an old man who is learning how to move again, he reaches for his mug of coffee. It's become a bit tasteless, so he grabs the bottle of whiskey next to it and adds a few hearty drops to his drink before gulping it down. He does this over and over until there's nothing left in the mug.

For what feels like a lifetime, he's been scouring through staticky footage from June 3, trying to find a skulking Nick Greene creeping back into Driscoll Street or boarding a bus out of town. There is only one rental car company in Quince, and they haven't seen him. He's been keeping an eye on Victoria, too, but it's like she knows he's watching. Her life is appearing utterly bland.

Abbott puts in his next tape, his next dead end. June 4, June 5 and June 6. Nothing.

He rubs at the eyes that have become so tired, so strained, and massages the folds of his wrinkles that have become so much more distinguishable. He tries to slap some sense into himself but it hurts.

Then, the phone rings, the archaic landline, and Abbott considers ignoring it, pretending that it doesn't exist. He sighs, and finds himself pushing off from the couch, rocking back and forward a few times to gain momentum. He barely makes it to the phone before the call disconnects.

"You there, Duncan?"

Abbott's voice comes out in a growl, a bear coming out of a self-imposed hibernation: "I'm here."

"Good." It's his sister. "How have you been?"

Katherine. Kathy. Five years younger and Abbott's only sibling and family member left alive. They're not close, and yet she has the foresight to call, as if she senses he needs her petulant reassurance now more than ever.

"I'm fine," he grumbles.

"And how's Franny?"

"She's fine too."

His sister waits on the other end of the phone, hoping the silence will be enough for him to continue, to elaborate, to offer up a better adjective than 'fine'. There's no such luck.

Kathy sighs. "I've been following your case. Seems like a toughy."

Abbott wants to crumble, to spread himself along the kitchen counter like melted chocolate. Kathy was around all those years ago, for his failed case. She saw what it did to him. Now, he understands the purpose of her call. She's scared what happened then will happen again.

"Last time," she says unprompted, "what made you miss it last time?"

Abbott lets out a sigh; this one weighs heavy.

"I didn't look enough," he says. "But this time I am. I am looking everywhere."

"Maybe you're looking too hard," Kathy says, then, a pause. "Do you think this kid killed the guy?"

Abbott thinks to the newspaper photo of Nick Greene lying on the ground in a heap. Could he have killed him? It just doesn't make sense. Where's the motive? Where's the connection? Abbott asks himself these questions over and over until the letters scramble and all sense is lost.

"No," he finally says, though he feels like he's betraying himself.

"Well, then… do you need to keep chasing him? Maybe you should let this one go?"

Abbott slams his fist on the counter, though he's not angry at Kathy. Letting go, wouldn't that be like giving up?

"I did that last time," he shakes his head. "I can't do it again."

"What does Fran think you should do?"

The fridge continues to rattle, seemingly louder now. Abbott can hear the plastic milk bottle hit the inside of the door like a passenger on a plane in the midst of take-off. When he doesn't answer, it's Kathy's turn to sigh, perhaps even slam her fist on a countertop.

"You haven't talked to her, have you?"

"What would I say?" he mumbles.

Kathy, who as a child was always intuitive, who could sense ghosts down the hallway and easily befriend elderly neighbours, seems to have retained her second sight. She knows Abbott is hurting, and that his lonely heart burns with a longing like the fiery glow of an autumn sunset. She knows he's a good man, deep down.

"She never stopped loving you," she whispers.

Abbott once admired Kathy's ability to see the best in people but now, he bounces awkwardly on the balls of his feet.

He doubts that very much.

*

Abbott pulls himself together long enough to head into the station that evening. He hopes to see Rowan, but it's late and the young officer is out, doing normal people things like walking the dog or having family over for dinner. He had shaken away his whiskey haze and put on a clean shirt, but as soon as he steps inside, he realises the effort was wasted.

"Look what the cat dragged in."

In one of the corner cubicles, Cole sits with a smirk on his face. It's highlighted by the dim glow of a lamp to his left. He's flicking through documents and there's a cup of

165

joe within touching distance of his right hand. Abbott tries to smile but it comes out more like a wince.

"Where have you been?"

"Working," he lies.

Cole continues to smirk, stretching upwards so his back clicks. His yawn is obnoxious, too. "And what have you found?" he asks.

The Quince detective knows it's a trick question, yet still he answers, despondent. "Nothing. You?"

Cole pauses a moment, before standing up to walk towards Abbott. Wrinkles on his forehead start to form and for the first time, he looks as dishevelled as he does.

He sighs. "Nothing. Can you believe it? We've got nothing. Nothing that connects that fisherman with the kid."

Abbott isn't surprised, but he is pleased. Pleased to hear that a seasoned detective like Cole hasn't come up with the clue that ties the case all together. He doesn't think he'd be able to bear it if he did.

"That's a shame," he lies, sinking into his desk chair. He wants to mention the newspaper report, wants to tell him it was unfair to bring up his past, but he says nothing.

Cole retreats back to his desk to grab the cup of black coffee he left there. He sips on it like a child. "Actually, how are you placed tomorrow?"

Abbott looks up, puzzled.

"Because we did have a tip come through from someone in Abercrombie. Might be a bit of a stretch but... here."

Abbott stands with a jolt and snatches the piece of paper Cole has in his hand. He reads the printed text and Cole laughs when he sees the confusion on his face.

"From that list of stolen items we released after Driscoll

Street. I know, that's it." Cole's teeth are showing, that's how funny he thinks this is.

"The green jacket? That's all this is going on?"

"The dad's jacket, yep." Cole pops his lips.

"You want me to go all the way to Abercrombie and find someone with a similar-looking jacket?"

The lips pop again. "Yep."

Abbott scratches at the corner of his nose. He feels like tossing the piece of paper in Cole's smiling face. He feels like following Kathy's advice and throwing in the towel. He feels a rage bubbling deep inside him, but then all at once, it stops itself from overflowing. There's an anecdote of calm that washes away all his hate, all his bitterness, and he thinks about '97 and what he wishes he could've told himself back then: *Hang on.*

"Alright, I'll do it," he says.

Cole looks bemused. He slurps on his hot coffee and watches while Abbott walks back over to his desk.

He switches off the computer he had only just restarted, collects the pieces of paper he had only just removed from his briefcase, and dusts off the shirt he had only just taken out of the dryer.

He nods back to Cole, who says before he leaves: "Safe travels." Abbott's the one who smiles now. He's been given an out; an escape from Paula and the media and Cole; an escape from the long days and nights in his house where it's just him and his intrusive thoughts.

He hasn't left Quince for years, is unsure what the rest of the world is like, and while the unknown usually fills him with dread, there's another feeling in his stomach, and for the first time in a long time, the feeling is a welcome one.

23

JUNE 20   DAY 47

Nora Bassett once worked with hair for a living. Thin hair, curly hair, and hair that would at times disobey. She excelled at colouring, had a knack for layers, and was never afraid to tell a lady what styles best suited her bone structure. With a comb in her hand, Nora felt formidable. With a snip of the scissors or a shake of the hairdryer, there was nothing Nora couldn't do.

For 15 years, she worked at a suburban salon, and the women she'd see were some of the most demanding and difficult, but Nora always had the ability to smooth things over. She never let herself feel intimidated, never gave a refund or did a client's hair again for free. Working with hair made her the person she is today. Older, wrinklier, but still tough as nails with a perfect blow-dried bob.

The self-assured woman often finds herself reflecting on those days when it's quiet at Sub Rosa and the rain drips down from the gutters. She sits in her office and faces the far wall, which displays photographs and accolades from this life and the last.

Next to a certificate for hairstyling sits an award the motel received from the city's Business-After-Five event, some years ago now, when the motel was new and her husband was still alive. It has a gold star stuck to the side of the glossy piece of paper and a signature from a person Nora can't remember meeting.

Back then, she and Neil were considered pioneers. They were brave for ditching their regular, run-of-the-mill careers to become moteliers, and good moteliers at that. For a while, people swapped the luxury hotels along the main strip for her cosy accommodation with all the accompaniments, but when Neil died, it was difficult to maintain the place. She was good with hair; he was the handyman. Eventually, people went back to their hotels with strong water pressure and room service, and Nora has since had to provide long-term accommodation for those who need it most, in order to make a living and to keep a roof over her head, no matter how leaky.

At times she misses the early days. She felt like she lived at the centre of the world. Now, the world passes her by in the form of lost travellers, desperate couples, and cheap businessmen who keep 'Do Not Disturb' signs on their doors.

Still, she enjoys the people, as varied and unique as hair is, and dealing with hair, she learned, was not so different from dealing with humans. There were times when the frizz wouldn't subside, or when box dyes would come out in different shades than expected. There were some stubborn curls and wild fringes, and over the years, she had encountered people with similar traits.

But Nora Bassett deals with people now the same way she dealt with hair back then: she listens, she smiles, and she's never afraid to cut something off.

It is this mantra that Nora keeps at the forefront of her mind as she walks across to the gentleman on the night of June 20.

The man is already impatient before she can make it to the front counter. His wet shoe taps on the motel's floor and he's too consumed by thought that he doesn't notice the drop of rain falling from his hair and sliding down his weathered cheek.

"Good evening," she says, though she can tell it hasn't been a good one for him.

"I'm looking for someone," the man answers back, and Nora takes issue with his tone. She brings her hands together and rests them on top of the counter.

"I doubt I'll be able to help."

The man retrieves a damp photo from his pocket and Nora smacks her lips, shaking her head at the stranger's persistence. Before she can answer him, he holds his police badge in her face.

"What's this about?" she asks, her nerves unshakable.

"He goes by the name of Nick Greene."

It isn't the first time Nora has been in the presence of a tenacious police officer. The kids who stay here are often running from some sort of charges, usually small ones, like petty theft or a drunken assault. The motel has become the first place cops scope out, even if they have nothing to go on.

"There's no one here by that name," she tells him, sucking in her lips so that her mouth is a tight line. "Not all my guests are felons."

"He could have been here up to a month ago. Does the face seem familiar?"

She shrugs. "I don't think so."

"Could you look again, please?" the man asks, pushing the image, snatched from an old photo album, across the front counter.

Nora sighs and picks up the photo with tender fingers. She barely glances at it before she recalls the days when she was once handed cut-out photographs of models from magazines for reference. The hair was always the most unusual style, worn on women who in no way resembled the world of Abercrombie.

Instead of focusing on the image in her hand, her mind drifts off to the dreams she's been collecting for some time now, the dreams that consist of her buying her own small piece of land and building a salon with checked titles and pink walls. She sees herself flitting about, in her happy place, her safe haven with a pair of scissors in her hand. She knows nowadays it'd be hard to compete with the young girls that do hair in an assortment of bold colours and styles, but Nora knows she has the talent, a cup of tea for clients, and good conversation to make it work.

If she did that all, though, if she fulfilled her wild dream at an age when it's easier to finish things than start fresh, she'd need to sell the motel. She wouldn't get much for it now, what with its leaking roof and stained carpet, but perhaps she'll find someone who can see the potential she once saw in it, someone who can return the motel back to its former glory. She smiles to herself, feeling comforted by the pictures playing inside her mind, but the man at the counter clicks his teeth impatiently.

"Ma'am?"

Nora is pulled from her trance. She hands the photo back to him. "I'm sorry I couldn't be of more help."

The officer begrudgingly places the image of Nick Greene back inside his pocket but pulls out a small and dated business card and hands it to her instead. "Call me if anything changes," he says.

Nora watches as he shoves his hands into his coat pockets before he heads out the door into the perpetual deluge. She watches as he skims his feet over the loose chips of gravel as he makes his way to a rundown old vehicle. She watches as he shakes his head at a male passenger inside the car.

Her nosiness allows her to be intrigued by the men for a minute, but when they retreat from the parking lot and move out of sight, Nora Bassett sinks back into more attractive thoughts.

*

The following morning, when the rain has subsided long enough for the birds to stretch their wings and spiders to crawl out from the comfort of their webs, Nora walks along the parking lot towards the west end of her motel.

She's been told the guttering outside Number 16 has filled with sodden leaves, and the weight of it had brought down the plastic piping in the middle of last night's deluge. She wears yellow rubber gloves on her hands and carries a matching bucket. On her feet are gumboots with polka dots, and she's wearing her favourite paisley-print skirt. She trudges towards the room like a gold miner heading towards paydirt, her eyes squinted in focus and her mouth a stoic line.

When she gets there, she drags a short ladder from the laundry utility closet and climbs up three rungs to get her short frame in sight of the problem gutter. It rattles and shakes as she pops it back into place, although she knows it'll be only temporary, as more rain is on the horizon.

She starts scooping out the leaves with her rubber-covered hands, and as she throws them to the cobbled ground a few metres below, aiming for the bucket as best she can, a man approaches her, hands in pockets and with a humoured look on his face.

"Oh, it's you," she cries down. "Anything I can help you with, dear?"

"Actually," the man calls back up, "I was going to ask you the same question."

Nora chuckles, but then she throws another fistful of leaves to the ground as if to say: no need. The man side-steps the incoming gunk. "No help required, Rick, thank you."

"Come on, I don't mind."

She pauses at the top of the ladder. Her heart is feeling a little heavy, so she sighs before taking a few steps down towards the ground. Her legs wobble as she lands. She looks at Rick, has the urge to cup his face, but then remembers the grey-brown residue left on her rubber gloves.

"It's been a long time since I've had the offer of help, you know," she says, as Rick replaces her spot on the ladder. He pulls at the leaves with bare hands and Nora can see he is cringing, but he makes good work of it. "Where are you from again?"

"Ormiston."

"Must be a town of gentlemen," Nora decides. "Will you be heading back home soon?"

Slop. Another leaf pile falls. "I don't know. I'm not sure if I'm ready to leave just yet."

"Well, that's nice." She smiles, thinking to herself that it must be the motel's charms keeping him here, like a hug, hard to pull away from. "I had that same feeling when I moved here, too. Though, I think that feeling is beginning to fade."

Rick pulls his face away from the gutter. "Really?"

"I have family a few hours away. It might be nice to move a little closer. Granted, they've never come to visit."

"You should go see them," he calls down. "I'm sure they've missed you."

Nora glances up at him and the two exchange quick grins. She pulls the gloves off her hands and Rick, seeing this, takes it as a hint to keep cleaning. She rubs at her forehead with the back of her hand and then places both fists on her hips.

"I'm sure your mother misses you, too."

Above her, Rick holds a ball of wet leaves in his palm, staring down at the faint veins like they're ribs of a fish. He tosses them to the ground without looking and they get a little too close to her. She lets out a raucous laugh.

"Sorry."

Nora can see he's grown a little quiet. "Have I upset you?" she asks. She'd hate it if she had. One hand pulls away from her hip and hovers over her heart.

"No, no, of course not," Rick stutters. "She does miss me, you're right."

The occupant of Number 16 comes outside to inspect the clean-up. She talks with Nora for a time, complaining about the television picture and the mildew on the shower curtain. Nora promises she'll see right to it, and she mentally adds two duties to her already-burgeoning load.

After successfully cleaning his section of pipe, Rick steps down off the ladder and helps her pack the mess into the yellow bucket. He says he'll carry it to the bins out back for her, but she refuses his second offer of help.

"Nonsense, you go out and enjoy yourself," she says. "I'll be fine here."

He hesitates and she ushers him on with a stubborn wave of her hands. He wanders back to Number 24 and Nora finishes up her task alone.

After clearing the gutter, wiping down the shower curtain, and smacking the back of the TV set to try and improve the picture quality, Nora waddles away from Number 16 and back to her office. Dark clouds are forming overhead and she fears she'll have to do it all again tomorrow morning.

She leans back in her chair and ponders for a moment, thinking of all the guests she's ever had: the ones that gave her a basket of questionable baked goods over Christmas; the ones who managed to get on the motel roof on New Year's Eve; the ones who stayed for a year but never tried to learn her name; the ones who kept noise to a minimum, and the ones who offered to clean out the gutters. She worries about them. She wonders where they'll go and where they've already been.

A sudden desire rushes forward and Nora quickly shuffles the papers on her desk to the side, in search for something she knows is buried underneath. At last, her fingers feel the familiar surface, and she pulls the business card to her eyes. She purses her lips as she reads the officer's name printed on the front: A-B-B-O-T-T. Helvetica font.

She taps away at the keys on her computer, pulling up a search engine and clicking through its contents. One page leads to the next, and the next, and the next. Finally, she flips the card over and jots down a phone number in red pen, the tip of it flicking with the hurried movement of her wrist. She picks up the landline on her desk and takes in a deep inhale.

There's three rings, maybe four, Nora can't keep track. She's looking around her small office, at the framed awards, the accolades, the memories.

"Hello!" A sing-song voice answers the phone.

Nora hesitates. Around her, the motel seems to buckle and creak. The dark clouds that were forming are now well and truly on their way. The ceiling light flickers and an advert falls from the noticeboard in the foyer.

She inhales, preparing herself like a swimmer awaiting the starting gun. "Hello," she says. "I need to sell my motel."

24

Cole can feel his body become tired. It's done good work so far, ducking under mischievous branches and regaining balance when he's lost his footing in the mud, but now it's as if the fuel tank is on empty and he's sputtering to a stop.

He chooses a bank to rest on and he sits, ignoring the dew dampening his trousers. He yanks a daisy from its root and twirls it around in his fingers. Being at the river reminds him of being a kid. The weak sun on his shoulders is reminiscent of the heat that bore down that summer before Happy went missing.

He had been here with him before. School was out and all the kids gathered at the forest park for a refreshing dip or to read a book under the long arms of the pine trees. On that day there must have been 30 of them, stretched across all corners of the park. Some kids were throwing stones, attempting to skim them, others were slacklining on a rope tied taut between two bent bushes. Happy was sitting on the grassy verge, aimlessly picking daisies from their weed beds and handing them to a girl sitting slightly below him. She was making a daisy chain and, once completed, she stuck it on the top of Happy's head like a crown. Cole walked over to them, nervously smiled. Happy grinned and nodded at the spare patch of grass by his feet, indicating it was okay for Cole to join them.

They sat in silence for a while, and Happy wore that daisy crown like it was the real thing. Soon after, the girl left their small group and went to join her friends by the river's edge. She yanked off her t-shirt and underneath she wore a halter-top stitched in the colours of the rainbow. Cole could see the freckles on her pale shoulder.

It was nice, feeling part of something. Although he was one of many, he preferred it over the solitude at home. Here, he could blend in and yet be noticeable enough to warrant coy looks from his female classmates and sit in Happy's shadow. Cole heard him say: "This is the life, huh" and he didn't know how to respond.

He looked at him. Happy was squinting under the afternoon sun, gazing out at the river like he was admiring a newly sowed lawn or sparrows bathing in a bird bath. To be fair, their outlook was fortunate, looking back on it now. In a town as small as Quince, everyone could rally together, could revel in the good things. Together. They also felt heartache together.

"Happy?" he said in the smallest of voices. "Do you think it'll always be this way?"

With that, Happy shook his head wildly. "Na, no way man," he answered casually, waving his arm through the air. "Good things never last."

Cole can't quite believe that this was the last time he saw him.

He sits now where they sat all those years ago; the outlook has changed. Winter has sapped all the vibrancy out of the forest park. The river is murky, the sky is dull, and the trees no longer provide shade. There are more daisies now than there were that February, though, and Cole considers collecting them all, making a crown, but he's forgotten how to connect the delicate stalks together. He leaves them to fill the grassy bank with colour instead.

Somewhere behind him are a couple of his colleagues, but their bodies wore out quicker than his did and they lost sight of him early in the piece. They are good men, but their hearts aren't in the case like Cole's is. They didn't know Happy, so they don't know how desperate he is to make sure Nick Greene doesn't share the same fate.

"Cole?" One of them creeps up onto the embankment. "You want us to search anywhere else?"

He tilts his head towards the sound of the man's voice. His mouth is in a tight line. He wants them to look again but this time, look harder, but he stops himself from uttering the command. He knows they've done their best, and he knows this isn't the first time the forest park has been searched for Nick Greene, but he hoped, boy, had he hoped, that he'd find Nick, dead or alive, and be able to bring him home.

"It's okay," he calls back. "I think we can call it a day."

The two men share a relieved look between them and sit down on their own grassy knoll, a few metres behind Cole. One pulls out his phone and proceeds to show the other photos of his wife and newborn daughter. They chatter among themselves but all Cole hears is babble, like his head is underwater.

He doesn't want to believe Nick Greene has run away on his accord, like Abbott suggests. That's what they all thought Happy had done and they were wrong. No, this time, Cole wants to be the advocate that Happy never had, to be the man that vows to bring him home when no one else made the same pledge.

179

Then a phone rings, it's one of the officers'. The high-pitched tone reverberates through the calm serenity of the forest park. He fumbles to answer it.

"Yello? Yes, this is Alex. Yes, he's with me."

Cole turns his tired body around so that he can see the officer, and the officer is looking straight back. His eyebrows are raised and he nods towards the phone. Cole heaves his body up and extends out his hand.

"I'll put him on."

When the phone is at Cole's ear, he mutters a greeting.

"This is Debbie," the voice on the other line says.

Cole has to mentally scan through the list of new names he's had to learn since coming to Quince, and he finally finds Debbie some way down the order. She works at the station; does something less important than he does.

"Right," he says. "What is it?"

"A call has just come through, I thought you'd want to know."

"What call?"

"Nick Greene has been spotted in Abercrombie."

An immediate lump the weight of lead forms in his chest, taking up valuable space inside his ribcage. It's hard to breathe, so he blinks furiously as if that will help but it doesn't.

"What do you mean? Are you sure? What do you mean?"

Debbie sighs. "A call came through from someone certain they saw Nick Greene in the city about a week ago."

"A *week* ago?"

"A week ago."

"Why not report it sooner?"

"They said they weren't certain."

"But you just said they were certain."

"They weren't, but now they are."

"And who is *they*?"

Another sigh. A rifle through papers. "I've got an E. Spelling."

Cole pulls out a pen from his pocket, prepares to write something on his hand. "Can you spell it?"

There is a notable silence on the other end of the line. Cole can't picture Debbie, but he can envision her rolling her eyes. "There's something else," she says, ignoring his question.

"What?"

"This E. Spelling, he's the worker at some internet café. Said Nick Greene came by to use one of the computers. He left behind a wallet."

"Go on," Cole presses impatiently.

"Well, inside the wallet was an ID. We haven't confirmed it yet, but I just thought you should know." Debbie pauses to talk cheerily to a friend who has called into the station for lunch.

Cole is about to burst. "Whose ID?!" he yells down the receiver.

A pause. Debbie is not impressed. "The name *they* gave us was Fir. Hugh Fir."

Cole can't even summon enough strength to end the call. He simply sticks his arm out and waits for the officer to collect the phone and do it himself. They stare at him, concern in their eyes, knowing by the look on his face that it isn't good news. No, just news that confirms their hours-long search through the forest park has been for nothing.

Cole falls to the bank like a collapsed building. He stares out at the river, the daisies, the vast woods ahead of him. How he hoped he'd find him here.

"Nick Greene's in the city," he whispers as if to no one.

The men move awkwardly. Neither know what to say, until: "Are you sure?"

"He had the fisherman's wallet. Which means…" He can't bear to say it. "Which means he either found this guy's dead body and took it, he was there when the fisherman fell, or…" His throat goes tight. "Or, he killed him."

Cole looks down at the daisy he plucked from its root, now lying limp within the blades of grass. He doesn't want to believe in Nick's guilt; he never expected that he'd have to. Nick is meant to be one of the good ones. Cole was supposed to help.

The daisy seems to lose all colour, all fragrance, all strength, and in front of his eyes, it dies.

25

The two men sit in the dark car eating burgers out of paper wrapping. Lettuce falls from a mouth and onto the upholstery. One of the men apologises through a mouthful of meat and mayo.

"Don't worry about it," the other says.

They're sitting across the road from a strip of small stores, each covered with differing themes of graffiti. A tattoo parlour is closed but houses a small party of men and women, and the officers can hear a medley of rock and rap music escaping from the brick and mortar store. Every so often, one of the partygoers steps outside for a cigarette and shouts across at a neighbouring business or punter looking for a late-night feed. They all seem to know each other here, along this small strip of a big city.

The only light in the car is coming from the instruments on the dash. The clock reads close to midnight, the fuel tank reads empty. The odometer has increased by a few hundred. The younger officer stuffs his last bite into his mouth and sighs when he finally gets it down. He reclines his seat as far back as it can go.

"What now?" he asks.

Abbott stares down at his own meal; he hasn't enjoyed it as much as he thought he would. He can feel the heaviness of the food fall into the pit of his stomach and tuck in for the night. He doesn't know the answer to Rowan's simple question, either.

The men have been out on a limb for the past two days, heading in whatever direction their noses took them. It was the same technique that led Abbott to the fisherman's body, so he hoped that logic would result in another – even greater – find, but it hasn't.

In front of them, a man from the tattoo shop lets out a loud, thundering laugh as his mate arrives with a case of beer.

"Where haven't we looked?"

Rowan pulls out the brochure the men picked up from the city's information centre that morning. It lists all of the hotels and motels and orders them by price. They started from one side of town and ended at the other, scrawling out each lodging with a thick black pen as they went.

The page was covered in ink.

"We've checked them all," Rowan says, defeated.

Abbott snatches the brochure off his young colleague, needing to see it for himself. He's dismayed to find they've crossed off every hotel and motel and backpackers in Abercrombie, and the closest they got to Nick Greene was a man telling them he had seen someone of similar appearance looking through their lobby window more than two weeks ago. In other words, they had learned nothing.

"I don't want to give up so quickly," Abbott confesses, staring out the window. Next to him, Rowan nods.

"I understand."

The men on the street start cracking open bottles of beer where they stand. The parlour door swings open and the music pulsates louder. The tattooist steps outside.

"Is that because of what happened?"

Abbott ignores the men on the street and turns to look at Rowan, who sheepishly glances in his direction.

"Chris mentioned a case of yours. Said you– well, he said you fucked it up."

Abbott clicks his teeth. He looks back outside and spots the small liquor store the man on the street retrieved his beer from. He takes a long breath, like a diver ready to take the plunge. If he's going to strip himself bare, to excavate bad history in order to ensure Rowan doesn't make the same mistakes, he cannot do it empty-handed.

*

It was the night of February 14, 1997. Abbott remembers the date clearer than anything because it was Valentine's Day and the crowd of men in the station kitchenette were making crude remarks about an officer's latest squeeze.

A man named Johnstone was to meet up with his new girlfriend later that evening, a woman named Lucy, and a couple of old colleagues were giving him schtick.

Abbott was too busy listening to the jibes when he tipped the jug of boiling water into his mug. It splashed wildly over the rim and scalded the skin below his thumb, causing a pink splotch to form. He reached for a paper towel to dab the mark and leaned in closer to the cohort.

Johnstone was telling the men around him that it wasn't going to last with Lucy, that she was too needy, too desperate for a relationship, and he only wanted a fling. His colleagues jeered and laughed while one commented on how women were too highly strung, but Abbott, sipping innocuously on his coffee, knew it was all a farce. Because although he'd deny it, Johnstone's face lit up at the mere utterance of Lucy's name. His rebuttal came out too forced, too scripted, and when the other men made snide remarks about Lucy's appearance, Johnstone stared wistfully into space, as though reminiscing about tender moments, compelling the memories back into existence.

Abbott rolled his eyes ever so slightly at the bravado the men were urged to display. Back then, they wanted to keep up appearances, to show off as men befitting a position in the police force. To express love for a woman would be to admit they had a sensitive side, and the officers in the kitchen, though nearing middle-age, weren't ready to confess to such a thing just yet.

Abbott patted Johnstone's back as he passed him, leaving the man to his uncomfortable conversation. He walked over to his desk, dentless and clean, and sat down at his chair. He clicked his teeth. The station was full of his accomplices, some, he would even call his friends, but there were times he needed silence, to have a space where the thoughts inside his head could roam.

He barely got comfortable when a man behind him cleared his throat, and the gruff action was at once recognisable. Abbott stood and anxiously tugged at his jacket, bright blue and in perfect condition.

"Sir."

The head of the precinct back then was a man named Boyle. He was just a few years older than Abbott, but already he had the round nose and weathered face and bushy eyebrows of a middle-aged man.

"Abbott, I need you to look into something for me. Could be nothing, could be something." He peered down at a pile of papers in his hand. "It's a missing persons report.

The kid's mother has just filed it."

"Absolutely, sir." Abbott received the papers from Boyle and wanted to express his excitement but remained indifferent. Excitement fell into the same category as sensitivity: non-existent, in these men.

Boyle pulled Abbott in. "There's not many cases like this that come up in Quince," he said. "Solve it, and it could bode well for you."

Abbott nodded his head, and when Boyle wandered on, he dove into the paperwork, gorging himself with the detail like it was wagyu steak smeared in butter. He read the file four times, careful that he didn't skim over even an ounce of information.

*

Rowan pulls the bottle of whiskey from his colleague. He takes a quick swig before handing it back. "Go on," he urges.

*

The missing boy was 14, gone for little over three hours. Because he was a minor, they had to move fast. He was last seen riding his bike through his neighbourhood, so that was where Abbott began.

That night, a team was established and sent to Drury Road, a nondescript suburban street in the centre of Quince. Abbott spoke to the boy's mother in the family living room. There were chairs with lace antimacassars on the backs and a cuckoo clock on the far wall. The mum was flustered, panicked, said her kid would never stay out so late. If he did, he would call, she said. She said it again and again.

Abbott looked around the property: in the boy's room, the garage out back, even under the house where a stray cat had given birth to a litter. He questioned the neighbours and nosy people gathered on the street, whispering behind cupped hands. He logged every detail into a pocket-sized notepad.

The next day, the kid's bike was located on the main street that connected Quince to the outside world. His mum ID'd it through bloodshot eyes. Abbott was in charge of leading the search party around the site, and he meandered through the bush on either side of the road. He remembers his boots were squelching in the mud. He was looking, he swears he was looking.

Abbott grew anxious at the ongoing case. He was desperate to impress Boyle, desperate for a rise up the ranks. He started looking for reasons to call the kid a runaway, and soon, the reasons found him.

The school told him the kid was a troublemaker, bad in exams and a bit of a show pony. He was a child of divorce and he had stolen money from his mother's wallet in the days before his disappearance.

In the end, Abbott deduced that there was no mystery to the young man's vanishing after all, rather, he was a boy who hitchhiked his way out of Quince, psyched for an independent road trip like one he'd read about in a book. He broke it to the boy's mother and brothers, and they all cried. They didn't believe him, but they had no choice.

The case took its toll on Abbott, too. By the end of it, he was run-down and worn-out, irreversibly aged, but he was admired among the precinct for wasting little police time searching for a no-good kid who'd voluntarily run away.

It was all looking up for Abbott, and as the months passed, the case became a blip in his memory. But then, another call came in. The person on the other end of the phone was vague, he remembers, and that was never a good sign.

It was late autumn at that stage, when there were more leaves on the ground than grass, and he showed up to the edge of a ravine wearing new black boots and a wedding band. Johnstone was there, his head tilted down, a sour look on his face.

Abbott recognised the area. They had been here little under three months ago, searching for the Price kid. His bike was found an s-shaped bend away. Abbott walked the route himself. He canvassed the area himself.

"What are we doing here?" he asked.

No one answered. There was a foul smell in the air that did all the talking.

Looking down, Abbott saw the crook of an elbow. A foot with a shoe. Dirt-stained jeans. The rest of the figure was shrouded in a bed of wet orange leaves. His stomach heaved and his body convulsed, and Abbott was propelled forward as if his breath was kicked out of him. His vision turned blurry and his head spun but he willed himself not to faint.

"They reckon it's the kid from Drury Road," Johnstone said, barely audible. "The shoes he's wearing match the ones his mum described him as having on the day he went missing."

Abbott looked over to him, tears stinging his ducts. He couldn't believe him, but he had no choice.

"There's an abrasion on his head. Forensics are on their way."

189

Johnstone stood stiff. He played with his fingers and his shoulders were slouched low. Abbott hardly recognised him. Gone was the man who had eyes full of longing and a heart full of love that Valentine's Day in the station's kitchen. He had been replaced by someone who had seen what no one should have to see.

"I can't believe we missed him," he said, his voice breaking. "I can't believe we missed him, Abbott."

*

Rowan is silent in the passenger seat, Abbott has another drink, and in front of them, the rowdy crowd takes their party indoors.

Rowan wants to press for more, Abbott can tell, but he seems to know when he's pushing his luck. He feels his face distort, agony likely obvious in the wrinkles on his forehead and in the bags under his eyes. He picks up the brochure that had come to a rest in the car's centre console and considers tossing it out the window.

"We could try again?" Rowan says, holding back Abbott's arm. He takes the brochure off him and opens to the page covered in black ink.

Abbott releases a small smile, though it seems to take a while to form. *There's no harm in trying again.* Isn't that what he said to Rowan at the coffee shop all those days ago? When they were both deflated but still had enough air to carry them through what was to come? Those days seem long ago. Now, it feels like there is very little air left to breathe. He sighs, clicks his teeth.

"We could."

In the morning, the two men, dressed like the party's invitation read 'smart casual', prepare to recycle the previous day's events. Rowan clutches the crossed-out map like it's a lottery ticket and heads down to the hotel's foyer to check out. Abbott hangs back a few minutes longer to steady himself.

A good night's sleep has added another gust of momentum into solving the case, and he feels close to something, like the shoreline lies just beyond the fog, but when he meets Rowan downstairs, the feeling shifts.

"What's wrong?" he asks.

Rowan leans against a console table next to one of the hotel's grand windows. As Abbott gets closer, he has to squint until his eyes adjust to the light.

"They have a paper here," Rowan says. "Did you know about this?" He pushes the newsprint towards Abbott, who reads the full story though a pit forms in his stomach after the first sentence.

A Quince man thought to have run away willingly is now the prime suspect in Hugh Fir's murder case.

Fir was found dead at the Quince Forest Park on June 7, and late last night, Police revealed they were looking for only one person in relation to the case – Nicolas Greene.

Greene was pronounced missing by his family on May 5 and it was quickly determined that the 23-year-old medical school student voluntarily disappeared. Now, police believed the two men crossed paths at some point.

Detective Senior Sergeant Chris Cole told the Star that Fir's death could not be ruled out as a homicide. He said

Greene was wanted for questioning.

"We only want to speak with him at this point," he said. "There's still a lot of questions that need answering."

Cole said the police's focus had now shifted to the city of Abercrombie, and while he had no reason to believe Greene was armed and dangerous, he urged the public to contact police if he was seen.

The family of Greene could not be reached for comment.

"I can't believe this," Rowan says, flustered. He's shaking his head fast and rolling his eyes like following a pinball around a machine.

Abbott thinks back to his interaction with Cole: *Nothing. Can you believe it?* He supposes he shouldn't have. He pulls out his phone from his pocket and checks for any missed calls from Cole. There aren't any.

He leans on the console table and Rowan keeps shaking his head. "Why would he keep us in the dark?" he asks.

Abbott picks up the article again. He has an answer for Rowan, but it isn't polite. He decides not to say it and instead focuses on the final line in the story. It sticks out to him like a sore thumb. Like a bruise on a pale knee. It's hard to ignore.

The family of Greene could not be reached for comment.

26

Paula clutches the trolley's handle like the bar of a rollercoaster ride: knuckles white, veins protruding. There's no great drop approaching her, no sweeping twists or bruise-inducing turns, just the shadow of the Super Saver, all red and white like a candy cane.

She's still in the car park, next to the beige sedan, deliberating whether she really needs food all that much. It really wouldn't be the end of the world if she waited another day or two. But at home, the cupboards are bare and the milk has gone stodgy, and the same thought that led Paula to the supermarket car park returns to her now: that a home cooked meal could be just the trick to rid the family of their blues. It *has* worked in the past, she thinks.

When Edwin was made redundant from the first job he really cared about, there was a slow-roasted leg of lamb and scalloped potatoes waiting on the table for him when he got home. When Mollie had her heart broken by a boy whom she thought was her true love, there was a garlic and herb stuffed porchetta with her name on it for when she felt ready to eat. And when Nick was first declared missing, nothing had relaxed the family more than a flaky chicken pot pie hot from the oven.

If anything, Paula knows how to use food to forget

things not worthy of remembering.

As flavours flit about her head, so too do ideas of lasagne, or pan-fried snapper. Paula's stomach growls and she eyes up the supermarket like a roast on a spit. If she can conquer cooking eight steaks medium rare for a neighbourhood dinner party at the Taylors, she can conquer the Super Saver, and whatever may hide among its aisles.

She marches towards the store, the trolley squeaking as she goes. One of its wheels is off-kilter and rattles and rolls like a mechanical toy in need of new batteries. She presses on through the turnstiles at the entrance and pops out in the fruit and veggie aisle. There's a stack of the day's newspapers on a display to her left but she steadfastly ignores them.

Hurriedly, Paula grabs a handful of items here and there: navel oranges, vine tomatoes, white-washed potatoes, and then she's out and down a new aisle. She grabs a few more tins of coffee, Belgian biscuits, sugar, and bottled water. She makes good time as she approaches the dairy section and heaves a 3-litre bottle of milk into the wobbly trolley. She then throws in a week's worth of meat, a large pack of toilet paper, and an even larger variety of tissues; boxes that have an assortment of colours and patterns.

Paula glances down at the watch on her wrist. She's never been so prompt. Usually, a trip to the Super Saver is a time to mingle, a time to gossip with the ladies from bridge club, to compare recipes and question the freshness of produce. Usually, Paula can spend up to an hour in its aisles, reading the backs of packets or assessing prices. But today, she pays no attention to best-before dates or discounts. Instead, she grabs at items almost compulsively and her trolley is in disarray because of it, when usually it is a clean stack ordered by size. Today, she doesn't want to see the ladies from bridge, or to ask for Leslie Draper's mint sauce recipe. She wants to be invisible, to navigate the supermarket's aisles so stealthily no one would ever know she was there.

Unfortunately for Paula, no one ever really gets what they want.

"Paula! That is you, isn't it, Paula?"

The noise comes from Aisle 12, where Paula is attempting to go unnoticed as she reaches for a block of dark chocolate. Her hand freezes in mid-air when she sees Linda McAssey peering at her down her glasses.

"I hardly recognised you, Paula!" Linda says, stepping closer.

Paula plays bridge with Linda on Wednesdays. Linda always wins. If she doesn't, she'll argue black and blue with the club director, accusing the opposition of being cheats. The ruling always seems to go her way. She's the type of woman who likes to let everyone know that her husband is a successful businessman and that her three sons have all moved out of home, are married, engaged or promoted, and are starting families of their own. And to Paula's jealousy, she always looks impeccable, with pearls around her neck in the summer and a scarf matching the colour of her shoes in winter. Today she is wearing a yellow cardigan over a white blouse, capri pants and expensive-looking loafers. She pats the scarf that sits against her breastbone while Paula pats at her unwashed hair.

"Hi Linda," she says meekly.

"I missed you at bridge this week. Under the weather?"

"No, no," Paula says, rubbing at her cheek. "I just had a few errands to run, is all."

"Oh, that's right!" Linda exclaims, puckering her lips. "I heard about your son."

Her stomach pangs but the hunger pains have long subsided. Her hope that no one had read the front page of the morning's paper quickly diminishes with Linda's pejorative stare. Still, in typical Paula Greene fashion, she decides the best solution is to pretend everything is fine. It's what she did when Edwin lost his job and when Mollie got dumped, after all.

She stares at the block of chocolate she had earlier craved but it no longer looks appealing. "How are your boys, Linda?" She forces a smile but her face feels like cracking stone.

"Well, Robbie just got a big promotion at the oil company, Sean just proposed to his girlfriend, and Tyler and Amelia just returned from their honeymoon in the Maldives!"

It's a good distraction, but the question only diverts Linda for a moment. After staring down at the items scattered within Paula's trolley, she says: "It is a shame about Nick, though."

Paula gulps down the saliva that has been building in her throat. She nods twice; that's all she can bring herself to do.

"I could not have picked it. I simply could not have picked it."

"I have to head home now, Linda," she whispers, turning the trolley sharply, the bad wheel emitting a squeal.

"Although," Linda snaps, "wasn't there that little incident with Ed?"

She slams the trolley to a stop. The hairs on her arms and at the back of her neck stand erect. She slowly turns to look at Linda, who has her lips pursed and her eyebrows raised.

"What incident?" she asks.

"The camping trip when Nick was, what? Twelve, thirteen?"

Paula feigns ignorance, though she knows the trip Linda alludes to. There is only one, and he was fourteen.

"That must have been so traumatic for Nick. For the both of them," Linda sighs. "I cannot imagine. Trauma can have many consequences on a young mind."

Linda steps forward so she is back at Paula's side. She grasps her shoulders with both hands. "It's such a shame," she says again. "Nick was such a good kid."

*

She bursts from the Super Saver like a hurricane. Leaves get trapped beneath her feet and brochures get tangled up within her gait. She still clutches the trolley tight, as if letting go could spell disaster. Her bottom lip quivers and her eyes fill with tears but she does not let them fall. Not yet. Not when Linda McAssey could still be in earshot. Not while there are prying eyes peering across at her like spotlights.

At the car, she abandons her shopping into the boot, the bottles of wine she picked up after her encounter with Linda clinking together madly. She kicks the sedan into gear and careens out of the car park, the candy-stripe colours of the supermarket quickly disappearing from her rear-view mirror.

She makes a few turns, then another right, and as she heads towards the main highway, she moves well above the signposted speed. She passes the entrance to Quince, passes East Chapel and eventually, she passes through Albertan. She wants to keep driving forever.

She hasn't thought about the camping trip for a long time. It had been an attempt at bonding, but whatever happened that day drove a further wedge between Edwin and Nick. She still remembers getting the phone call. *There's been an incident.* Ed didn't talk about what happened until a few days passed; he didn't want to worry her. When he did talk about it, he spoke of it simply, like reading a script.

"That kid could have damn near killed me."

Paula keeps driving while up ahead, a speck on the horizon, is the sign for Abercrombie. It's the grandest of the signs she's passed, with twinkling lights that come on in the darkness and colourful lettering as if to say: we're happy here. Paula feels her heart pull in that direction, but, as if fate happened to be watching her drive haphazardly along a highway she isn't familiar with, the light on her fuel gauge suddenly glows bright. She turns onto the next off-ramp, puts her car into idle at a rest-stop, and finally starts to cry.

It's an outburst unlike any other, and Paula loses breath and coughs out wads of mucus.

"Why would you do this to me, Nick?"

She asks the same question over and over, her voice eventually wearing thin, while outside, the world continues to move. Cars meander past her, the occupants smiling or talking or listening to music. Sometimes, she can hear them laugh. They're all heading to the city, as if it's the only place one can be at peace.

Life goes on, unless you're the Greenes.

27

JUNE 22   DAY 48

Cole has one of the other officers drive him to Abercrombie. He knows the roads a lot better, and he could get there a lot quicker, but his mind isn't in focus and today he prefers sitting slumped against the window.

His body looks small in the middle of the passenger seat. The driver of the car keeps glancing over to him, an awkward look on his face. Neither speak and the ride stays silent; gentle bumps cause the cell phone in the centre console to shake.

When Cole heard that Happy was missing, it was all just a joke at first. None of the kids believed it. They thought he'd played hooky from school or was down at the river swinging off the rope that was hanging there, and they all planned to give him shit about it the next day. But when the next day came and Happy didn't show up, Cole knew something was different. The teachers at school were frizzier than usual and kept leaving their classes to whisper in the halls. The kids all craned their necks to hear. They couldn't, but nobody thought it was a joke anymore. They no longer thought it was funny.

There was a search for Happy that afternoon, so when the last bell chimed, they all hopped on their bikes or scooters or in their parents' cars to help look. Cole searched too, on his own, so as not to get distracted.

He muddied his trainers clambering over banks and peeking into bushes. When he passed people on the street, he asked if they'd seen him.

"Happy?"

"Oh, right. Harvey, I mean."

It got dark early and Cole had to go home and help his mum with dinner. He aimed the potatoes and the peeler towards the window, just in case a shadow of a kid on his bike came riding past. It never did.

The days went on like this, and Cole swore he could see the Quince sky glaze over. He reckoned the day Happy went missing was the day the fog rolled into town and never left.

He remembers seeing Happy's mum when he went to pick up a bottle of milk and a lottery ticket from the dairy; she'd been stopped on the street by someone, a woman with a scarf that matched the colour of her shoes. It wasn't long before Happy's mum burst into a sob that Cole could hear from the other side of the road. He scrunched the Lotto ticket into his balled fist and headed for the police station.

Yanking open the door with his young might, he marched up to the counter, a plexiglass shield over the front of it. He stuck his face near the gap cut at its centre and demanded to see a detective.

It took a while to be seen. At one point, he thought he was forgotten about, so he went up to the counter to ask again. The man at the reception rolled his eyes and went out through a door that had a window you couldn't see through. He came back a few minutes later, a youngish cop in tow.

"Are you a detective?" Cole asked.

The man raised his eyebrows and laughed a little. "Sure am. What's it you want?"

"I want to help you find Happy – I mean, Harvey. Harvey Price."

"You want to help us find Harvey Price?" the man repeated. Then he said: "We don't need any help, kid."

Cole yanked him back by his sleeve. "Yes you do! You haven't found him yet, have you? It's been a month!"

"Look, I can't discuss the case with you, kid."

"But I'm not a kid! I'm his friend!"

The detective juggled on the balls of his feet for a few seconds, then he crouched down to Cole's height. He needn't crouch far; Cole was big for his age.

"We've looked everywhere for your friend, okay? Trust me. I don't think he's been put in harm's way. If anything, he's off on a little adventure, alright?"

The cop stood up, folded his arms, and chuckled with the guy at reception. "Now, off you go," he told Cole. "We've got work to do."

He was spun around and ushered back out of the station. He turned to protest, but the detective was waving him goodbye.

"Hey, Roy," Cole heard him mutter. "Keep the door locked, will ya?"

*

The phone in the centre console rattles from more than just the bumps in the worn-out road. Cole looks down and he can see the screen is lit. He reaches for it, peers at the name that's come up, and sits straighter in his seat.

"Can we pull over?" he asks the driver.

"Perfect timing. There's a gas station on the left and I need a Red Bull."

The tyres of the car skid along the gravel accessway and Cole answers the call but leaves the ringer waiting until they've come to a complete stop. When he lifts the phone to his ear, he can hear Abbott repeating his name, flustered.

"Yes?" Cole snaps.

"What the hell?" is Abbott's response. "We leave town for one day and now Nick Greene is a suspect in Hugh Fir's murder?"

"That's correct."

"Why? Since when?"

"Since a witness called saying they saw Nick in Abercrombie with the fisherman's wallet."

There's silence on the line. Cole can see the other officer talking to the female gas station attendant. It reeks of petroleum.

"Were you going to tell us?" Abbott asks.

Cole pictures his stomach like the inside of a volcano, dark red magma bubbling with all the hate and all the rage he's felt for 20 years. He can feel it all, in there now, moments away from eruption. He thinks back to the younger Abbott he met at the station two decades ago and inhales a lungful of cold air that dampens the hotspots deep below, holding off the explosion for however long. He is in charge now, not Abbott, and there is a pride in him that placates his desire to explode.

"Eventually," he says calmly.

He can hear Abbott's angry breath through the line. "Well, what are we supposed to do now?"

"Continue with what you're doing. We're heading to the city. I'll call you later." Abbott starts to say something but

Cole ends the call.

They get to Abercrombie five minutes after the internet café has closed, and this E. Spelling is standing at the door, cross-armed, angry at their lateness.

"Take us in," Cole demands, not giving him any time to protest.

The lights flicker on and the room is painted in white fluorescents. Cole and his driver are joined by other officers who arrived before them, and their bodies take up a lot of the cramped space. It's a shabby old building but today, he doesn't care about appearances.

"Where did he sit?"

The worker points to the closest set of desks and Cole reaches them in seconds. He shakes the mouse, presses keys on the keyboard. When the screen stays black, he turns back to Spelling. "How do I get this on?"

"Press the 'on' button," the clerk answers, rolling his eyes.

The computer screen lights up but even so, Cole doesn't know where to go from here. The screen shows a generic blue background and a prompt encouraging him to enter a code to connect to the internet.

"How do we find out what he looked for?" he asks.

Spelling shrugs. "Don't you have guys for that?"

Cole looks at the PC. He's right. This is outside the realm of his powers. He turns to a few of his men behind him and gestures to the machine. "Unplug it. Take it away."

Before he departs, Cole makes Spelling hand him the fisherman's wallet and he collects it in a plastic bag. Another officer pulls out a fingerprint card and dusts the clerk's fingers in powder. They're gone before the clock hits half-past.

He sits in the passenger side again. He holds the wallet in his hand and peers through the plastic to see its scuffs and marks. He digs into his jacket pocket and pulls out a latex glove which he sticks his right hand into. Opening the bag, he pulls out the wallet and flicks it open. Inside is the fisherman's driver's licence. His photo resembles the corpse brought down from the forest park.

"Why the hell would Greene take this?" he thinks aloud.

The officer next to him has a theory. "Maybe it was a trophy. You know? A reminder of his kill."

He raises his eyebrows in disbelief. "You think so?"

"Well, the only person who will ever know for sure is the kid."

When Happy was found no one could say what had happened for sure. Kids would sometimes tell ghost stories about 'The Quince Killer', a deranged man who murdered Happy for the hell of it. Cole hated that story. Others came to the conclusion that Happy's bike got a puncture, so he abandoned it to walk the rest of the way home but he fell and hit his head. Cole didn't buy that one. He knew Happy wouldn't leave his bike. He knew he'd drag it the whole way home, through hell or high water, because that bike was his prized possession. That bike, you could say, was his best friend.

There was no forensic evidence, either. That's what Cole read in the paper, anyway. No one had seen anything, and in such a small town like Quince, that was the strangest thing about it. Not one person reported seeing Happy that day, and not one person had found him. Because of that, Cole left Quince. How could he live in a town where the people had eyes but chose not to look?

"It's strange no one spotted Nick Greene leaving town,

don't you think?"

"Hmm?" The driver is looking for another place to stop to empty his bladder of the Red Bull.

"He was alive and walking around Quince for a month and not one person saw him. Isn't that a little hard to believe?"

The car stops. The driver turns the ignition off. "I don't know," he shrugs. He heaves his body out of the car and when he shuts the door, the whole chassis rattles. He pokes his head through the open window. "People have never been good at looking for what's right in front of them."

28

There's a section of Abercrombie's city where the concrete makes way for water and the cramped storefronts are replaced with white, ornate buildings. People meander along the boardwalk or have picnics on the grassy ledge, and Marina comes here sometimes just to watch them. She ignores her reflection in the expansive shop windows and pretends she's someone else: a worker nipping out for a coffee run or a dog walker with poodles and terriers.

They're all so lucky, the people she stares at. So lucky to have been born into a world where money isn't an issue, work is guaranteed, and family is a sure-thing. She doubts they know what fear is. Or hunger.

"Can I ask you a question?"

Rick's standing a few feet behind her, looking out over the water. She brought him here for an ice cream, said it was her treat after another successful pawn. He shrugs. "Sure."

"What will you do when your money's all gone?"

He shoots her a glare but it's a genuine question and she tells him she's not trying to pick a fight.

"I haven't thought about it," he says, his tone curt, his shoulders back. "Why?"

She continues along the pavement, dodges the cracks

that try to sneak under her feet. "Maybe we should start to think about it."

"We?"

She looks back for a second. "Yes. We."

The ice cream parlour appears busy but perhaps it's because it's so cramped. Only five or so bodies can fit in the line, while the rest of the space is taken up by a large cabinet showing an assortment of odd flavours: blueberry buttermilk, toasted marshmallow, and orange blossom. Marina tries to poke her head above the queue, surveying the selection and the cost. Her latest pawn fetched an alright price: little more than $200 for a G-Shock watch she stole from a gym bag. Danny didn't know it was nicked, of course, though he did know more about her than most. When she first found his little family-owned store, she told him the truth, that she has a history of theft. She told him that because of it, she hasn't been able to find a job and Trev's wage, while enough for Sub Rosa, isn't enough for the do-over they so badly deserve. That's when a lie crept in. She promised him she wasn't a crook, she just needed to pawn stuff Trev didn't need anymore. Danny suspended disbelief and allowed the trade. He did so again and again.

When they get to the front of the line Marina asks for a cinnamon toast and Rick gets a coconut choc chip. They sit on the boardwalk but the sun disappears as soon as they rest, and they lick their ice creams while shivering, lips turning blue.

"I think Nora's selling the place."

Rick's tongue freezes mid-lick. He draws it back in. "What makes you say that?"

"She's been doing a lot of maintenance lately."

"So?"

"I heard her talking on the phone."

"And?"

"Trust me," she says. "It doesn't look good for us." She watches as he flattens the ice cream atop its cone, which he now seems disinterested in eating. He holds it in two hands down by his knees while the wind picks up and causes the water to overlap the boardwalk's edge. "Where will you go?"

"I told you, I haven't thought that far ahead."

"Will you go home? To your parents?"

"No."

"Then you should come with us."

Rick lets out a puff of air in place of a laugh and she feels hurt by the action, rejected, almost.

"Why not?"

"I don't think Trev would like me hanging around."

"This isn't about Trev," she insists. "It's about the three of us, sticking together."

"Why?"

"Because I like you, that's why." She feels bad about saying it. She feels like a con. Marina never cares about the people she steals from, never feels remorse about telling a lie, but manipulating Rick while he's so weak feels like kicking someone who's already down. She watches his face for a reaction but he gives hardly anything away.

"You want to form a misfit gang or something?" he asks, deadpan.

She grabs hold of his elbow. His ice cream drips from the soggy tip of the cone. "Why not? Trev likes to think he's got it all figured out but we don't have a fucking clue."

Two friends pushing strollers saunter in front of them. Close behind, two young girls toss bits of bread to the gulls.

"I'm not saying we leave right now," she continues. "I'm just putting the idea in your head. You can't stay at Sub Rosa forever."

"I know that."

"And whatever money you do have, it's gonna run out eventually."

Next to her, Rick gulps. She reiterates that they'll be stronger together, that with the three of them, everything will work out fine. She stands and snatches the uneaten ice cream from his hand and tosses it into a nearby bin. When she's back at his side, she says the five words she knows he wants to hear: "I feel safe with you".

He melts like the dessert.

Walking back to Sub Rosa, a new wad of cash in her wallet and a wary excitement in her chest, she inundates Rick's mind with talk of the future, hopeful visions of life in a new city: a quaint but clean flat, living anonymously but luxuriously. He laughs at her more than once.

"I think you're over-estimating me."

"I think you're under-estimating yourself."

She continues with her dream-like fantasies, clutching the crook of his elbow and absorbing him into her, all the while secretly planning her betrayal.

*

Trev's waiting outside their room when they arrive back at the motel. Him being there frightens her – he's working the day shift this week and he's meant to be gone for hours. She leaves Rick's side and darts across to him, falling a little too quickly into his torso.

"What's happened?" she asks, panicked, and he pulls

her inside and slams the door. "You're scaring me." She notices his heavy gait as he walks to the back of the studio, to where it's dark. He returns carrying a newspaper and he almost hits her across the face with it.

"Read it!" he yells, but she doesn't need to. She scans the headline and drops the paper to the floor.

"I already know."

"What?" Trev hisses. A vein on his forehead looks ready to burst.

"Just let me go talk to him." She starts to turn but Trev yanks her back by the arm.

"There's no way I'm letting you over there, he's a murderer!"

"How do you know that?"

He bends down and repeatedly stabs his finger at the newsprint like it's a knife. "It says so right here!"

"I don't care."

"You don't care?"

"We need him."

"Like hell we do. I'm calling the cops."

Neither have cell phones so Trev walks over to the motel's old landline and puts the receiver to his ear. He can't work out how to make an outgoing call so he slams it back down and Marina's sure Rick can hear the noise through the wall.

"We can't call the cops yet. He has money, babe, I know it. We can't push him away."

"Fuck his money." Trev's back in front of her. His hands shake with rage. "We don't need it."

She scoffs. She walks over to the bed where Trev has thrown the day's paper. She calmly folds it in half so the headline no longer screams at them and tucks it under her arm. She isn't going to let this ruin her shot at redemption, her chance for a better life.

She exhales slowly. "I'm going to talk to him. I'll be right back, okay?" As she passes Trev she pats his shoulder and he lets out a frustrated gruff.

Besides, she thinks, the man next door is hardly a killer. He's naïve, yes, easily led, and she knows he will listen to her.

29

JUNE 22   DAY 48

It's a few minutes later when there's a knock on Nick's door. He's sorting through clothes which are in desperate need of a clean and the TV set is on, an old movie playing in the background. He throws a long-sleeved shirt onto the bed and waltzes over to peer through the peephole.

She's only just raced into her own room but Marina has returned, standing flustered on his stoop. She's chewing her bottom lip and stamping her foot impatiently, darting her eyes either side of her to make sure no one is approaching. Nick shakes his head as he turns the knob to the right and Marina throws herself into the room.

"He knows," she says. The door ricochets off the wall. It swings a few times but stays open so that the sky, now approaching dusk, makes a frame around her.

Nick raises his eyebrows. "Who knows?"

"Trevaughn knows."

"Okay," he nods. "And what does Trevaughn know?"

Nick walks back to his bed and to the pile of sweat-smelling clothes. He folds a jumper in two and tosses it back down, waiting for Marina to answer. She hasn't moved from the threshold.

"He knows you're Nick Greene."

There's a sting. The quiet music from the old-time

movie suddenly sounds like a scream. There's an uncomfortable familiarity when he hears his real name, not the Rick Brown he's become used to. It doesn't sit right, like a piece of expensive art on a dirty wall, or a kayak close to capsizing. The anticipation of falling sends a shiver up his spine.

He hastily grabs an armful of unwashed clothes and darts across to the other side of the room, losing a sock along the way. He reaches for his rucksack and hurriedly throws things inside it, tripping over himself. It's a mess. His arms and legs flail about in a panic. He tries to do so much that he does nothing at all.

Marina walks into the room. "Wait, Rick, wait," she cries, using his fake name. A habit? Perhaps. "He won't tell, he told me he won't tell."

Nick scoffs but he's panting so it sounds like a grunt. He doesn't respond, doesn't know what to say.

"Rick, just stop." She's trying to cling hold of the rucksack and although she doesn't have a tight grip, the bag tumbles and loses half of its contents. Nick struggles to pick it all up again. "Just listen to me!" Marina cries. She reaches forward and places a hand on Nick's chest. Heart beating, blood pumping.

He finally comes to a stop, like she's a sorcerer controlling his every move. His mind flicks through images of cop cars, handcuffs, his mother's tears, a town's scrutiny, Nora's disappointment.

"He promised me he wouldn't tell."

Despite Marina's reassurance, Nick doesn't believe her. "How'd he find out?"

"He drove to Quince today for work. He stopped off at a gas station for lunch and you were front page news." She hands him a folded newspaper and Nick darts his eyes across the page. "I already knew."

His heart stops beating now. It falls right out of its cavity and lands on the floor by his feet. He stomps on it. It squishes. Blood spurts out the pulmonary artery. "What? You knew?"

Marina lets out a puff of air and the noise takes Nick out of his self-induced panic for just a moment. It's like she's blowing his problems away. "What did you expect? Rick Brown? It's not exactly a genius deception." She sniggers. "I think we all knew. Trev's just a bit slow."

"All? Who is all?"

She shrugs. "Suze, Rico... that mum who has the two cute kids in Room 4... Pretty sure Nora knows, too."

Nick drops the pair of shoes he just picked up. He thinks of his encounter with Nora cleaning the drainpipe. Did she know then, and if she did, how come he didn't pick it up, see the signs, gauge her suspicion? Has he become that lazy?

He bends down, tries to grab the shoes again with both hands but they're shaking. He sits on the motel's soft bed instead. He presses his hands into a praying position and squeezes his nose in between his sweaty fingers. In front of him, the black-and-white movie depicts a couple dancing in what looks like a ballroom, smiles on their faces and soft voices speaking in that old-fashioned way no one does anymore. His breath is a vibrato, and he can hear it playing in his ears. Then, he realises again: Marina knew.

"How long have you known?" he asks weakly.

"Since the first night I met you."

Nick thinks he's going to vomit. He forces himself off the bed but his body drags him back down. He rocks back

214

and forward like an addict. He feels betrayed by her. He has never felt so exposed.

"You've known for that long? How? Why?"

"Why didn't I rat you out?" Marina sits next to him. "Because I don't care what you did."

"How is that possible? I killed a guy." The words come out like a howl in the distance, undistinguishable between a cry for help or a cry of laughter. Nick corrects himself quickly. "I mean, I didn't *intentionally* kill him. He fell, he hit his head, I swear."

"I believe you."

They sit in silence. Eventually, Nick stands up and tries to gather the items he lost in his haze around the room. His brain is still foggy, his hands have a tremor in them. Then, Marina says his name, his real name.

"Remember when I told you I had done something bad? Something I regretted?"

Nick nods. "You kill someone, too?"

It's a joke, but neither laugh. Marina gulps down saliva and stands to join Nick.

"I ran away from someone," she says. "Like you."

And then she tells him everything.

She tells him about her stepdad, a hot-headed chain-smoker who used to hit her and her mum. She tells him how Trevaughn always knew about it and wanted to do something about it, but she begged him not to. But then it got really bad.

She tells him how one night, when Marina's mum was out at the pokies, her stepdad, in a rage, threw a plate at her from only a foot away. It sliced her nose and bruised both her eye sockets. But it didn't break. Marina bent down to pick it up – it was still wobbling on the old wooden floors

– and she smashed it against her stepdad's head, hitting his temple first.

He fell to the ground like a bag of sand. Marina stepped over him, used the home phone to call Trevaughn. He arrived within minutes. Trev told her that it was their chance to leave, the only chance they'd ever have. They packed a couple of bags with clothes and items they could pawn and whatever cash was left in the house. They emptied her stepdad's wallet and took the gun he left lying on the coffee table.

"His name was Navy. Stupid fucking name, I know," she says. "We left town that night, we came here, and that's that."

It's taken a while for them to get through the conversation. The old movie has long ended and infomercials have taken its place. Nick listens with his head in his hands. He can't believe it. Two runaways living next-door to one another under the same motel roof; Nora the mother hen of young criminals.

"He died?"

She shakes her head, rolls her eyes. "I wish. They reported it to the police, said I attacked him and took all his stuff. They issued a warrant, spoke to Trev. He told the cops he wasn't a part of it, didn't know where I was and he's kept up the lie. For me."

Nick purses his lips. "It was an accident, then. You shouldn't have run away."

"Yours was an accident. You ran away."

"That was different, I had to go."

"Oh, right. Because you'd already faked your disappearance for god knows what reason."

He rises, frowns.

"I'm sorry," she says quickly. "I need you to do something now, Rick."

Nick laughs. For some reason, flashes of the forest park and the fisherman appear in his vision. All of that has led him to all of this. If he could, would he go back in time and erase it all?

"No, absolutely not," he tells her. "No."

"You don't even know what I was gonna ask!"

"Fine. What is it?"

"Well." She starts moving around the room, drumming her fingers on the TV cabinet and the chest of drawers as she passes them. "What I talked to you about today… you're gonna have to promise me."

"Promise you what?"

"That you won't leave without me. Without me or Trev."

He clicks his neck and then it's his turn to start pacing. This time, when he collects items that were flung to the floor, he slings them over his shoulder. "Where will we go?"

"You're the genius, Rick Brown. I was hoping you'd tell me." She smiles at him. "You're the one who has been invisible for a month."

Nick shuts off the TV. He can no longer stand the bright animations and high-pitched jingles playing low in the background. He leans against the cabinet and thinks about his options. Is a misfit gang such a bad thing? Is it such an insane idea? Sure, he'll have to put up with Trev but Trev is a small price to pay if it means keeping Marina safe. Like him, she doesn't want to be found. They could lay low. Together. For a time.

"Trev's job," he says. "What about that?"

"It no longer matters," Marina tells him, shrugging.

"The paper mill's shutting down. He won't have a job soon anyway. That's why I was upset the other night. And now with Nora selling… No one is gonna let us stay here for practically nothing. It's all becoming too hard."

He makes a noise with his tongue. "It's only going to get harder."

"I know. But with you I think I can survive it."

He knows she's trying to charm him, and he knows he's a fool because it's working. He walks into the bathroom for a drink of water and returns wiping his lips. Marina is sitting on the bed.

"If we do this…"

She jumps straight up. Nick hasn't even finished talking but she wraps her arms around his tense frame and hugs him so tight he loses breath. "Thank you, thank you, thank you!" she squeals.

Nick lets her squeeze onto him but his body is hot and shaking. He's panicked by the prospect of leaving the city, heading to god-knows-where with Marina and Trev in tow. But at the same time, there is something thrilling about it because she was right, he has been invisible. He has been a ghost walking under the shadow of skyscrapers and Scots pine. For more than a month, no one has come close to finding him, and a part of Nick wants to know – how much longer can he keep it up?

"If we do this," he repeats, unwrapping her arms from him, "you have to do what I say."

"Of course we will," Marina says, happy now. She dances around the room like she's just won the lottery, tossing notes like tissue paper up in the air. "We'll go wherever you wanna go. Just think about it and let me know."

She spins on her heels and quickly exits, leaving Nick standing in the centre of the room trying to clear his head of all that has happened. Then, she immediately returns, holding something in the pocket of her sweatshirt.

"This is to show we're not fucking around." She pulls out a gun from within the pocket and Nick falls backwards with a yell, landing hard on his tail bone.

Marina laughs erratically, bends down to help him back up. "I'm sorry!"

"What the fuck!"

"It's Navy's. I think it's full. Trev says you can tell by the weight of it. Neither of us know how to use it."

"What makes you think I do?"

"Well, do you?"

Nick pauses. That camping trip with his dad. He gulps down the memory. "Sorta."

"You take it." She forces the gun into his hands. "This is to prove to you that I trust you completely. Wherever you go, I go, okay?"

There's silence for a few beats. Someone slams a door in the distance. The clock on the nightstand reads 6:11. Nick doesn't like holding the gun so he tosses it to the bedspread and stares down at it like it's cursed.

"We'll talk more tomorrow." Marina heads to the door and her high energy almost frightens him. How can she be so damn calm?

"Marina?"

She turns when she hears her name. "Yes, Rick?"

A part of him wants to stay watching her, the glow of the patio light shining dimly behind. The other part wants to grab the gun and pull the trigger, just so his thoughts can shut up for one fucking minute. He does neither.

"Tomorrow," he says. "We'll talk more tomorrow."

30

JUNE 24   DAY 50

It's a rare warm day; a random 20 degrees squashed in between days no higher than 16 and stormy. The sun is out and a thin layer of clouds provides insulation between atmospheres.

In his motel room, Nick strips off his usual layers of heavy thermals and tosses them into a plastic bag that arrived last week carrying polystyrene containers of Chinese food. He wears his father's coat over his thinnest of t-shirts. He collects his trainers from their spot at the door and steps into them, hardly bothering to tie the laces. Looping his hand through the bag's handles, he departs the motel room, curtains drawn to reveal the sporadic winter sunlight, and locks the door with a flick of his wrist.

He first sees Nora dusting away cobwebs from the foyer's facia that are so old they've caught a layer of dust. She whips at them with a broom and the weak banging echoes around the parking lot. Nick watches her, trying to read her face. Does she know he's not Rick Brown? Does she know there's a killer sleeping in one of her motel rooms? Her eyes don't move from the webs on the wall and Nick doesn't hang around to ask her.

There are a few other guests around, loitering outside their rooms with cigarettes between their fingers, and others heading towards the vending machine for an early morning soft drink. None of them look too hard at Nick. Maybe Marina is right, he thinks, maybe everyone knows who he is and doesn't care. Maybe there really is nothing to worry about at Sub Rosa because the place is already full of degenerates? Maybe that's what unites them.

Usually, on a morning like this inside the forest park, Nick would head out for a fish, and when he'd been adequately warmed up, he'd wade waist-deep into the water, running the palms of his hands on the surface, leaving tiny whirlpools that would ripple back to shore. He'd be in no rush for a capture, he'd let the fish take their time. Then upon snaring one or two, he'd sit on the rocky riverbank and bask in the forest's serenity, feeling powerful at being so close to civilisation, but seemingly so far away.

There are days he misses the park, like today, when he misses feeling on top of the world. The only things he had to fear out there were the defensive possums and relentless thunderstorms. He didn't have to fear people, and they are what scare him the most.

Nick steps off the wooden veranda wrapped around the frontages of the motel and onto the gravel carriageway. He swings his bag of clothes like a child on the way to school. He heads into the motel's communal laundry, where he is, gladly, the only one there. A few yellow-coloured washers and dryers sit against the plaster walls, and a bench that has been written on and chipped and stained is stationed in the centre of the room. There are instructions written on sheets of laminated paper tacked to the walls; some have fallen and lie face-down on the damp floor.

Nick throws his items into the closest machine and reaches into his pocket for a couple of bucks change and the small packet of cheap laundry powder provided by the motel. That goes in, the coins follow, and with a whir of a contraption being brought back to life, the washer kicks into gear.

He's heading out with Marina later. That's the plan anyway. They're gonna go pawn the last few items she and Trev have stashed away – a flask with the initials D.A and an old world encyclopaedia – and maybe grab a bite to eat.

They talked last night underneath the awning of their rooms, just like he said they would. He asked her if she knew what she was doing. Running away for real was difficult, he told her, and he should know. Once she took that first step, there'd be no turning back, and Marina nodded enthusiastically and with a grin of pure glee.

He told her he hadn't thought that long or that hard about where to go, but because no one had looked twice at him while he'd been in Abercrombie, they should probably stay put, just for now. She said she understood and repeated that she'd follow him, no matter what, and Nick's stomach grew butterflies.

He thought then, in preparation for the unknown, that today would be a good day to give his clothes a much-needed spin cycle. He reads instructions on laminated pieces of paper that say a load of washing will take 30 minutes, and he's wary of the clothing's safety left alone in the laundry room. He deliberates waiting on the plastic chairs that line the closest wall, but they too make him apprehensive; they don't look as if they can withstand his weight – almost back to normal after weeks of fast food.

There's the day's paper lying with its sports section facing up on one of the chairs and Nick bites his lip and contemplates opening it, scanning through the pages for his name or his face, but the routine has become tiresome, a morbid game of *Where's Wally.*

He decides instead to leave the newspaper and his laundry to chance and gazes up at the clock on the wall. Its batteries have run out – or have been pinched – and Nick, rolling his eyes, departs.

Outside, it remains relatively quiet and Nora is still clanging about with the broom, but a car on the street has its blinker on and it slowly pulls into the parking lot. Nick watches as it brakes outside the foyer, surprising Nora and causing her to stop sweeping away the webs. She rests the broom against the building and walks towards the car. Upon recognising its occupants, she flaps her arms and stomps her feet.

Nick can hear her raised voice but the banter is muffled and so, being curious, he takes a few steps away from the route to his room and towards the dark vehicle whose driver is still shielded.

"Look, I'm very busy, I'm expecting someone actually," Nora says, her hands on her hips.

There's an indecipherable response that seems to ruffle her feathers further. Her mouth hangs open and Nora stomps her right foot again, the gravel erupting from her heel like ash from a volcano.

Nick steps forward. "You alright, Nora?" he calls out to her.

The motel manager quickly looks up and, noticing Nick, she waves her hands in front of her face. "Oh, yes, Rick, all okay. Thank you, dear."

Nick nods and turns away, heading towards his room. He looks back to see Nora seemingly give in to the driver's request. Sighing, she gestures them to follow her into the foyer, and the car's brake lights turn off. Out step two men and they both take their time scanning their surroundings. They gaze up at Sub Rosa's old roof, stare across at the small rooms, and when guests saunter into view, the men eye them up like ants under a magnifying glass.

It takes Nick mere seconds to figure out who they are.

He recognises the taller one, Abbott, dressed in plain clothes but still evidently clear he's a detective; he drags his feet along the gravel, as if he really can't be bothered. The younger officer wears Top Gun aviator sunglasses and follows in his superior's footsteps. Both men move their eyes around the small parking lot and Nick, whose stomach has jumped into his throat, quickly retreats.

In his haste, Nick's departure is too loud, too panicked, and the strident sound of the gravel crunching underfoot makes his movements more noticeable. He doesn't turn around to see the two men gazing after him, the younger one peering out from behind his sunglasses. He doesn't look back to see them tilting their heads, smacking their lips, wondering if this is just another motel guest with a bad rap, or the man in the green jacket they've been looking for.

He reaches the door to his room and gazes up at the rusted '24', the irony of the number slapping him across the face. He tries to open the lock, but he finds his hands shaking and uncooperative.

In the slightest of movements, he turns his head to the right, hoping to see the two officers tucked away inside Nora's foyer. Instead, they are both looking towards him, and Abbott now has both hands firmly attached to his hips.

"Hey there," one calls.

Nick curses under his breath. He slowly pulls his key out of its hole and clutches it in the palm of his hand. He knows he can't enter the room while the officers are standing by, knows he can't answer their call or run away, arms flailing wildly, feet kicking out to the side. He instead takes a breath so deep his lungs balloon under his chest. He puts his key in his pocket and casually begins walking back to the laundry room. His heart pounds with each step. His feet smack one by one onto the wooden porch and then crunch atop loose gravel. He decides to swing his arms, reaching his hands up to a clap. When he rounds the corner of the building, Nick runs.

He can hear the officers calling after him, their obsessive voices excitable and strained. He hears nothing else after that. For the next few minutes, the only noise Nick can hear is the blood pumping in his head and the odd gasp of breath.

He winds through the building's twists and turns, running as fast as his feet can carry him, faster than the day he fled the forest park. Rounding a corner, he trips on his untied shoes and skims his right knee across the gravel. He stands, limps for a moment, but fear maintains his speed.

The motel is small and Nick quickly finds himself facing a barrage of trash cans and a brick wall. He ascends the wall but on the other side there's nothing but a field of dead grass, so instead of rushing out into the open, he follows the wall for a few metres, scratching his palm across its rough surface. When he sees an opening, he jumps back over and into the bounds of the motel.

Lurking behind each room like a voyeur, he crouches down when he sees a shadow in a bathroom or hears the draining of a sink. He ends up at the side of the foyer, next to the vending machine where Marina stood that very first night.

"Oh. It's you."

Nick looks up to see Trevaughn cracking open a can of Coke; spray is sent into the air with a fizz. He eyes up Nick's knee, where blood is beginning to seep through the fabric of his jeans. Fuck.

"What are you up to?" he asks suspiciously. "You're not leaving, are ya?"

Nick sticks his head out to inspect the parking lot. The officers' car is still there, windows down, but Nora is now showing a lady wearing an A-Line skirt and blazer around the motel, arms pointing here and pointing there. Nick knows he doesn't have much time.

"No, of course not," he says. "I'm just doing some laundry. You?"

Trev grins. He jabs at Nick's ribs with his elbow. It's supposed to be playful, but Nick is already out of breath and it stings. "You are some guy, you know that?"

Nick looks around again. "Huh?" he says, not really listening.

"Of all the places you hide out, you hide out here? Making friends, talking to people like you didn't just kill somebody?"

Nick bites at his lower lip, dry and begging for moisture. He stares at Trev, the man he never got round to liking, and shakes his head. "I didn't kill him."

"Right, that's what Marina keeps telling me," he says. "Is that why you stayed for so long? Is that why you wanna leave with us? You have a crush on her?"

He could laugh if the situation wasn't so perilous. Marina's face flashes in front of his eyes. "No."

"It's okay, man, I won't be mad. And I won't tell the cops, either," he says. "I was going to. I actually had the phone in my hand ready to call them."

Nick gulps.

"But then Marina talked me out of it. She said you could help us somehow."

"Huh."

"I'm not sure if she told you but… we have our own shit that we're running away from. We just aren't as well-off as you are to keep doing it alone."

Nick frowns at him, wants to push his head into the brick wall to his right. That'd be the easier option, he thinks, but he talks himself out of it.

"She says we might be leaving soon," Trev continues. "My job will dry up in a week. Got any idea where we're going?"

He shakes his head. The pounding in his skull gets harder and heavier. "No. I have to go."

Trev nods, purses his lips, but after a beat, he ushers him back and Nick rebounds like a rubber band stretched too tight.

"Marina says I should trust you. Can I trust you, Rick?"

That's when he gets the idea. The worst idea he's ever had. If he does it, Marina will never forgive him. If he does it, there'll be no running away together. The sinfulness is tantalisingly sweet. His capture is drawing nearer and nearer.

"Take this." Nick starts pulling away his father's green jacket. Goosebumps appear on his arms as soon as the fabric departs the skin. He throws it at Trevaughn and Trevaughn catches it, confused. Nick storms away and Trev calls after him.

"What's this for?"

He shouts back: "Trust."

Behind him, Trev puts the can of Coke down on the ground and wraps himself in the coat. He pops the collar, looking pleased with himself. He swaggers along to the bus stop opposite Sub Rosa's parking lot. He's heading into work. Any minute now.

Nick quickly rushes to his motel room. His hands are still shaking when he rams in the key, but this time he's successful and he lets himself fall to the carpeted floor. The clock on the nightstand reads 9.57 and Nick gets a knowing feeling that he won't be meeting up with Marina in an hour. No, he expects her day will be much different now. He slams the door shut and yanks the drapes closed, just in time to see the two men round the corner, panting but undeterred.

Peeking through a gap in the curtains, Nick watches as the officers look left and right. His heart freezes with the thought that at any moment, their fists could pound on the door of Number 24. But then, Nick's plan pays off, and the cops look over at something in the distance, across the other side of the parking lot.

"Stop!" the men yell. "Stop!"

Across the road, Trevaughn is climbing the stairs of a bus, his body encased in the distinguishable green jacket.

Nick, wide-eyed and rabid, watches from his room as the men run across the parking lot, shouting and waving with their hands in the air. When the bus departs, the men throw themselves into their car and chase after it, and all the while Nick sighs, a fateful moment of reprieve before the thrashings of a long-awaited storm.

31

JUNE 24   DAY 50

Of the eggshell-coloured washing machines lined up in a depressing row, the one that Nick Greene's clothes sit in, damp and bleeding, is by far the ugliest.

They each have their blemishes – a dent from someone's foot, a scratch from an impatient user – but the one Nick Greene chose was caked in grime and dust; one more load away from death.

The machines whirr and rattle so furiously and the sound is like a blender in Abbott's ears. There's a girl chewing gum and leaning on the counter in the centre of the room, seemingly oblivious to the noise. She's staring up at the men with a sullen indifference, frustrated by their appearance in the old laundry room. Abbott looks down to her, his gaze unfaltering, and eventually the girl rolls her eyes and turns her attention towards a months-old magazine, gum tossing underneath her tongue.

"Well?" Abbott presses.

"Hang on a minute."

Nora waddles over to the washing machine and tugs on the handle. It sticks, so she tries again. Abbott can feel his pulse quickening, beads of sweat forming on the nape of his neck. When the washer door swings open, he lunges towards its innards.

Nick Greene's assortment of long johns and thermals pile into a damp heap on the floor and Abbott rummages through them, unsure what he's looking for but hopeful his fingers connect with something of importance. He pulls a shirt in towards his eyes, searching the material for the smallest of blood drops, but he spies nothing.

With Abbott's nod of approval, Rowan bags up the items, careful not to be too boisterous as the senior detective stays crouched, his knees shaking.

The men had caught up to the stranger wrapped in Edwin Greene's jacket, had boarded the bus only to discover the wearer was not Nick Greene after all. He had kicked up a fuss, caused a commotion, but when the officers quizzed him about his choice of outerwear, they learned the coat had only just come into his possession, and when threatened with a night in the cells, he quickly spilled the beans. He told them all about a guy named Rick Brown, and another guy named Nick Greene.

Abbott's heart went thump, thump, thump the whole way back to the motel. Dragging Trevaughn by the elbow, the officers hollered for Nora and stood facing the closed door of Number 24. Abbott gazed at the rusted numbers; poetic. A crowd formed to watch as the recent arrivals from Quince prepared themselves for an ambush.

Abbott reached down to an empty holster. He lunged forward with Rowan close behind. He scanned his eyes around the dark room, noticed the mess, noticed the emptiness, but didn't give up straightaway. He slinked towards the bathroom, kicked open the door. It ricocheted back and hit the porcelain toilet bowl. He walked over to the wardrobe, pulled that open too, and when all other dark corners were searched, he sighed.

The officer sighs again as he stands up from the puddle on the laundry floor. He kicks out his feet to stretch his legs and his knees click. He stands with his hands on his hips and Rowan, Nora and the nosy girl with the gum look to Abbott as if he has something to say.

When he called Cole, informing him that the impossible task he sent him on resulted in the locating of Nick Greene, there was silence. Abbott had to repeat himself.

"We found him."

"I heard you."

Cole showed up almost immediately and looked at Abbott with more disdain than ever. Abbott thought he'd get more of a kick out of telling him he had found Nick, but he didn't, because the news wasn't all good. What immediately followed was Cole asking where Nick was now, and when Abbott said he lost him, Cole let out a pitiful laugh.

Abbott and Rowan walk towards the motel room. The crowd has dispersed, presumably bored by the lack of blood and gore on site, and all that remains are the tired officers ready for the long drive home. Nora follows meekly behind.

"You say the kid was using an alias? Rick Brown, is that right?" Abbott asks her, and she nods. "You didn't think that was a little too obvious?"

"I didn't know he was on the run," the manager insists.

"You don't watch the news?"

"No," she says. "It's too upsetting."

Nick Greene left one wad of cash for Nora, and another for a girl called Marina. A note was left beside it with her name written in shaky writing. When Abbott saw it, his nose wrinkled. He didn't like the thought of Nick Greene making connections while he was a man on the run. It wasn't fair, not when Abbott felt like he'd lost part of himself searching for him.

The motel manager told Abbott who Marina was – the girl in the room next door. He walked straight back outside and pounded his closed fist on the door of Number 23. She opened the door with a flourish, as if she was expecting someone else.

"Marina?"

"Yes," she answered, her voice low.

Abbott waved the wad of cash in front of her face and Marina's eyes grew wide, like a woman hypnotised. She allowed them into her small studio room and, sitting on the bed, she steadfastly denied knowing Rick Brown or Nick Greene. But then Rowan got a phone call.

He'd earlier called an officer back in Quince, asking him to look up the names Trevaughn Casey and Marina Kirk. Turns out, there was a result for the woman. She had a warrant out for her arrest following an attack on her stepdad, some guy called Navy Bluett. When Rowan walked over to the pair of them, his maturity and competence increasing by the hour, Marina started crying before he could even open his mouth. She and Trevaughn were loaded up in a car and driven to the Abercrombie police station, and Number 23 was left as it was, Marina's faded slippers at the door.

In Nick's room, Rowan stares down at the frayed carpet. The night has turned dark and the brass light hanging from the ceiling does little to replenish their sight. "Thanks, you can go," he tells Nora, and she departs with a nod.

The other officers leave too, and eventually it's just Rowan and Abbott standing in the centre of the room.

Rowan swings the bag of laundry. It hits the door, edging it shut. "It's not your fault," he says aloud. "We'll get him next time."

"Next time? And where do you suppose he'll be next time?"

"He's got to stop running at some point."

The second book Nick checked out before his disappearance, *The Rime of the Ancient Mariner*, sits on the bedside table, and it dawns on Abbott that Nick must be walking around with a much lighter load. Only Ed's rucksack and a few items of clothing had been scooped up in his most recent absconding.

"I guess we better head off," Rowan says. "Start fresh in the morning."

The thought unnerves Abbott, and he tires of Rowan's positivity. Instead of starting fresh he wants to rot away. Instead of waking in the morning to another day destined to fail, he wants to shoot himself with a tranquiliser dart, the strongest of its kind, and only rise when his thoughts are no longer his enemy.

Without waiting for Abbott to answer, Rowan clicks off the light switch and the room turns a murky black. The young officer is right, Abbott thinks, they do need to press on, and whether that be to a bottle store or to bed, is up for them to decide.

Suddenly, there is a gentle rap on the door. A boot kicks it open a nudge and in steps Cole, his face half-shielded by the encroaching night. Abbott's annoyed to see he's still here, but then Cole opens his mouth to speak and the words come out sluggish, like his vocabulary has been walking uphill.

"Nick, uh, searched for an address. In Google, uh, he

looked for bus tickets that'd take him to Bellevue."

"Bellevue?" Rowan questions.

"It's a town two hours from here."

"Why would he go there?"

Cole can't be bothered answering. He only shrugs. Abbott walks over to him and looks at his face. It shares the same withdrawn expression as his own. He decides not to press too hard.

"Let's call it a night." He sighs.

Then, a dim light adds brightness to the room. Abbott's cell phone, half poking out from his pants pocket, lets off a blue glow, big red and green buttons appearing on his screen. He clicks his teeth before dragging the phone out slowly. He tries not to sound too defeated as he speaks, but then his tone switches dramatically.

"Are you sure that it was him?" A pause. "Positive?"

Rowan and Cole stare through the dimly lit darkness. When Abbott ends the call, the room returns to its eerie shade and the men stand like statues in the night. From outside, a woman lets out a high-pitched laugh as her heels slide across the loose chip of the parking lot.

When Abbott next speaks, there is a change to him. He moves not optimistically, not overwhelmed, but his body lingers somewhere in the middle.

"Nick Greene isn't in Bellevue," he says.

"How do you know?" Cole asks.

"Because. He just hopped off a bus in Quince."

32

JUNE 25   DAY 50

One day morphs into the next as the tyres on Abbott's rustbucket roll through town boundaries with the steadfast determination of a steam train. The rush of light streaking against the windows is the only indication that they've arrived at another town, but each time the blurs appear they disappear just as quickly. Not their destination. Not Quince.

Shortly after departing from Abercrombie, they were passed by a car-load of teenage boys who jeered as they overtook Abbott's Audi 90, and the officer cursed under his breath, but other than that speeding cargo of infringements, the rural highways don't host a steady stream of travellers at this time of night, and for the most part, it is only the two of them on the road.

One of Abbott's windows is stuck open about a millimetre, and it's never bothered him until now. He doesn't drive enough to notice, or care enough to get it fixed, but tonight the wind seeps through the crack and fills the car with an uneven whistle, and Abbott now wishes he'd done something about it sooner.

Rowan doesn't mention it, though his eyes keep darting back to the window in question, as if he's wondering whether a simple tug will fix the issue. When he's not sneaking a look behind him, he's staring at the dust stuck in the centre console, or at the dirt stained into the floor mat. There's nothing complimentary to say about the car, though Rowan finds a compliment, nonetheless.

"Comfortable ride," he says, shuffling in his seat. "Where'd you get it?"

Abbott yawns as they pass the sign welcoming them into East Chapel, meaning Nick Greene is only half an hour away. The anticipation is making him anxious, and perhaps Rowan is feeling it too. Perhaps that's why he is clutching at straws, desperate for conversation to lighten the mood.

Abbott quickly glances towards his colleague, along for the ride and doing a fine job as a sidecar to his motorcycle. Though used to silence, and becoming more tired by the kilometre, he's grateful for Rowan's unfaltering ability to find something to say.

"It was my wife's," Abbott tells him.

Rowan pauses, then stutters; the usual reaction. "I didn't know you had a wife," he says.

Nowadays, nobody knows. The presence of Frances was so long ago that she has become a myth, an urban legend, and sometimes Abbott has to convince himself that she was once really there. Now, when he makes his coffee in the morning, he no longer reaches for two mugs. He no longer has to keep the volume of the TV turned low so as not to wake the woman sleeping soundly in the bedroom. There's no more tripping up on the purple pair of slippers outside the door.

"Did she…?" Rowan doesn't want to say it, and Abbott doesn't let him.

"No," he says quickly. "She lives in Australia."

There's another pause, longer this time, and the wind's whistle seems louder and somehow exaggerates the silence.

237

"When did she leave?" he asks.

"Not long after the wedding."

Rowan sniggers but then swallows his laughter when he realises Abbott isn't sharing the same jest. He stares back towards the bad window as if needing to look at something, and he plays with loose skin on his finger.

The lights of East Chapel disappear and the two men are back on the deserted highway, dodging (for the most part) potholes and taking the corners 10km above the signposted speed. One of their stomachs rumbles. Abbott clicks his teeth.

"Do you miss her?" Rowan asks cautiously. When he doesn't get a response straightaway, he continues talking. "I only ask because I had a girl once, not a wife, I know, but… it didn't work out. I mean, does it ever?" He sniggers again and this time Abbott lets a smile release from his mouth's stony clutches.

He doesn't think things ever work out.

Take a look at the Greenes, for example, a loving nuclear family by all appearances until one of them turns up missing. Unsurprising, really, because life, more often than not, doesn't work out. Not for careers, not for families, and certainly not for marriages.

Still, he doesn't want Rowan, who is not yet 30, to wind up as cynical as he is. There's already too much pessimism in the world, he thinks.

"Everything works out in the end," he says slowly, like reading off a teleprompter. "You just have to wade through shit to get there."

Rowan smirks and discards the skin on his finger. "How much shit?" he asks.

"Depends on the person."

Rowan doesn't ask any more questions throughout the rest of the journey, except whether or not he can turn on the car radio, to which Abbott flatly declines. As they edge closer to Quince, the roads become more familiar and they can recognise the dark outline of the trees and hilly terrain. Their eyes droop, their joints ache, but as if the road ahead is made up of nothing but excrement, the two men press on.

*

When they arrive at Driscoll Street, they are surprised to see the house at the end of the cul-de-sac lit up like the sole lighthouse at the end of a rocky shoreline. The rest of the neighbourhood is nestled under the early morning's protective blanket, and it'd appear an eerie scene – leaves blowing, streetlights humming – if not for Number 24.

Cole got there first, but he waited patiently at the end of the driveway, his posture menacing, his mouth puffing out smoky air. Abbott nods to him as he passes. He taps lightly on the front door, his knuckle hardly making a sound, but Paula soon appears, wrapped in a teal dressing gown that comes to a rest above her ankles. Surprisingly, she lets them inside the house without much of a fuss.

The Greenes' grandfather clock reliably ticking away is the only noise coming from inside the home until Paula clicks the jug on to boil. It builds into a crescendo of ripples and bubbles before it settles down, clicking again once done. She hands the three officers a cup of coffee each, and when she speaks, her voice comes out in a whisper.

"Have you found him?"

The men glance at one another. They came to deliver news, but now they couldn't tell it. They came to scope

239

around, to catch Nick hiding in a closet, but now, looking at Paula's face, they knew they needn't have to.

She waddles into the living area and the officers follow. She flops herself down into her usual chair and clutches at her mug with both hands. There's a wine glass and an empty bottle of merlot on the side table next to her.

"Have you been sleeping, Paula?" Abbott asks as he falls down into the low armchair opposite her.

As defiant as ever, Paula assures that she is, but the dark rings under her eyes tell a different story. It's clear that even now, as she faces the three men, her mind is elsewhere.

"How's Edwin? Mollie?"

"Upstairs," Paula says, her eyes looking towards the sky. "Mollie wants to leave tomorrow, wants to go home, even though I tell her this is her home, really. Not that other place."

There are a few grocery bags sitting on the kitchen counter. A handful of ingredients have been pulled out as if someone was preparing a home-cooked meal. There's a 3-litre bottle of milk that hasn't been put away into the fridge and its dew has left a puddle on the island.

Abbott notices there is no longer the family photo tacked onto the refrigerator door, and when he scans the room looking for the image of a smiling Nick Greene, he can't spot it.

"We did find him," he says, and for the first time tonight, Paula's eyes meet his. "He checked into a motel in Abercrombie which is popular with down-and-out kids and the unemployed... used a fake name and paid for everything with cash."

Paula swallows down her drink. Her tired eyes stretch as wide as they can go.

"We're pretty confident it was him," Abbott continues. "We found a jacket that fits the description of the one that was taken from here, and also a couple of books with his initials; *The Rime of the Ancient Mariner...*"

"Oh!" Paula interjects. "He read that in high school."

Abbott nods slightly, before saying: "He fled the scene."

Paula deflates back into her chair, nodding to herself as if replaying the conversation over in her head. She lifts her hand to her chin and taps her cheek with her fingers. Rowan slurps more of his coffee before he excuses himself to the bathroom. In the hall, the grandfather clock continues to tick.

"So, you haven't found him," she says bluntly.

Abbott leans forward and slings his arm across his knee. "No," he says, "but we think he's come back to Quince."

Paula's eyes flicker and the tapping of her fingers cease. A pained look appears across her weathered face and her lips open and close like a fish sucking in air. Abbott thought the news would please her, would reassure her that her son was at the very least in a place he knows, a safe place compared to the likes of Abercrombie, but it appears to have done the opposite. She inhales sharply like an asthmatic dependent on every breath, before composing herself with a gentle sip of her drink.

"I suppose that makes sense," she says. "I suppose he's coming back for me."

There's a flush from the downstairs bathroom and the running of water through pipes. Rowan returns to the tense living room where he relaxes back down into his seat, appearing more comfortable than before. He looks between Abbott and Cole and Paula and realises quickly that the atmosphere has changed for the worse since he took a leak.

"Why would he come back for you?" Cole asks.

Paula's voice returns to no more than a whisper. Her eyes look everywhere but to the three officers hanging off her every word.

"I always expected so much from him," she says. "I always wanted him to do better, try harder, work faster. It's as if I wanted him to prove his worth."

Abbott can see Rowan looking at him from the corner of his eye.

"Why?" he asks, but Paula doesn't listen. She may be desolate and sleep-deprived, but she's stubborn and tells the story how she wants it to be told.

"I wanted him to be perfect, and he was, for a time, the happiest little kid. But I convinced myself that he wasn't, and when he started getting into fights and running away, I thought: 'This is it. This is why he isn't perfect. We made a mistake; he wasn't worth it'."

Paula sips her tea again and Abbott can feel the muscles in his neck tensing up. Goosebumps form under his shirt and he just now realises how cold the room is, the winter chill welcome here. He's growing impatient and Paula's dramatics are wearing thin. It's late, he hasn't slept, and his stomach is still making noises beneath his layers.

Rowan leans forward. "What do you mean, he wasn't worth it?"

Paula ignores him still. "When you told us it was him who broke in, I didn't want to believe it. But I knew, deep down, it was. He wants to punish us, that's why he's back in Quince."

Abbott can't help but scoff. He's thought many awful things about Nick Greene, but dedicating his disappearance to playing mind games on his mother? It just doesn't seem plausible. He has to give him more credit than that. Still, Paula looks genuinely concerned. She's watching the door now, as if her son is going to burst into the room at any second, spiteful after years of worthlessness.

"I don't see that happening," he says.

"You wouldn't know," Paula answers, then she pauses, as if awaiting a sound. The neighbour's dog starts to yap. The three officers look at each other; their weariness after the drive from Abercrombie compounding following Paula's cryptic conversation.

She finishes off her drink and carefully places the mug next to the drained wine glass next to her. Finally, with her fists clenched, she says: "I'm not his mother, not really. Nick's not really our son."

There's a very quiet intake of breath, so quiet, an ordinary person wouldn't have noticed, but three in the room hear it loud and clear. Abbott lets his head sink into his hands and he rests there a while, pressing his palms into his ears so that the sound of thunder rumbles through. The revelation of Nick's adoption doesn't shock him; it's a common circumstance he knows all too well. It's the aftermath, the thought of a child being made to prove his worth, that leaves him feeling wretched.

He thinks of Nick, outside somewhere, sleeping in another lonely motel room or walking aimlessly through the forest park. He thinks of the boy in the photograph, wearing his school uniform and badges with pride just to discover that his efforts weren't good enough. No matter the goal obtained, the work put in, nothing was ever good enough.

"You told him? Before he ran away?" Cole says slowly, testing the waters.

243

"He found out, yes."

"And then what?"

"What do you mean 'what'? He ran away, clearly."

Cole looks at Abbott and Abbott clicks his teeth. His focus is on Paula, who sits there, sucking her bottom lip, while Rowan shuffles in the seat opposite.

"What did you tell him?" Abbott asks. "What did you tell Nick when he confronted you?"

Paula faces away. She looks disinterested. "There was hardly a chance for me to speak. He was very upset."

"Of course he'd be upset," he snaps. "He's a kid."

Abbott thinks of Frances, dressed in ivory lace under a maple tree, her rounded belly a perfect curve. His eyes meet Paula's and the mother begins to lift herself from the plush chair, as if noticing the growing tension in the room. She lets out a gentle moan as she rises.

"I think you should be going now."

33

It's past 9 when Abbott wrestles himself awake, a throbbing feeling akin to a mid-week hangover pounding in his head despite not touching a drop of alcohol, at least, none he can recall.

He's had the feeling before and it wasn't caused by drinking too much liquor. That self-destruction came too easily. This is a different feeling, like being crushed under a concrete truck; a weight on his chest that makes it too difficult for him to drag himself out of bed. So, that's where he stays.

There's been no sign of Nick Greene and for the first time since his personal investigation commenced, he doesn't care. He doesn't care about keeping up with the chase and he doesn't care about the fisherman, though he knows that makes him a bad guy. But he also doesn't care about redeeming himself, about making up for the wrongs in his past, so does that outweigh the terrible?

When the kid from Drury Road was finally laid to rest, buried under a different patch of dirt, Abbott offered the parents his condolences, dressed in black and genuinely mournful. The mother had aged years in just a few short months, and Abbott realised upon walking across to her, that while he was getting married and expecting his first

245

child, she was living through hell. Her round eyes had sagged into pockets of tired skin; her already meagre frame was reduced by half, and her breastbone could be seen beneath the delicate fabrics of her charcoal dress, as if barely able to contain her broken heart.

She looked up to him, her face pensive at first, but then it twisted into a terrible form; wrinkles so thick they appeared drawn on; nasolabial folds dark and deep.

"You don't care," she said to him. "You never cared."

His first reaction was anger; he cursed at the woman under his breath, wanted her to know that he did care, does care, but then a realisation hit. A realisation that left him bedridden with an unknown illness. An illness that had Frances, third trimester at that stage, nursing him back to health. He felt so sick he couldn't move, and he didn't want to, really, didn't want to go back into the precinct and have the men look at him with the same sorrowful stare he presented to the kids' mother. *First missing persons case in two decades and Abbott fucks it up*. No, he didn't need what was inside his head playing out in front of him, too.

Because back then, Abbott realised he did care – about himself, about advancing through the ranks, about his beautiful wife, but not about some runaway. He didn't care enough to really look, to be on the hunt, to tie up loose ends because loose ends are frayed and cause even more damage. The realisation made him sick to his stomach, and every time he closed his eyes he saw the decomposing 14-year-old boy buried under soggy leaves and rotting sticks. Maybe he could have helped him? He'd never know and that alone was torture.

One night, it must have been close to 11 because their neighbour at the time worked evenings and had already left with a slamming of her door, Abbott was lying in bed and Franny, the angelic Franny, whose long auburn hair was pinned up in a reckless manner, who always rubbed her belly as she walked, came into the bedroom. She bent down to kiss Abbott on the head, to hand him a glass of water, and when she turned, Abbott reached his hand outside of the covers and grabbed hold of her wrist.

"Franny," he whispered, and his wife returned to his side.

"What is it, my love?" she said, running her palm across his damp forehead.

"I can't do it."

"Can't do what?"

Abbott looked at his new wife, his childhood sweetheart, the only woman he had ever dated, had ever lived with, had ever loved. "Be a dad."

Fran let out a small laugh, then sighed. She was expecting this at some point, a pre-fatherhood panic. She continued to run her palm across his head.

"You'll be a great dad," she whispered into his ear.

"No," Abbott groaned and his grip tightened around her wrist. "I don't want to be a dad."

There was noise in the background, he remembers, there was noise. The television – a late-night rerun of *Murder, She Wrote*. He remembers because elsewhere was silent. Fran was silent. Abbott gulped down spit that had been collecting in the back of his throat but even that was too afraid to make a sound. Frances pulled her hand away.

"You're telling me this now?" she said quietly.

Abbott pictured the boy, dead, lying under shrubbery with no soul attached. It was true, no one cared; it wasn't them, it wasn't their loved one. It was easier to claim he ran away and it was a story easily believed. But he didn't run away in the end. He went out for a bike ride and never came back. Still, he left this earth and people pretended not to notice.

"Yes," Abbott whispered. "I don't want to be a dad."

Tears pricked Fran's eyes. "You don't mean it," she said. "You're unwell."

But Abbott did mean it. He couldn't bear the thought of being a father; couldn't bear the thought of having a child to love and look after for 14 years only to find them dead in the most haphazard sense. He couldn't bear the heartbreak, couldn't love something so much and be forced to let it go.

So, Abbott did what he thought was best at the time. He convinced Frances that he wouldn't be a good dad, and that she wouldn't be a good mother, and eventually the idea took hold. With every bill in the letterbox, Fran realised the child wouldn't be well-supported. With every late-night shift at the police station, she realised the child would hardly know their father. With every argument and quarrel, she realised she and her husband were growing apart.

Abbott lies star-fished under cotton sheets. He breathes in the cold air and sends it back out in thick puffs, envisioning himself as a beast, a super villain; an adult playing children's games.

The mother called him an impotent man and, after 20 years, the woman is still right. Impotent, indolent, incapable. He couldn't bring Harvey Price home then, and he can't bring Nick Greene home now.

Abbott scoffs when he thinks of Nick. The man doesn't want to be found, so why hunt him? After the conversation the other night with Paula, Abbott doesn't blame him for wanting to stay away. But then there's the fisherman, and like the kid from Drury Road, he was left to rot. He clicks his teeth, an old habit, and remains torn on finishing what he started or accepting the fact that he is the man everyone says he is.

His cell phone rings as if to give him no choice.

Moving his legs for the first time in 12 hours, Abbott shuffles to the side of the bed. Rowan's name comes up on the screen and Abbott lets the call linger. When he eventually answers, Rowan's voice comes out ragged and breathless.

"I need to see you," he says.

Abbott scrapes off the plaque on his teeth. He balances the phone between his ear and his shoulder. "I'm busy," he lies.

"It's important. It's about Nick Greene."

Abbott stops what he's doing. He forces himself to take in a deep breath, one that makes his lungs expand to capacity. A quick flash of Franny walking out the door gives Abbott an iota of enthusiasm.

"I'll unlock the door."

*

Abbott has thrown a cable-knit jumper on top of the shirt he wore to bed. He's wearing old trackpants with holes at the hems and slippers on his feet. He avoids the mirror in the bedroom; he knows how bad he must look and he doesn't care. He asks himself: what's the point? He lives alone.

Rowan knocks once but doesn't wait to be summoned indoors. Instead, he flies across the threshold and almost collapses into the living room. He's brought with him a stack of papers and nothing else.

"I need to show you something," he says, taking a seat on the timeworn couch. Ordinarily, Abbott would be self-conscious of his surroundings, he may have even tided up a bit, but today is different and today Rowan seems not to notice the dishes in the sink or the musty odour in the air. Today, there are more pressing things at hand.

"I couldn't stop thinking about what Mrs Greene said the other night."

Abbott nods. He's been thinking about it too.

"I did a little research, wondered whether Nick had requested his original birth certificate. Turns out, he didn't. So, I found it for him."

Rowan flicks swiftly through his masses of paper. Some pages drop to the floor in his haste. One document grabs his attention and he clutches at it, crinkling the edges. His rush has Abbott a little wary. He hasn't seen Rowan like this before. There must be something scrawled on that piece of paper, something that demands this urgency.

"When you get adopted, you get issued a new certificate, right? But the original birth certificate always includes the name of the biological mother and, sometimes, the father, too.

"Now, Nick's only has the name of his mother, and she used her maiden name, but…" Rowan's voice trails off. He extends the piece of paper across to Abbott. "That's the part I think you should see."

Abbott frowns at Rowan, but he humours him, taking the sheet of paper and squinting down at the words typed on its surface.

He stands suddenly, knocking the television remote

from the arm of the sofa onto the floor. Its batteries fall out of its back. He reads the piece of paper three, four, five times. He reads it until the writing becomes blurry. He wipes away tears from his eyes with a shaking hand. He walks around the living room, stomping on the pieces of paper abandoned in the journey to deliver the message. His head continues to throb as it did when he woke. This time, the pounding is indescribable.

"I have shown this to no one," Rowan insists.

Abbott's eyes dart to him then back down to the paper. Through his blurred vision he sees Rowan looking meek. Abbott thinks he must look worse. He nods furiously and the movement agitates the pounding. Clutching hold of his kitchen bench, with the piece of paper secure, yet crinkled, in his other hand, Abbott collapses and he cannot be raised for some time.

54

Nick wakes but wishes he hadn't.

Almost immediately, his lower back starts to ache and the worn-out muscles of his legs begin to throb. He rolls onto hands and knees, stretching his shoulder blades forward and back, arching his spine forward and back. He stares down at his hands. His fingernails are teeming with dirt and there are scratches, some he's never noticed before, spread out across his knuckles. He rolls his head, his neck clicking like popcorn in a microwave, and with a final thrust for reverence, he rises.

Standing from his resting place – a bed of sodden leaves – Nick is grateful for the slumber that had him, for a short while, in another place. He dreamt he was in Victoria's flat but the flat was floating on a sort of barge in the middle of the ocean, and the ocean was wide and blue. People were looking for them and though the shore was out of sight, they could hear their desperate cries. Still, that didn't force them to turn home. Instead, they continued to drift out into the endless blue, gentle waves like creases in a mink blanket, allowing them to rise and fall. It felt so real, and when Nick woke it took him a few seconds to realise his true surroundings. There was no bobbing ocean but a damp pile of soil for a pillow, and in the distance, a gentle stream of water gracefully weaving around sharp rocks. The sound of his mother's wailing was left behind in the dream.

Nick's lips are dry, purple, and chapped. He rolls them into his mouth and sucks on them, hoping to fill them with warmth. His body is covered in goosebumps and his brain is frazzled from lack of food. He knows he doesn't have much strength left in him. He needs to continue moving forwards and at a faster pace. He can't bear to imagine sliding back into normal life if he ever gets found, the life he once resented.

It was a photo that led him to the upstairs hall cupboard that first week of May, two days after Victoria told him she no longer loved him. It was a photo of the four of them, and Nick found it after he'd told his mum of his heartbreak. He remembers her saying 'that's a shame' and nothing else. In the image, he's sitting with folded legs on the floor, his parents and Mollie stand behind him. They're all smiling forcefully and three out of the four of them have dimples in the centre of their chins. He pointed down at his young face, showing Paula what was missing. She shrugged and told him to put the photo back in the album, but he didn't. He tacked it to the mirror of his old bedroom so he could analyse it while staring into his reflection.

Growing more and more concerned and sure of his suspicion, he walked into the hall and stood on tiptoes to reach for the box labelled 'Nicolas' before carting it back into his room. He didn't need to look hard, didn't need to dive deep. One of the first sheets of paper stored away recklessly was a birth certificate, and in less than a minute, Nick knew the truth.

He sighs. As he heaves himself along the park's incline, he stops to grab at trees, to caress the leaves, to feel their grooves and their veins. He feels more a part of the bush than he ever felt down below, in Quince. He rounds a slight bend where there are marks and paths he recognises and an excitement brews in the bottom of his belly. Two more great strides and a push of a branch and the scene opens up onto his old campsite, his old home. Of course, there's nothing left of it.

The tent has been pulled down and his towels, utensils, and the pillow stolen from his parents' house have all been whisked away as evidence. But there's a dent in the forest floor where the fire pit used to be, and the tree branches that spent their time swinging with the breeze, dropping leaves into Nick's lap, remain as they were overhead.

He walks into the camp's centre. The wind picks up as if to welcome him and he responds with a slight grin. He feels so comfortable here, but then the rock to the left of him catches his eye, its sharp edge standing out like stitches along smooth skin. Nick's bliss drops and he can almost evoke the fisherman's dead body into existence, lying where he last saw it. He walks over to the rock, to make sure there's nothing but disturbed soil at the angler's final resting place.

The vision of the fisherman's lumbered fall plays back in his mind. Some nights he dreams about the moment, and in the dream, Nick rushes forward across the fire pit to try and catch him. Each time, he fails, and still the fisherman falls.

He knows he can't stay here. Hugh Fir haunts the campsite like a ghost, and as much as Nick feels like the forest is his home, so too is it the angler's. There's a solemn feeling in the air even now, like Fir's walking alongside him, and though the trees drop their leaves in support, they're also begging Nick to go.

He turns sharply on his heels and returns to the old fire pit. From there, he takes three measured strides to the right and bends down. He digs into the soil like a dog in sand, intent to sniff out a bone, with his hands scratching on loose stones and the dirt sending itself up under his fingernails. Dark earth flies every which way. It gets on his jeans and into his shoes and it paints his hands black. Finally, the fingers on his right hand pummel into a small box. He lifts it to the surface and blows away the dirt which has moulded itself into the velvet.

He opens it, sighing happily when he sees the ring is still inside. It's a 1-carat diamond set in the centre of an 18-carat white gold band with a halo of delicate sparkles, and it cost him more than a year of med school course costs. It was the ring that Victoria was supposed to wear on her left hand, the ring that took Nick a painstakingly long time to pick out, the ring he went to Abercrombie more than three months ago to get.

Nick holds the box under the light of the sun and watches as the diamonds glitter. He buried the ring at the campsite after the angler's untimely death, partly as a backup plan, as he knew pawning it off would give him another few months on the road, and partly because he wasn't ready to let this place go. The ring, being here, safe under the watchful eyes of the stars, meant there would always be a reason for him to come back.

The box shuts with a pop. Nick stands and stuffs it inside his pocket where Marina's gun also waits. He takes a last, long look around the campsite. The memories flood back to him and he shuffles through them wearing rose-tinted glasses. He doesn't see those difficult first days, cold, hungry, and afraid. He doesn't recall how difficult it was to light a fire or catch the fish. He doesn't dwell on the nights he spent lying awake, hearing strange noises just outside his door, or waiting for a wild storm to pass. He sees none of that. Instead, he sees a home, one that taught him how to persevere through the hunger and the cold, one that forced him to be victorious over his fears, that showed him how to fish, to light a fire, to figure out what were friends and what were foes, to navigate with the stars. This was his and his alone.

The gun hangs half-out of his jeans pocket, and, with his index finger, Nicks rubs at the cool metal. He wasn't lying when he told Marina he sort-of knew how to use it, except, his dad's gun was a hunting rifle, and it wobbled in 14-year-old Nick's grasp.

On their camping trip – at the forest park of all places – Nick's dad thought a couple of practice shots at empty beer bottles would do his son good. Ed lined them up on boulders along the riverbank, about 30 metres away. He stood alongside them, yelling back at Nick to stare into the scope, then pull the trigger.

Nick looked at the bottles through the lens, the heavy gun shaking in his hands. Then, he moved the scope so that his dad was in its crosshairs. He could see the greying stubble on his usually cleanshaven chin. Through the viewfinder, he watched as his dad waved his arms, pointing down at the row of bottles. Then Ed's mouth drooped open and a frown appeared on his forehead.

"Nick?" he called. "What are you doing?"

Nick could hear the whistling of birds in the trees above his head, as well as bubbles rising from the water as if the fish were coming up to get a closer look. His dad began to yell, palms outstretched in front of himself, warning Nick not to fool around. The noises tripped over one another so that it all sounded like one, loud, high-pitched ring.

"Nick!" his father screamed, terrified for what could have been the first time in his life.

He really thought he was gonna do it, squeeze the trigger, but then he remembered that if he did, his dad would die, and Nick didn't want that. He only wanted to wield a power he thought was non-existent within him. So, he lowered his arm, aimed the gun at the first bottle, and fired a shot as his dad stood frozen to the left of it. Offering no congratulations for hitting his mark, Ed instead marched over to Nick and held him up by the scruff of his shirt.

"What the hell were you playing at?!" he hissed.

A young Nick stammered. He could feel his father's spit as it splashed onto his cheek. He still held the gun in his hands and gave it a little shake, inched it forward a little, and Edwin fell backwards like a slingshot released. He landed in the flowing river, which was moving at a much stronger pace than they realised, and he was struggling to make it back to the edge. He hollered for Nick to help him, to extend his arm or grab a tree branch, but with all the thoughts rushing through Nick's mind, he took a while to react. His dad was tired and drenched and, on a wild day, he might have been swept down with the current, but Nick, though he was tempted to let his father fall victim to the elements, eventually dropped the gun on the rocks and helped Ed heave his body onto dry land.

An ambulance was called. The police showed up, too. Ed told them that his fall was an accident, but he looked at Nick a little differently from then on, as if he could read his son's mind and found the hesitation within it.

He takes a deep breath to fill his lungs with fresh forest air. Nick doesn't know where he'll head next, but he does know that this time, now that the ring is safe in his pocket and all presence of him is erased, he won't be coming back.

He climbs to the top of the forest park. It takes him an hour to get there, but he's not deterred. The struggle of climbing through dense bush without a path has warmed up his body, and the lack of many personal belongings means he isn't being dragged down. He reaches the peak just as the mid-morning fog lifts away from Quince. He can see gorgeous shades of green; a canopy of diverse trees that have been left undisturbed for centuries. Beyond that, he sees the colourful roofs of many houses he's been inside: Victoria's, Gary Gray's. He can see the hospital, his old campus, the police station. He swears he can even see Driscoll Street.

Nick stands right on the edge. Below him, a 200m drop down into the forest. If he fell, no one would find him.

There's a large gust of wind travelling through the park and it rises to meet Nick at the precipice. He stretches out his arms, he raises them above his head, and his body starts to shake with weakness. He closes his eyes. Then, slowly, as the wind subsides, he brings them back down to his side. His gaze opens onto Quince. The town still looks like shit from above.

Suddenly, there's a break in the silence: a snap of a twig. Nick stands rigid, on top of the world. Coming out of the canopy is a man, arms raised, palms outstretched. He flinches each time his black boots make an impression in the dirt. As he takes each sturdy step away from the bush, the shadows are removed from his face and Nick can see him clearly.

Over-dressed for a morning hike, but at the same time looking like he's just rolled out of bed, is Abbott, and his whole body tremors, from his wrinkled chin down to his weak knees.

Unbeknownst to Nick, Abbott had been ascending the forest park, calling his name, anxious to talk. Each lunge had Abbott clutching at his side, burning with a stitch, but his desperation propelled him forward. The news Rowan had left him with, news he hadn't fully absorbed, was sitting at the base of his stomach, an added weight to his already heavy load.

At the top of the peak, he hunches over, panting from adrenaline or the climb, it could be either. Nick, surprisingly, doesn't feel anything from his arrival. He doesn't feel panic or fear. He doesn't feel remorse or guilt. He doesn't move from the cliff's edge and he doesn't speak. The wind does the talking for him, and both he and Abbott's shirts slap wildly, the sound reminding him of his tent's canvas in a storm.

The officer eventually sputters out two words: "Nick Greene."

The man in question turns his body to look at Abbott. He doesn't want to be rude. It's taken them this long to meet face-to-face, so he might as well be cordial. He feels like he knows him and, for Abbott, the feeling is mutual.

"We need to talk," he says, after a few more ragged breaths.

Nick shrugs but remains where he stands, a good few feet away from the officer. "What about?"

Abbott gets a good look at the kid. The one who has caused all this trouble. It's the first decent look that he has had. At the motel in Abercrombie, there was only a fleeting

259

glance, a look over a shoulder, and prior to that, only glossy, over-exposed photographs on Paula's fridge. Abbott can see there's a resemblance to the missing persons posters plastered around town, but at the same time, Nick looks different standing in front of him, older than his 23 years, as if the past few months have aged him irreversibly. Nick seems to notice the staring and, concerned with the officer's blaring intensity, he turns away.

"No, wait!" Abbott yells, and he marches forward out of the bush, arm extended.

Nick stops and the men face each other. It's similar to the way Nick stood off against the angler. The only difference this time is that he doesn't have a fish knife tucked away in a backpack at his feet.

"Why did you do it?" The question erupts like ash from a volcano. It seems every second is a second too long for Abbott.

"Do what?"

His body shakes impulsively. "Any of it."

Nick scoffs, uninterested in explaining himself and doubting Abbott will even listen, but the detective looks even weaker than he does, his whole demeanour is deflated. It's as if he is clinging onto the smallest ounce of detail and it's as if that detail will give him life.

"I'm not planning on sticking around," Nick tells him. He wants to shoot straight from the hip.

Abbott smiles gently, and only for a second. He finally lowers his arm. The invisible gun remains inside its empty holster. "To be honest," he says, "I didn't expect you to."

35

The men cannot be mistaken as friends. They sit too far
apart and too rigid. They keep eye-balling each other too,
like opponents in a pool game, and anyone stumbling upon
the scene at the peak of the forest park wouldn't stay for
long. The air's too tense up here; there's a list of things that
have been left unsaid.

Abbott considers making the first exchange but it's
easier to stay mute. There's something in the pit of his
stomach – it feels like a ball of wool – and as he unravels
it, it's as if all the questions he's ever had drop into his lap.
Abbott imagines picking one up, trying to examine it, but
each piece of string is as frayed and undecipherable as the
rest.

Instead, he thinks of Paula leading him around the
upstairs bedroom, making sure he took note of the missing
items she was nervously pointing out. He thinks of her
crying on camera in the centre of the park. He thinks of her
that night, in the living room, tugging at the sleeves of her
dressing gown, eyes glazed over, lips chapped. He should
have asked her so much more.

Abbott lingers on his thoughts, tossing each one up into
the air but refusing to catch them when they fall. Not
knowing what to say, it makes him feel guilty, but it doesn't

matter because Nick mutters something under his breath and Abbott has to ask him to repeat it.

"Oh, nothing. I was just saying I'd offer you a drink but I'm a little unprepared."

Abbott notices the little amount of clothing Nick is wearing and he knows all too well why. Bad timing, or good timing on Abbott's behalf, meant Nick had thrown his winter gear in for a spin cycle the same moment he and Rowan had arrived at Sub Rosa, and now, winter's unforgiving bite nips at his bare arms.

He also notices how he speaks about the place. He talks as if the forest park is his home, equipped with all the amenities one could need. It perplexes him a little, for he sees only endless rock and dirt, but he supposes it makes sense. For more than a month, Nick had no one by his side but the oddities of nature.

"It's fine, I… I've caught my breath," Abbott says. "You did put on quite a chase."

Nick looks off to the side. He seems to be listening to the birdsong that has just begun from the branch of a pine tree. "How'd you know where I was anyway?" he says, his head still tilted to the sky.

"It was a hunch," Abbott replies. And a little luck.

After Rowan delivered the news, Abbott climbed into his car and raced to the forest park. There was nowhere else. After finding Nick's first camp on the 7th, Abbott knew it was the best place to find him now. He wouldn't be at Driscoll Street; he knew that much. No, it had to be here, where it all started.

"No one gave a shit about where I went until that fisherman died," Nick picks up. "I was walking around, right under their noses and they didn't fucking realise it."

"That's not true," Abbott says, shaking his head. "Your friends, your family, they were all worried about you."

"Bullshit," Nick spits. "I ran away because I knew how easy it would be."

Perhaps that is the same for everyone who runs away, Abbott thinks. He knows if he chose to leave Quince, there'd be no search party, no public gathering, no pleas in the newspaper. It would be as easy as hopping on a bus and that was precisely Nick's point.

"Why did you leave?" he asks, feigning ignorance.

Nick leans forward so that his hands rest on his knees. Abbott subconsciously copies the position, then fumbles around once he notices. Small stones and jagged sticks poke into his hands and leave their marks.

"It was always on my mind," Nick says. "I had always wanted to leave but I never had any reason to. And then…" He pauses.

"And then what?"

"I had a reason to."

Nick smiles tightly but it's an uncomfortable grin. He's bringing forward a memory that fuels him, Abbott can tell.

The conversation shifts quickly to less passionate things. Nick starts pointing up to the different kinds of trees above them and tells Abbott which are deciduous and which are evergreen. He talks about the long nights at the camp, the shooting stars, and when he witnessed the eye of a storm pass right over him. He talks about learning how to fish, how to gut them and cook them once caught. He tells him how he'd left the camp a handful of times and how each time, he went unnoticed.

Abbott listens intently. He catches himself hanging onto every word and it's not like him at all. He finds himself impressed with the man, and for a moment he ignores what he has done; he pushes it to the back of his mind. Nick is impressive, in his rebelliously misunderstood fashion, and it reminds Abbott of himself; a version of himself that went missing too, long ago.

Abbott asks questions about the tenacity of the weather and the solitude of the bush. The conversation flows as smooth as the river below them, but then talk turns to the toothbrush found with the other items taken from Driscoll Street, and the nagging question that has been ignored for so long climbs to the top of Abbott's throat.

"Why did you come back? I mean, why stay in Quince at all? You could have been gone, but you came back to break into your parents' home. Why?"

Nick seems upset that the serious discussion has resumed. He wants to stay talking about the birds and the sky, not about his parents and his reasons, but at the same time, Abbott knows it'll be good to get it all it off his chest, and he is the best person to hear it.

"That wasn't my intention," Nick says.

Still some distance apart, Abbott needs to crane his neck to decipher what he is saying. Each time the wind picks up, he loses some words within the sentence.

"I went to see her."

"Who?"

"Victoria. I couldn't sleep, so I woke up before dawn to try and catch her before she left for class. The busses weren't running yet; I had to walk the whole way into town. By the time I got there, she was with *him*."

"Who?"

"I was missing, and she was dancing around making coffee with another guy. Without a care in the world." He scoffs, and kicks at dirt with an already dirty shoe. He plays with something in his pocket. "So, I left something for her. Something that would make her realise I was watching."

The words come out monotone and malicious.

"I knew then that nobody cared, but I mean, I wasn't totally convinced. I told myself that when I got to my parents' house, they would be there, doing all they could to look for me."

Abbott sighs because he knows what comes next. He rubs harshly at his forehead, but the pounding inside doesn't stop. He can't imagine how Nick is feeling.

"They weren't there," he continues. "They were in Ormiston. The papers said they were visiting my sister but they were at the fucking Myers' barbecue, something they'd been bitching about going to for months."

Nick rises now and Abbott stands too, his knees letting out a click.

There's a drumming inside his chest, underneath his jumper and bed shirt. If he focuses on it, it sounds like it's trying to tell him something, but Abbott is too afraid to hear it. He looks across at the runaway, the runaway who would be the same age as his child, the child he made Franny give away. He looks again to see any similarities. Does Nick Greene look familiar? Does he look like him? Does he look like Fran?

Nick paces back and forward and Abbott can tell he's getting stressed. He knows he doesn't want any of this: to be here, with him, on top of a mountain overlooking the town that discarded him, but this is the closest Abbott has come to Nick Greene and he can't let him slip through his fingers again.

"Be honest with me – Abbott, is it?"

He nods.

"You're only here 'cos of the fisherman. When I was just some missing kid, you couldn't care less."

"That's not true," Abbott says, though the ghost of the boy from Drury Road is laughing.

"If that guy didn't care so much about the goddamn trout, I wouldn't be here."

"Is that why you killed him? To make people care that you left?"

Nick stops pacing. The tension has been ebbing and flowing and has come to a crescendo at the cliff's edge. The wind swirls all around them. He stares across at Abbott, his forehead thick with wrinkles and his mouth hanging open, like a door ajar.

"Kill him? I didn't kill him," he stutters. Nick shakes his head furiously and takes a step closer to Abbott. "Well, if I did, it was an accident. He fell and hit his head on a rock."

"How can I trust you?" he asks.

"Because it's the truth!" Nick backs away again. The wind picks up, unhappy with the change in atmosphere. The birds seem to abandon their stoops and the sky greys over with clouds. He looks through the trees as if he is desperately searching for an escape route.

Abbott's voice drops down into a whisper. He looks at him, as confused as he is. Neither are sure of the truth, or whether the truth means anything anymore.

"I need to know," he sighs. "I need to know why you did any of this. Were you that unhappy?"

Nick laughs across at the ageing cop. He rubs at the creases in his forehead. "What has that got to do with any of this?" He sighs, tired and fed up.

"Because I know about your parents."

Nick stops moving then, stands still like a statue. "What?"

"I know you were adopted. Paula explained everything."

The wind around them whistles once again and Nick lets out a small but powerful yell, one that comes from deep within his chest, frightening Abbott.

"Did she tell you how much she hated me?" he says. "How much they all hated me?"

"How did you find out?" Abbott presses.

"I got sick of being treated like shit. It wasn't hard to find. Upstairs. In a box somewhere. It's like they didn't even try to hide it."

"That's the reason," he says. "That's the reason you left."

Nick pats his pocket, this time wanting Abbott to see. "Among other things." He walks over to where he had been sitting and picks up the rucksack with one hand. Swinging it over his shoulder he says: "And now I have to leave again."

*

Nick turns his back and heads out of the clearing, into the dense bush. The cop calls after him, to no avail.

"There's nothing you can say that'll make me stay," he murmurs. "I'm sorry."

With that, Nick makes another desperate attempt to flee. He careens down, down, down into the bush where the wood is dark compared to the surface of the peak. He uses his hands to shield his face from any intruding branches as his feet fly forward and he gathers speed quickly.

There's a cry from on top of the cliff. A loud, mournful cry. Nick hesitates when he hears it and hides behind a wide pine, resting his head against the bark. He waits for Abbott to come closer.

Bending down into his rucksack, Nick feels for the gun he quickly stashed away upon Abbott's arrival to the top of the crest. He won't hurt him, he thinks, just scare him; make sure he knows that he doesn't want to be found. He drops the bag to his feet. His chest rises and falls. He holds the grip tight in his shaking hands.

Only a few feet away, Abbott appears. He looks left, right, left. He can't see Nick behind the pine. "Nick!" he calls. It comes out in a strained whisper. "Nick."

He keeps still. He can hear Abbott approach. He's about to jump out behind the tree and hold the gun in front of his face, but then he hears a different noise. A sob. A gentle sob that comes out in a bubble and pops.

He freezes, lowers the gun. He bends down to the forest floor and sticks it back inside his rucksack. The zip makes a noticeable sound when it closes.

"Nick?"

He takes off running again. Instead of going straight down the mountainside, he turns to the right and runs in that direction for a few minutes. Abbott bounds after him. He's much slower than Nick is, and the branches of the trees aren't acting in his favour. They poke into his side and scratch at his skin and obscure his vision. He slips and falls down the gentle slope of the mountain; he is spurred on by his son.

"Nick!" He cries. His fatigued voice echoes around the forest park. "Nick! Stop! Please...stop."

Nick keeps running. He heads downhill, hoping it will

get him out, send him into the open. Allow him to be free.

He turns once more to look back, but as he does so, his feet catch the top of a decaying log. His body is flown forward, his rucksack is sent flying, and Nick cascades down the mountain's side. His bare arms scrape along the surface of the ground. Loose stones burn against his skin and roll across his head like a cheese grater. Larger boulders jut into his lower back and he can hear himself crying out in pain. The forest floor and the canopy of trees above turn into a blur of green and brown.

He feels like he rolls forever. He tries to dig his hands into the soil, but his speed is too great and the momentum too strong. It's a horrible feeling, like being tipped upside down.

Soon, the wet ground makes way for a bumpy surface and a dip in the landscape sends him back into the air for a split second. As he descends, he hits another rock, this time with the side of his head, and the pain courses its way through Nick's nerve fibres. This time, he doesn't hear himself when he yells.

He comes to a rest on a stony shore. Behind him, he can hear the soft river flow. The sound is soothing, as all other sounds cease to exist.

There's blood pooling out of a wound by his right temple. He can feel the warmth of it drip down his cheek. Above him, the wind dies down and the trees stop moving. One last leaf falls onto Nick's chest.

He tries to move his legs, but he can't right now. He tries to lift his head, but it feels the weight of a bowling ball. There are no clouds to make pictures with, so the sun beams down unguarded instead. He tries to yell but he's out of breath.

The ring still lies in his pocket. He can feel the bulge. He tries to move his hand to touch it but his fingers only wriggle.

When he gets out of town, he'll pawn it off for cash. He'll use it to start a new life, maybe a life as Rick Brown. He might even catch up with Marina and Trevaughn. He'll apologise for what he put them through, but they'll forgive him, he's sure of that. Maybe this time, he'll move far away to a part of the world where people are too happy to run away, if such a place exists.

There's an object lying to the side of Nick and he struggles to make out its shape. Using all of his might, he turns his head to the side as pebbles roll into themselves underneath him. The object is white and pointy and looks odd among the smooth surface of the stones. After blinking through the blur behind his eyes, he realises what the object is and laughs gently. No noise comes out, and the snigger hurts all the muscles in his back.

It's a trout carcass. Its skeleton sticks up among the rocks. Nick looks back up to the sky and closes his eyes.

36

AUGUST 10

Abbott slips off a rock and into the path of the river. His ankle rolls and he lets out a groan. He places his hands on his hips and tries to catch his breath, but it's no use. His breath abandons him a lot these days.

He squints into the dying sunlight. It's been a good afternoon, but still it yielded no results. He's been out here day after day, often alone, wandering the rugged terrain in a fruitless effort to tie up loose ends.

He has since come to learn what Nick liked so much about the place. Being within nature is soothing, even though there's nothing but harsh thoughts nestled among a harsh environment. Being out here, he's come to learn things about himself, unpleasant truths that he once pushed away.

Nick Greene allowed him to do that, and for that, he is grateful.

"Feeling old yet?"

The jibe is made over on the shore and comes from the mouth of Rowan, whose eyebrows are raised behind those tinted aviator sunglasses.

Abbott clicks his teeth as if hurt by the insult, but he still has to let out a smile. He shakes off his boot and trudges back to where Rowan is sitting and sighs.

"No," he says. "I started feeling old that day we lost Nick Greene at the motel."

Rowan nods his head as the sun sets beyond his shoulder. He looks good, refreshed almost, wearing a glow one gets after a holiday on the coast. The sleeves of his shirt are rolled up to the elbows and the same can be said for his pants: hems folded into cuffs so as to prevent the wayward water from drenching them.

"Oh, yeah. Even I felt old," he says.

Abbott looks a little different too, though not as put together as his colleague. He's felt less inclined to pick up the razor than he has in getting to the forest park, and his search has led to the sacrifice of other daily rituals, like combing his hair and brushing his teeth and ironing his clothes. Still, he remains a staunch figure on the surface, an older, wiser version of his younger self, although inside he is wilted.

"Don't worry about it," he tells Rowan. "It's incredible how fast you can run when you don't want to be caught."

With that, Abbott looks up into the vast bush. From where he stands, the forest park looks endless, with multiple entries and exits, but with 1000 men, there'd be no path untraveled. With only two, someone can stay hidden forever.

Rowan stares up at him and watches as he gets lost in contemplation. He watches how Abbott's brow curves with a thought, and his mouth droops open as if speaking aloud to himself. For a moment, he is transfixed, and there is nothing that can break him from his trance. His mouth bobs, his jaw clenches, and then the trail of thought is abandoned.

Abbott doesn't realise he is doing it; doesn't realise his

questions are as obvious as they are hopeless, but it's been more than a month, and all remnants of Nick Greene have waned. People seem to have an easier time moving on than he does: cops go back to walk their regular beats, girls forget about a love they once cherished, and sometimes even mothers can adapt to a different way of life, but for Abbott, Nick clings to the cells of his brain like a sloth to a tree. He is as all-consuming as the scent of a fragrant perfume, and Abbott's mind no longer works the way it used to.

His days in the forest park are joined by thoughts of: What If? What if he had found the boy from Drury Road alive? What if he had grabbed Franny by the hand and asked her not to go? What if he had told Nick that he was his son? Would he have stayed? He wonders what his life would be like if just one thing had been a little bit different.

He asks these same questions now, staring up at the forest park where he last saw him, where he vanished through layers of thick bush. Abbott had followed him that day, followed him as much as he could, but he got lost through the repetitiveness of the forest and his knees were close to buckling. The further he descended, the more disoriented he became, and he was forced to retrace his steps back up the mountain, only to return down the slope along a clearer path, arriving at the park's entrance some hours later.

By then, of course, Nick was gone.

Abbott had returned the following day, and the day after that, to make sure Nick wasn't hiding out, though that, he admits now, is wishful thinking. When it was clear he had gone and wasn't returning, the fisherman's case was shoved into a box and put on a shelf, though Nick still remains a suspect in the random death – the only suspect, to be clear.

Eventually, all the missing persons posters were taken down, the newspaper articles ceased, and talk turned to other things. Cole and his squadron of men returned to their regular posts, Mollie moved back to Ormiston, and Paula lost Abbott's home phone number. All that is left is Abbott, balancing on pebbles like an unsteady toddler and with a boot now dripping with water.

To his left, Rowan yawns. He's been wanting to go for hours. He only came to be a pillar of support, to watch on as Abbott took one last look at the mountainside in all its mysterious glory. Abbott had told him not to come, in fact, but Rowan insisted, and Abbott is glad that he did. Otherwise, he thinks, it would be too hard to leave.

"You really think he's still here?" Rowan asks.

A group of teenage boys with fishing poles step out from behind the grassy bank and saunter past them. One is holding a tackle box, another, a four-pack of beers. They laugh about something and Abbott ponders through the list of 'What If's' again. What if he raised Nick Greene? Would he have turned out different? Would any of this have happened? Abbott waits until the boys pass.

"I can't explain it," he confides. "I just get the feeling he hasn't gone too far."

The squawk of birds flying in a v-formation overhead catches their attention. The pair watch as they head towards the mountain's peak, their wings moving rhythmically, silhouettes against a tangerine sky. Eventually, the naked eye loses sight of them. The birds disappear into the ether. The men look across at one another, their shoulders shrug, and their heads nod.

"Let's go," Abbott says.

The two friends march across the stony shore but Abbott can't break his glance away from the embankment: the mossy enclaves, the shield of the bush, the shadowy fissures. He makes sure to look at it all. With every step he swears he stumbles upon a strange stone, a suspicious piece of litter or a familiar footprint, and each time he shakes his head, blinks his eyes twice, and carries on.

Abbott went back to where the boy from Drury Road was found. Happy, that's what the kids had all called him. He sat down on the slope, his backside getting damp from the dew, and just stayed there a minute. He breathed in the winter's air, watched the black beetles crawl out from underneath leaves, and allowed whatever wanted to happen, happen. He couldn't help but think about when he searched that area for Happy. He wondered what he was thinking about back then, what had made him so preoccupied that he missed the boy lying in the ditch? As he sat, he thought about what his life would have been like if he'd found him. Closure for the Price family; Franny's slippers at the front door; Nick.

Abbott had gone to see Paula once more, but he didn't tell her about the forest park. Instead, he went to say goodbye, and Paula, as if realising the time had come to let Nick go, let him leave. He also didn't tell her that her son was also his. It was almost impossible to believe. Abbott did, however, come to learn that Paula and Edwin had adopted Nick while they were living in the beach-side town of Bellevue. Franny had chosen them to take care of her first-born. They moved to Quince when Nick was just a toddler; when Franny had long gone and Abbott was already a mess.

Cole also left relatively soon after Nick's second

departure. He said Quince still haunted him and for the first time, Abbott could relate.

He and Rowan return to the forest's main car park, where there are only a handful of vehicles positioned between the faded white lines: a convertible, a ute, the ranger's buggy with the ranger in it, Rowan's dark green station wagon, and Abbott's Audi 90. The rear window is still stuck open a chink. When they get to their vehicles, Rowan pounds his hand hard on the bonnet. Abbott would do the same, though he doubts his car's durability. He instead pulls his driver's door open and leans on it, although delicately.

"So, I guess this is it," Rowan says. He lifts his sunglasses from his eyes even though that means he's forced to squint. He moves from his car towards Abbott's and peers into the boot as he walks. Inside there are old canvas duffle bags, a tall stack of cardboard boxes, and a dehydrated plant that has already lost a few leaves. It's nicely packed and, for some reason, it gives the men a sense of reassurance, as if everything is going to be okay.

"You sure you got everything?"

Abbott gently nods. The question makes him uncomfortable, like he's a student moving out of home for the first time. He wonders if Rowan worries whether he's capable of looking after himself or not. Hell, even Abbott isn't so sure that he is.

The retiring detective holds out his hand; his young protégée reaches out to shake it.

"Be good," Abbott advises him.

Rowan smiles and the two men disperse. Abbott slides into his front seat but as soon as he sits, he rises.

"Oh!" he calls out. "Promise me something."

"What's that?" Rowan yells back.

"Unlock the bloody door."

The men gaze across at each other one last time; a knowing look, a final goodbye. Rowan nods before sinking into his station wagon, putting the car in reverse, and exiting the parking lot.

Abbott stares out his windscreen at the vista in front of him, an abundance of colour and texture. The forest has never looked so beautiful, the water has never been so smooth.

Winter is slowly disappearing, and with its absence comes new blossoms. Trees become vivid and bountiful again, the nights become longer and the mornings more plentiful. Soon, the park will become crowded with day trippers and hikers and fishermen. There will be children swimming in the river and bird watchers and photographers climbing the peak. There will be jogging groups and yoga classes and families having picnics on the verge. There will be swarms of people converging with nature, picking dandelions, and combing the shore for treasures.

There will be no site uncanvassed, no gully left undiscovered, and all the secrets of the forest park will be revealed.

THE END

Acknowledgements

It is never an easy feat to thank the ones who have helped you achieve something you could only dream of. No words seem to do the trick.

Completing a novel, trusting myself, and being brave enough to take the leap has only been possible because of the amazing supporters I have backing me. Firstly, my parents, Darren and Jackie. My first memories of writing stem from their simple actions of buying me notebooks and pens, giving me story ideas, and listening when I read out 'My Best Friend Brian', a comedic short story about a boy who believed he was a rock star.

We had book club together; evenings spent reading in bed. They let me bring my latest work-in-progress out to dinner. These simple gestures, these silent affirmations that reading and writing was a skill I was allowed to develop and enjoy, have undoubtedly shaped my life.

Thanks also to my husband, Matthew, who, on the other hand, is not a reader or a writer. Despite this fact, he has never once belittled my dream. I am forever grateful, and forever in love.

Finally, Cranthorpe Millner Publishers. A joy to work with from day dot. Thank you so much to Kirsty, Victoria, and the team for taking a chance on a Kiwi author and for allowing her to see her wildest dreams become a reality. I once interviewed a woman who told me that life was like a tapestry, and the people you met were the threads. I am so blessed to have such a vibrant, strong tapestry made up of wonderful moments such as these.